# UNMASKED

## BLOOD BOND SAGA: VOLUME FOUR
### PARTS 10 - 11 - 12

## HELEN HARDT

# UNMASKED

BLOOD BOND SAGA: VOLUME FOUR

PARTS 10 - 11 - 12

## HELEN HARDT

WATERHOUSE PRESS

# TABLE OF CONTENTS

*To those who walk by night...*

# BLOOD BOND SAGA

## PART 10

---

PART 10

# DANTE

I walked out the door to River's apartment. My father was nowhere in sight.

"The car, Dante."

His voice. I walked quickly to Erin's car and got in.

"This isn't going to be easy to say."

Again, only his voice. He did not appear.

"All right. Just say it, then."

A gruff sound—as if he were clearing his throat.

Then, "I concentrated all my energy on the darkness that has targeted you. I was determined, this time, to find its source."

"And...?"

"As I said, this isn't easy to say."

"For God's sake, Dad. Just say it."

"I double- and triple-checked my findings. I even conferred with a few other ghosts on this plane, and they agree with me."

Silence.

More silence.

My gums began to itch, even though I knew my fangs

would do no good against a ghost. Against my father. "Would you get to the fucking point?"

"I was able to pinpoint the source of the darkness. Bea was right. It's not a demon or a ghost. It's a dark energy."

And I knew.

Before he said anything more, I knew.

"You're correct," he said.

"You know what I'm thinking?"

"I can tell, just by your movements. Your canine nerve is responding. You're becoming angry, and there's no reason for it. No reason other than what you and I now know."

I bared my fangs, growling.

Growling at the darkness.

Growling at myself.

"Are you sure?" I snarled.

"Aren't you?" my father replied.

I gnashed my teeth at his voice.

The darkness was here. Now. In the car.

The darkness hadn't targeted me.

The darkness *was* me.

# ONE

# DANTE

I rubbed my forehead, trying to ease the sharp knifing that had erupted.

*Me.*

The darkness was *me.*

"I'm sorry, Dante. Believe me. I wanted to be wrong."

I'd gotten used to hearing my father's voice in thin air. But these particular disembodied words, even from a voice I recognized, slashed through me like a samurai's sword. They were horrid words. *True* words.

"It might have something to do with this power you're developing," he continued.

"Is this darkness...evil?" I asked.

Silence for a moment.

Several moments.

"For God's sake, Dad. Fucking answer me!"

"Dante, you know the answer."

"Say it! I want you to fucking say it!"

"Darkness, by its very essence, is evil."

"No. Not true. The night is dark. The night is not evil."

"You know as well as I do that we're not talking about shades of color here."

Yes, I knew. I already knew everything. Desperation clawed at me. I just wanted some tiny belief that maybe, just maybe, it wasn't what I knew to be true.

"You've learned a lot of control," my father continued. "You can control this as well."

Control? Was he insane? How was I supposed to control a dark energy when I couldn't control the ultra-glamouring ability? Erin was my control—Erin and my love and need for her—but she hadn't been able to help me control my new skills. "How?"

"The way you control everything else. Remember what is real. Nothing is black and white. All beings have a certain amount of darkness in them. Without the darkness, light couldn't exist."

"But this...part of me—it's not actually *me*. Is it?"

"I don't believe it is. I believe something happened to you while you were in captivity. I don't know what, but I think the answers might be found in the *Texts*."

I pounded my fist against the steering wheel, blasting the horn in Erin's car.

"Easy," my father said.

"No. This isn't fair. I finally found happiness with Erin. But now...what can I do? I need her and she needs me. We have a blood bond. But I'll have to leave her. I can't be around her if I have this evil inside me."

"No, Dante. If anything, you need to be with her even more. If not for her, the darkness might have taken hold of you by now. She is a source of light for you. A source of love and devotion. Take care of her, and take care of yourself. You won't be any good to Emilia and anyone else if you don't see to your own needs."

"But what if I—"

"You won't. You would never harm her. Don't forget that *you* have the power here. Not the darkness. *You.*"

"How is it that this part of me... How is it that I feel it? And it feels like a separate entity?"

"I don't know. I've felt the dark power too. I've warned you to flee when I've felt it. It's something new and different that we don't understand yet."

"I felt it the first time I was in Erin's home. Right after I escaped. It felt like something I had to scope out and eliminate. I didn't run from it then, and it went away."

"I wish I could tell you more. I don't want to frighten you, but it *is* growing stronger. Yet it's not as strong as you are, Dante. It never will be. I know that, and I believe, in your very being, you know that as well."

"What did that bitch do to me?" I clenched the steering wheel.

"I don't know. We will find the answers. I promise you. Whatever her plan was, she most likely wasn't counting on the blood bond with Erin. That is helping to keep you from succumbing to this evil."

*Succumbing to this evil.* The words played in my head like a discordant rhythm. "What if I can't ever shake it? Get rid of it?"

"Then you'll learn to live with it. We all have our own crosses to bear. Never doubt your strength, son. You are something special. Remember that."

Special? If special meant a special kind of evil, maybe.

"How am I supposed to tell Erin this? She'll run away screaming."

"Have faith in her, Dante."

Faith? That damned word again. Faith was believing without seeing, without knowing as fact. It went against logic, and now more than ever, I needed to draw on logic, on what was real.

Unfortunately, this dark part of me was real.

Faith. Faith in what?

I drew in a breath. If I could have faith in only one thing in the world, it would be in Erin.

She had accepted me as vampire, had accepted the blood bond between us. But could she accept the darkness that lived in me? That, in essence, *was* me?

"You have to tell her," my father said.

He was right, of course. *Have faith in her, Dante.* Faith that Erin wouldn't run from me. Abandon me.

"How, Dad? How do I explain something I don't understand myself?"

"You just do."

"That's not fatherly advice."

"I wish I had some concrete answers. This is new territory for both of us."

An unwelcome thought speared into my head. "Shit. What if..."

"What?"

"What if this new ultra-glamouring power I have is a dark power, Dad? What if I can do bad things with it?"

Then another unwelcome thought.

The levitation.

"There's something else."

"What?"

"This is difficult to say to my father."

"I think we've gotten beyond that," he said.

I sighed. "I suppose so. The last time Erin and I made love, we floated above the bed."

"Meaning?"

"Meaning exactly what I said. We levitated. I can't help but think that levitation is a dark power. Remember *The Exorcist*?"

"*The Exorcist* is fiction, son."

"Based on a real case, though."

"Let's attack this from a different angle, then. Buddha and Jesus reputedly walked on water. That's levitation. Do you think they were manifesting dark powers?"

"That's dogma, Dad."

"You were placing your belief in fiction. Whether the root of the story was based in fact doesn't matter. The book and the movie are fiction. Dogma is dogma. What's the difference?"

"I don't know. I don't fucking know anything anymore." Then, "Are you actually saying you believe me? You believe that I levitated?"

"I have no reason to disbelieve anything you say. My death has opened up a whole new world to me, so to speak."

"What if these new powers are dark? What if they make me do bad things?"

"Whether the powers manifest from darkness doesn't matter. Anyone can do bad things with any power he has. A good person can wield a gun and kill. That is within his power."

"It's not that simple."

"But it *is*, Dante. It is very much that simple. You may have a darkness within you, but you can choose what you do with that darkness and with the power that may come with it."

"What if I can't? What if it overpowers me somehow?"

"Believe in yourself. In your strength. Remember what you've gotten through."

"But what if—"

"Stop it. Stop going there. Your years in captivity didn't break you. *This* will not break you. Not if you don't let it."

I breathed in, held it a few seconds, and let it out. "Thank you."

"You don't need to thank me."

"But I do. You're dead, and I'm still so sorry about that, because it's ultimately my fault."

"Dante—"

"Please. Let me finish. It is. If I'd listened to you and Uncle Brae, River and I wouldn't have gone to Bourbon Street that night. None of this would have happened. But that's not even what I mean. Thank you for being *here*. For coming back as a ghost so you could help me. Dad, I don't think I'd get through this without you."

"I think you could. You have Erin."

"I know that. She's wonderful, and I can't live without her. But having you here, even if you're not really *here*, makes all the difference. Without you, I wouldn't know that the darkness is in me."

"You would have known eventually."

"Maybe. I did know before you actually said the words."

"Precisely. You'll get through this. I won't allow you *not* to get through this."

His words lightened my load a little. He might be a ghost, but he was still my father. No mistake about that.

"I didn't understand the magnitude of what your mother meant in the dream when she came to me. She said you had a nearly divine purpose to fulfill."

"Divine? When there's evil inside me?"

"She said 'nearly divine.'"

"What the hell is the difference? I'm hardly godlike."

"Godlike isn't the only definition of divine, Dante. It can mean, simply, 'supremely good.'"

"A supremely good purpose while I'm fighting darkness? Still doesn't make sense."

"You have something to do here. I feel certain. Your mother wouldn't have asked me to take my own life without some higher purpose."

"Not just to protect me?"

"No, son. I love you, and I will always protect you, but ghosts don't come back to the earthly plane just to protect their loved ones. If they did, they'd never cross over. The world would be inundated with wandering spirits. Who could resist staying around to protect the people they love? We'd be everywhere."

"You seem to be everywhere here in New Orleans."

"That has more to do with the supernatural veil here, a result of the voodoo and magick practitioners and the devout Catholic population. They draw down and send up energy. Energy attracts energy. I've told you this. But most ghosts still prefer to pass through the veil. Remember, I wouldn't be dead if it weren't for my dream of your mother. Your purpose may not be divine in a godlike sense, but she made it very clear that you needed to be protected. And I will make sure you are. You and Erin both."

A nearly divine purpose.

I didn't thank him again, though the words were formed in the back of my throat. He didn't want my thanks. He'd done what he did because my mother asked him to, because he was my father, because he thought I needed him.

And I did.

Probably more than I ever had when he was alive.

"Will I still be able to feel the darkness?" I asked.

"Why wouldn't you? I've felt it as well. I just didn't know it was coming from you. Be aware. When you feel it, learn to control it."

"What if I can't suppress it?"

"I didn't say to suppress it. Suppression only causes things to build up, and eventually the dam will break. I said to *control* it. Accept it as part of you and choose to take dominion over it."

"But it's growing, Dad. What if it takes me over?"

"You won't let it."

Faith. My father had faith in *me*. In my internal strength.

Could I have faith in me? It would be a lot easier if I didn't have a darkness inside me that was growing, that wanted to take me over. Perhaps I needed to think of this dark energy as my father did—as something that was inside me yet separate from me, something I could control.

"Why now, Dad? Em and the others are missing. I can't afford to deal with this shit now."

"We don't know the source of this yet," my father said. "But don't think of it as a bad thing, necessarily. Perhaps it can help."

"Help how?"

"These new powers you're exhibiting—maybe you can use them to find the women. To find my brother."

"Not if I can't control the powers."

"Then learn to control them. It's all part of controlling the darkness inside you. I have faith in you. Have some faith in yourself."

Faith. Again, faith.

"We don't know much about this energy," my father continued. "We know it's coming from you, but we don't know why."

An invisible brick landed in my gut.

*I* knew why.

*Her.*

*She* had done this to me.

*She* wanted something from me, was waiting for something.

Something big. Something powerful.

Something I had to fight—fight to the death, if necessary—to keep from taking me over.

*She* would not win.

I was not hers to use.

## TWO

# *Erin*

My cuticles were dry despite the moisturizing hand massage Sheree had given me at my facial a day ago. Or had it been two days ago? When had I last slept?

I scraped the nail of my index finger over the dry cuticle of my thumb, creating a hangnail. I engaged in the nasty habit when my nerves were on edge. Bill's presence had that effect on me. He'd been nothing but a douche since I met him. I wanted to believe that he cared about his son, his grandchildren, and the other missing women, but if he did, he should do everything within his power to help. That included helping us decipher the *Texts*, not throwing up obstacles every which way.

"Erin."

I looked up just as a drop of blood emerged where I broke the thick skin of my thumb. I quickly covered it by making a fist.

Dante's grandfather had said my name.

"Yeah?"

"Anything you want to tell me?"

Why would I want to tell him anything? "Not that I can think of."

"I find it curious," he continued. "Why can I no longer scent you? Or your brother?"

"It's no big deal, Bill," River said. "They're using a potion to mask their scents from some thug vamps who are after them."

"No big deal?" I said sarcastically. "Since when is this not a big deal? And since when is it any of his business?"

"No big deal to him, is what I meant," River said. "Of course it's a big deal for the two of you."

"Still not his business," I said. "Dante wouldn't—"

"Contrary to what you might believe, Dante doesn't always know what's best," Bill interjected. "Where did you find this potion?"

"Hold on, old man," Jay said, advancing toward Bill. "Why all the questions? Why do you care?"

"I may be an old man, but I could still take you down."

"Bring it on, Grandpa." Jay balled his hands into fists.

"Easy, both of you," River said. "Bill, Jay is one of the good guys. We're all tense because Em and Lucy and the others are missing. And they're right. I shouldn't have blurted out the stuff about the potion."

Bill smoothed his hands over the sleeves of his shirt. "Fine. To answer your second question, your sister is important to my grandson. Why *wouldn't* I care?"

My heart racing from the commotion and my anger at Bill, I went back to work on my cuticle. A drop of blood emerged, and I brought it to my mouth to stop the bleeding.

Bill's eyes went wide.

Shit. Was he hungry?

River stood. "I'll get us both a glass."

"Sorry." I rose. "Where are your bandages?"

"Bathroom," River said. "In the cupboard above the sink."

I hurried into the small room and bandaged my cuticle. Bill couldn't smell me, but apparently the sight of my blood made him hungry. I was thankful Dante wasn't here to witness it. The way he felt about his grandfather currently, that would not have ended well.

When I returned, River and Bill were sipping glasses of blood as my brother glowered at them.

"We don't drink from humans," River said. "You know that."

"Your cousin does." Jay turned to me.

"That's consensual." I sat back down.

Silence, then, the only sounds the sipping of blood by two vampires. I should be used to that by now, but the fact that the sight of my blood had caused their thirst bothered me a little.

Okay, a lot.

How long had Dante and Julian been gone?

Seconds turned into minutes into what seemed like hours.

My thumb throbbed beneath the thin bandage. *Dante, where are you?*

As if in response, he burst through the door.

I stood and raced into his arms.

He kissed the top of my head. "You okay?"

I pulled away slightly to meet his gaze, nodding. "Are *you*?"

"Fine." The word came out tersely.

He wasn't fine.

"Let's go home, Erin," he said.

"Sure. But what about—"

"It's taken care of."

The darkness that had targeted him had been taken care

of? Or did he think I was talking about something else? "If you'd let me finish—"

He placed two fingers over my lips. "It's okay. We'll be okay."

I sighed. He was acting—if not quite sounding—sure. "Where's your dad?"

He looked around. "Didn't he come in with me?"

"No."

"He's not here, Dante," River said. "Are you sure you're all right? You look a little frazzled, man."

"I'm fine," Dante said, again tersely. "I just want to go home. Now."

"Yes, let's," I said. "We'll check in with you guys later."

Once we were in the car, I turned to him. "We're alone now. Tell me what's wrong."

"I will. I'll tell you everything. When we get home."

⚜

As soon as we walked through the doorway, Dante pushed me against the wall, his eyes dark with desire. "I'll never hurt you, Erin. Tell me you know that. Tell me you believe me."

My heart lurched. "Of course I believe you. I know that, Dante."

"I won't. Ever. I'd die first." He crushed his lips onto mine.

I opened, and our tongues twirled together. Desire, passion, need—it was all there. Something else laced this kiss, though—something I couldn't quite name.

I didn't try. I simply surrendered to the kiss, to Dante, giving him all of me as I always did. It was a hard kiss, a kiss that demanded something from me.

I slid my hands up his arms, over his hard, broad shoulders, and threaded them through his soft dark hair. So silky, so perfect. Then I moved my hands, cupping his cheeks, his stubble prickly against my fingertips.

Still he kissed me deeply, and I pulled his face forward, trying to erase any tiny bit of space between us. If only we could be one body, stay together always.

He broke away quickly, drawing in a deep breath. He swept his gaze over me, from the top of my head down to my toes, and then he met my eyes.

His lips were swollen and glistening from our kiss, and his eyes...oh, his eyes. I'd never seen them so dark. So magnificent. The perimeters of his irises burned like rings of fire.

Again, I saw something new. Something I didn't recognize. Yes, the desire, the passion, the lust, the love was there. But so was something else.

"Are you...hungry?" The words came out timidly, and I had no idea why. I turned my head, giving him access to my neck.

He snarled as he bared his fangs. "Hungry. For you."

The tickle between my legs intensified. His teeth, the huskiness of his growl. It was all as attractive as the rest of him. This was Dante in his element. Dante as vampire.

He tossed me over his shoulder like a sack of potatoes and carried me up to the bedroom.

My nerves skittered. A sliver of fear rippled up my spine, but desire and the lust swarming around me soon displaced it. I thumped against his hard body with each clomp up the stairs. I became more aroused with each step closer to the bedroom, each movement pushing the texture of my clothes against my clit.

He laid me on the bed and then hovered over me, his

cuspids bared, a low growl—which I felt more than heard—still vibrating from his throat.

He stared at me, raking his gaze over my entire body until—

Quick as lightning, he ripped through my blouse with his teeth, tearing it in two.

I gasped, but he didn't stop there.

Next went my bra, another casualty of his teeth.

My chest bared, he lowered his head and inhaled, moving his nose over my throat, over the swells of my breast, until he got to my nipple.

"Mine," he rasped, before he took it between his full lips and sucked.

Tingles shot through me. He sucked and sucked, and though he didn't draw blood from me, he sucked with urgency, as though he were taking true nourishment.

I brought my hand to his head, his hair soft beneath my palm, and I caressed him. Stroked his hair, smoothing it, hoping I was soothing him at the same time.

"It's okay, my love," I whispered. "It's all okay."

His urgency against my breast softened then, and his sucking became more of what I was used to—an integral part of our lovemaking that we both enjoyed.

He released my nipple with a soft pop and slid downward over my belly. He removed my jeans slowly, no ripping this time, and then my panties. He inhaled, his eyes closed.

Our arousal.

Not just my arousal, but *our* arousal. The feminine musk came from me, but the fragrance was all us—a lusty perfume that fed my libido as well as his.

He spread my legs and inhaled again. "God, baby. My

God." With his fingers, he massaged my folds, lubricating them with my juices. "Tell me again. Tell me you know I'll never harm you."

Where was this coming from? I reached toward him, clasping his hand to mine. "I know that, Dante. I swear to you that I know that. I believe it with all my heart."

He leaned down and punctured my inner thigh, a satisfied groan emanating from him.

As he took my blood, as we were joined in body, I closed my eyes and lay back. He needed me, needed this sustenance. This was what both nurtured and nourished him, made him whole.

I made him whole, just as he made me whole. Whatever this man needed, I would give with my whole body and my whole heart.

When he licked my wounds closed, he stood and hastily removed his clothes. Then he was on top of me, inside me, pumping into me, giving to me and taking from me.

He thrust against my clit, and within a few seconds my orgasm mounted.

"Don't be afraid, love," he whispered against my ear.

Never afraid. Never.

We floated from the bed, our bodies joined, our hearts joined, our souls joined, as he pumped into me furiously and then climaxed, each one of his contractions quivering into me against my sensitive walls.

We flew together, like two hawks gliding over the wind, and when our orgasms slowed in tandem, we came gently back down onto the bed.

When I could speak, I said only, "How?"

He rolled off me. "I don't know, love. I can't explain a lot of what is going on with me. But I know one thing. I will never, never harm you."

I cupped his cheek. "I know that. Why do you keep saying it?"

He closed his eyes. "Because I need you to know it. To know it within your very being." Then he opened his eyes. "Promise me something."

"Anything."

A pause as he drew in a breath and let it out. Then, "Promise me you'll leave if you ever think I'll harm you."

"Dante, you won't. You just said—"

He silenced me with two fingers over my lips.

His eyes shone with such torment I wanted nothing more than to hold him close to me forever, show him how much I trusted him, believed in him.

Then something dawned on me. A recognition.

That emotion in his eyes that I didn't recognize at first?

It was fear.

# THREE

# DANTE

How?

How could I tell this beautiful woman I loved more than anything that the evil targeting me...was *me*?

Couldn't I have just this night with her? This one night, before I turned her already turbulent world further on its axis?

Yes.

I'd have this night.

I inhaled, letting her scent infuse every cell of my body. My cock hardened, and I grabbed at the emotions—even the dark ones—whirling through me.

I wanted this night. This one night. And I knew exactly how I wanted it.

I'd give her what I'd planned to give her when we were interrupted days ago, when my greatest desire was to take her forcibly.

With her begging me, pleading with me, for more, more, more...

I needed it now. Even as I thought about it, my dick

hardened further and my fangs descended. This was part of who I truly was. This night would have a purpose other than intense pleasure for Erin and for me.

If she could take it—take who I truly was—perhaps she wouldn't run away when I told her the source of the darkness.

I rose from the bed and walked into the extra bedroom where I'd stashed the stuff I hadn't had the time to unpack yet. I didn't have a lot, having been gone for ten years, but I'd had the chance to pick up a few things before Lucy, and then Emilia, disappeared.

Guilt knifed me. How could I be thinking about making hot love to Erin when my sister was missing? My uncle was missing?

*Take care of her, and take care of yourself. You won't be any good to Emilia and anyone else if you don't see to your own needs.*

My father's words sounded wise. Erin and I both needed this night.

I smiled at the items I'd stored in a plastic container River had given me. He'd been with me when I purchased most of this stuff, more than happy to show me what I'd need. Funny that I hadn't been embarrassed. He understood. Turned out sexual dominance was a male vampire trait, something I'd have known if...

I shook my head to clear it. Not going there tonight.

I regarded the box's contents.

The synthetic rope.

I fingered its rough yet satin texture and recalled the first time I'd bound Erin's wrists to her headboard—the first time I sank my teeth into her sweet flesh and drank her intoxicating blood.

The rope had served a valuable purpose. It had kept her from escaping while I fed from her the first time. So much had occurred in the short time since then.

She was willing to obey me in the bedroom. That much she'd made clear. But would she obey me if I told her to flee and never return?

Because, if I ever thought I might cause her harm, that was what I would command her to do.

I retrieved a cardboard box from the plastic bin.

Leather bindings I hadn't opened yet. I removed the tape securing the box, opened it, and pulled out the bindings. They'd been treated with silicone to ease the roughness, to not mark the wearer.

I couldn't help looking down at my own wrists, the faded marks upon them.

*Her* bindings had not been treated. They had chafed, made me bleed, caused markings...until the day when my skin toughened as all skin does eventually, like when you finally wear in that new pair of shoes.

No more blisters. No more broken skin.

Only a broken man.

*She didn't break you, son.*

My father's words. No, he wasn't here. The words were only a recollection, a memory I needed at this moment. Had he ever said the actual words? Didn't matter. He'd made them clear, and he'd say them if he were here. He'd help me chase away the darkness, say hello to the light.

*Thanks, Dad. I love you.*

Why had I purchased leather bindings? Yes, they were more secure and probably better suited to what I had planned, but I could never use them on Erin. Just looking at them, touching them, was a horrible reminder of *her*.

I quickly returned them to the box and tossed them in the wastebasket.

The next thing I pulled out of the container was a silk blindfold. It was deep red, the color of Erin's blood.

My fangs sharpened.

Erin's blood. The substance that made me whole. *Kept* me whole. Chased the demons away.

Could Erin's blood chase away the darkness that was determined to plague me? That wanted to break me?

It would help. Its essence gave me strength and nourishment.

But it could not chase the darkness away.

Only *I* could do that.

*You're strong enough, son. Remember that.*

My father.

*I'm counting on your strength, Dante. Your strength is what I need, what is required for you to become all that you're meant to be.*

No! Not *her* again.

Not now.

I closed my eyes, concentrating, trying to bring all the elusive power I held to the surface.

My skin tingled, my teeth hungered to break flesh. "Get out!" I yelled. "Get the fuck out!"

And...nothing.

*She* was gone. At least for now.

And I was hungry. Hungry and horny and ready to take what was mine.

With force.

Four pieces of rope. I'd bind Erin's hands *and* her feet this time. She'd be splayed open, ready for me to do what I wanted.

The silk blindfold. Perhaps I'd take away her vision, keep her at my mercy. Take away her sense of sight so she didn't know what was coming.

Two more toys.

A paddle, leather on one side, faux fur on the other. I could start with the fur and work her up to the leather.

And a riding crop, also of leather. Not necessarily for spanking but for teasing. Unless she got feisty. Then it would come down on her flesh with a whiplike ferocity.

The remaining toys—a butt plug with a large jewel on the end and a pair of fur-lined handcuffs—would wait.

All were new to me, save for the rope.

I growled, my groin tightening as I regarded them displayed on the carpet.

I would prove something to myself with the help of these instruments.

I would prove that *I* was in control of my actions. No one else. Only me.

I could stop when I wanted to, or when Erin wanted me to.

I would be forcible as long as it was pleasurable for the two of us, but if it was no longer pleasurable, I *would* be able to cease my actions.

Control.

Everything came down to control.

A soft hiss escaped my throat. Then a snarl.

I was ready.

Ready to exercise control over my woman.

Ready to exercise control over my*self*.

## FOUR

# *Erin*

"**E**rin."

Dante's voice was commanding—low, erotic, and commanding.

"Erin."

I opened my eyes. "Are you all right? I heard you yell..."

He didn't answer. He stood above me, his dark eyes blazing, demanding, almost menacing.

My nipples hardened.

He was magnificent.

No...he was *majestic*.

If the vampires had a king, Dante Gabriel would wear the golden crown.

"You're mine, Erin Hamilton. Mine to do with what I want."

More moisture pooled between my legs. I opened my mouth, but he gestured for me not to speak.

"No words," he said. "Only speak if I give you permission."

King of the vampires, indeed. I would gladly make him my king. Right now. I'd drop to my knees if he commanded it.

"You're so beautiful, Erin. So flushed, your blood so close to the surface of your milky skin. I love it when you're naked. My only regret is that I can't tear your clothes off again with my teeth."

I let out a soft moan and moved my fingers toward my nipples, their ache for touch nearly blinding me.

"No."

I stopped my hand on my belly.

"Only *I* will touch you today, Erin."

This time a groan left my throat. The throbbing in my pussy had become unbearable. My eyes shot wide when Dante whipped out the piece of rope.

I had seen these ropes before. I grasped two rungs of the headboard.

A part of me—a very big part of me—hoped for his punishment. He had bound my wrists to the rungs of my headboard before.

He regarded me sternly, the fiery amber around his irises blistering me. But he said nothing and only secured my wrists to the headboard.

A veil of arousing warmth surrounded me. I closed my eyes, embracing it, embracing the hot arousal between my legs, the warm fluid clinging to my thighs.

"Open your eyes, Erin. Open your eyes and watch me. Watch everything I do to you." Dante removed his clothes quickly, his cock springing forward in all its majestic beauty.

He wrapped his fist around it, squeezing it and letting out a groan. "I'm hard as a fucking rock for you, Erin. Do you want this big hard cock? Do you want it inside that sweet, tight pussy?"

I bit my lower lip and squirmed. Should I speak? He'd asked me a direct question, so I decided to go for it. "Dante, I want everything you can give me."

"You will have it. You will have it all." He picked up two more pieces of rope.

Although my footboard didn't have rungs, he quickly bound the rope around my ankles, and then stretched it, securing it with a little bit of slack to each side of the foot of the bed.

I was bound—completely immobile, completely at his mercy.

He licked his lips lasciviously and then bared his fangs with a low growl. Had his cock grown even larger? As I stared, it seemed to be made of flesh-colored marble.

He turned again once more and then held up a piece of red fabric. Goose bumps erupted on my flesh. He would either blindfold me with it or gag me. I didn't know which, and the suspense was killing me.

As he came forward, he held it in front of me. "Maybe for later." He laid it next to me on the bed. "Right now, I want you to watch what I'm doing to you. I want to see every reaction in those beautiful green eyes, Erin."

I nodded timidly.

"I'm going to do things no one has ever done to you, my love. I'm going to do things I've never done to anyone." He stroked his cock once more. "And when I'm done, when you are completely on edge, I'm going to force this hard cock inside your cunt as violently as I can."

I shivered, an erotic mixture of warmth and coldness consuming me. My nipples strained forward, aching for the slightest touch. I pulled up the bindings on my wrist, wanting so badly to touch those nipples, to give them the relief they needed.

To no avail.

I was completely at Dante's mercy.

He could do anything to me, and I had no defense. No escape.

He turned once more, coming up with what looked like a leather riding crop.

He brought it toward me, stroking it down the apple of my cheek, over my lips, and then over my chin. From my chin onto my chest until he stopped between my breasts. He guided the tip of the crop up over the swells and then traced around my areolas.

My skin wrinkled further, pushing my nipples out into two hard currants.

"Please, Dante."

He swatted my nipple lightly. "Who said you could talk?"

If talking got me another swat on my nipple, I was going to talk all night. The light tap had my two tight knobs straining.

"Again," I said softly.

The tip of the riding crop came down on my abdomen this time.

Warmth scattered through me, but what I'd been longing for was another slap to my nipple.

I opened my mouth again, but he touched the crop to my lips. "I think you're enjoying your punishment a little too much, Erin." He moved the tip downward and traced my areola once more. "I'll give you everything you want—everything we both want—in my own good time."

In his good time? His cock was rock hard. This must be killing him. He wanted to fuck me. I could see it in his eyes. I could see it between his legs.

God, my nipples. They were so hard.

Dante's lips were full, his fangs completely descended. What I wouldn't give for him to take my nipple between those lips, nick it with his teeth, draw some blood, and truly feed from me.

But the tip of the crop continued its path downward over my belly, over my vulva, until he tickled my clit ever so lightly.

My back arched as I strained forward, trying for more—more of the emotion, more of the feeling I desired. My lips parted, and I let out a soft moan.

"Easy, baby. No talking, or I'll stop."

I gritted my teeth. He was out to drive me slowly crazy. Slowly and beautifully crazy, and I was more than happy to go along for the ride.

The tip of the riding crop drew softly over my inner thighs, down my legs, and over the tops of my feet.

My pussy throbbed, aching to be licked, sucked, filled.

I pressed my lips together, lest pleading words tumble forth. My nipples were straining, reaching toward his elusive touch. My entire body tingled with shivers. I turned my head toward my pillow, closing my eyes.

"Keep those eyes open, Erin." He swatted my abdomen with the crop. "Open. And on me. On what I'm doing to you."

I obeyed, opening my eyes and meeting his hot gaze. His dark masculine beauty mesmerized me. I could look at Dante Gabriel forever and never grow tired of his magnificence. His hair was wild around his shoulders, his eyes on fire. His lips full and firm, his cheeks and chin laced with dark stubble.

And his body. Oh, God, his body...

His fair shoulders so broad and strong, his chest hard and

magnificent with the perfect amount of black hair scattered over the muscle. His abs a perfect six-pack, and then his hips, his bush of black hair, the perfect nest for that amazing cock.

Though my gaze didn't want to leave that source of my pleasure, I scanned downward, over his muscular thighs and calves, down to his feet that were also perfect.

Dante.

God, Dante.

I yearned to kiss him all over, trail my lips over every part of him. I wanted to make him suffer, kiss him everywhere but avoid his cock. Oh, it would be torturous for me, but even more torturous for him, like the way he was torturing me now.

His gaze was hot. Scorching. Melting even. Just his eyes were turning me into a puddle of goo, making my pussy pulse all the more.

*Swat!*

The crop came down over the top of my breasts.

"So beautiful," he breathed. "Brings the blood to the surface even more." He closed his eyes and inhaled. "Your musk, your blood, all of it. You drive me insane, Erin."

Me? I was doing nothing. Lying there. He was the one driving *me* insane. I nearly said the words but managed to keep my mouth clamped shut.

When he opened his eyes, a new bloodthirstiness glowed within them. "Get ready, Erin. We're going for a new ride."

# FIVE

# DANTE

Her skin glowed with a sheen of sweat, making the pinkness from her blood all the more enticing.

I held the leather crop, my fingers curled around the handle. Black and sleek, it was an extension of me, of my arm, of my fingers. I felt what it felt as it landed across Erin's milky skin. Yes, now I understood why toys excited people so much. A toy added a new layer of texture, of pleasure.

Erin lay helpless before me. Helpless and beautiful, always so beautiful. Her hair was down, splayed across the white pillow like an ebony curtain, like a dark waterfall.

Her nipples, dark pink and turgid, were hard and peaked. I traced them again with the tip of the riding crop, amazed at the sensation. The texture of her skin zapped through the leather into my fingertips.

She bit her red lower lip, moaning softly. I'd told her not to speak, but now I wanted more than anything to hear her sweet voice, hear her beg.

"Speak now, baby. Tell me what you want."

Her reply was another soft moan. "Everything."

My lips curved into a semi-smile. "Everything?"

"Whatever you want to do to me, Dante. All of it. All. Of. It."

I brought the crop down harder on her nipple. "Be specific, Erin. Tell me exactly what you want me to do to you."

"That was good. What you just did."

"What did I just do?"

"You slapped my nipple." She arched her back. "God, it felt so good. Again, Dante. Please."

*Slap!*

I brought the leather crop down on her other nipple.

She arched once more, trying to writhe but failing under the restraints.

So beautiful. God, she made me ache inside. Ache that anyone could be so perfectly formed, so beautifully sculpted. Could move me physically and emotionally and spiritually the way she did.

I brought down the crop once more across her perfect breasts, and blood rushed to the surface of her skin. I inhaled. Perfect fragrance of Erin.

I wouldn't be able to hold out much longer without taking more of her blood. But for now, I wanted to tease her, make her want me all the more before I forced my hard cock into her.

*Slap!* Down onto her rounded belly.

*Slap!* Onto her perfectly shaved vulva.

*Slap!* Onto her hard clit.

Her lush fragrance wafted toward me, wrapping around me like a warm hug. And the notes, the soft jazzy musical notes...

*Slap!* Onto one thigh.

*Slap!* Onto the other.

Yes, the blood rose once more to her creamy skin, once more to make her scent that much more luscious, full of blackberries, dark chocolate, rich coffee.

I turned and eyed the paddle sitting on top of her dresser. It would wait for another time.

I could hold out no longer. I threw the riding crop to the floor and climbed atop Erin. For a moment, I gazed at her, baring my teeth and growling.

She gasped, but her eyes darkened to a light emerald.

"Do it," she said through clenched teeth. "Do it hard. Do it violently. Take what you want. What we both want."

I thrust into her heat.

"Mine!" I shouted.

Thrust again, this time harder.

And harder again.

"Dante!" she screamed.

Her walls clamped around me, perfectly formed to me as I thrust and I thrust and I thrust.

With each thrust, a grunt left her throat.

*Mine. Mine. Mine.*

*Mine for all time.*

My fangs lengthened, the nerves within them tingling, searching. In a flash, I turned Erin's head harshly and sank my teeth into her milky neck.

And I drank.

I drank of her blood, her soul, her very essence, as she clamped around me in orgasm.

As the red nectar streamed over my tongue and down my throat, I plunged once more into her warm pussy, releasing.

As I flowed into her, she flowed into me.

Every part of me.

Just what I needed to drive away the darkness.

✣

*"Fight!" Her voice again. "Fight to the death!"*

*In a flash, the other vampire had overpowered me and pinned me to the ground.*

Thud. Thud. Thud.

*Fist to my cheek. My chin. My forehead.*

*My nose.*

*God, my nose.*

*Blood spurted out of it as the crushing of cartilage forced a searing pain across my skull.*

Thud. *To my eye socket.*

Thud. *To my Adam's apple.*

*Breathe. Couldn't breathe.*

*Couldn't...*

*Couldn't...*

*Then nothing.*

*Nothing for what seemed like an eternity and then only an instant.*

*"Get up, you piece of shit! Get up and fight!"*

*Her?*

*No.*

*The words came from the vampire in the pit with me. He was shaking me, blood spurting from my nose and coating him in red droplets.*

*No. Hurt too much. Couldn't move. Couldn't.*

Let me die. Please let me die.

*My throat ached, and searing pain knifed through my nose*

*as it continued to bleed.*

*"Get up! Get up!"*

*Something unfurled inside me. Something angry. Something vengeful.*

*Something dark.*

*My teeth snapped downward, slicing through my gums with sharp pain.*

*The other vampire's eyes morphed into circles of fear. "What the fuck?"*

*I snarled, tossing him away from me like he was nothing more than a small child. He landed with a plunk on the dirty ground.*

*"Yes, that's it. Show him. Show him your strength. Show me your strength. Show me what you are meant to be. Let the rage take you. Let the rage consume you. Only then will you become what you are meant to be."*

# SIX

# *Erin*

I awoke, stretching. Dante slumbered fitfully beside me. I caressed his cheek, and he relaxed. I smiled to myself, loving that my touch gave him comfort.

I rose and walked into the bathroom. The tops of my breasts were pink from Dante's riding crop, and I smiled again. He'd driven me slowly crazy, and then when he took me forcibly while I was bound, I'd experienced rapture I'd never imagined. He'd released me before we fell asleep. Now, as I rubbed my wrists, slightly chafed from me pulling against the rope, trying to touch him, I understood more about this vampire I loved.

He liked control.

He *thrived* on control.

Most likely because he'd been denied control for that decade he'd been held captive.

But something told me his need for control stemmed from something bigger. Something more important and more profound.

*Promise me you'll leave if you ever think I'll harm you.*

He would never harm me. I knew that as well as I knew anything. Still, the fear existed in him—probably another reason control was so important to him.

I didn't know why. He'd had me bound and at his mercy, and he hadn't lost control. I hadn't been afraid. To the contrary, I'd been so turned on I thought I might explode.

I walked back into the bedroom. Dante was sleeping more peacefully now. I pulled on some panties and a tank and went downstairs. The two books on the coffee table drew my attention. The one on the left was the phony. I picked it up and put it away in my coat closet. Then I sat back down, and even though I'd already touched it earlier, I tentatively touched the other.

Nothing.

Yup. Whatever was going on with the book affected only Bill. Bea's shield was a success.

I gasped when Dante's father appeared. "Julian! Stop doing that. Shit." I covered myself. "I'm in my underwear here."

"I'm sorry." He turned his head. "Go get decent. Then I need to talk to you."

"Do you want me to wake Dante?"

"No. Let him sleep. He needs it. I've been working him hard with our glamouring exercises."

"All right." I hurried upstairs and hastily pulled on jeans.

When I got back, he was gone. "Julian?"

"I'm here. Just using my energy for other things. Give me a couple seconds."

I waited impatiently until he manifested.

"Sorry about that."

"No worries," I said. "What do you need?"

"I want to talk to you, Erin. About this Dr. Bonneville."

"Okay."

"If she's indeed a vampire, it's unlikely that Bill wouldn't know about her."

"Why is that? I thought you all existed in plain sight and couldn't smell each other."

"True. But Bill is an elder and a member of the council. They keep track of all the vampires still alive."

"Which means he knows about the ones stalking me."

"Yes, he does."

"Why hasn't he stopped them?"

"First, he might not know what they're up to. The council keeps track of vampires, but they don't spy on them. It's not their place. The council isn't a law enforcement entity. It's simply a group of vampire elders who keep and hand down our history and secrets."

"I'm sorry."

"For what?"

I felt foolish. "That didn't come out right. I meant that I'm sorry you'll never be an elder. Not just because you died before your time, but because you'd be an amazing elder, Julian. You'd be a positive influence on any council, with your wisdom and sense of justice."

"You flatter me. But don't be sorry. I'm absolutely fine with my fate. I am here for my son and my daughter. They are my priorities, and they *will* be elders. I will make sure of that."

I understood. He was going to find Emilia no matter what he had to do. And he was going to make sure Dante got through what had happened to him.

He continued. "I fear, though, that my brother may not be as fortunate."

I gasped. "I thought you said he's alive."

The ghost nodded. "He is."

"Then what makes you think—"

"Bill calls it 'the twin thing.' Brae and I have had a connection since we were kids." He shook his head. "He's alive, but time is running out. I feel it very strongly."

I bit my lip. "Maybe I should go wake Dante."

"No. Don't. He has enough on his plate right now. Trust me."

"But he'd want to help you."

"Please, Erin. I can't burden him with this. And I can't burden River. Braedon is his father. I'm sorry I have to burden you with it, but I fear I have no other choice."

"Why is that?"

"Finding Emilia, Lucy, and the others must be our first priority."

"But...?"

"But...my brother is running out of time. So my question to you, Erin, is—just how certain are you that this Dr. Bonneville is involved with the missing women?"

"I..." I sighed. "It's just a feeling, Julian, and believe me, as a rational person, I know how ridiculous that sounds."

"Tell me about her."

"She's brilliant, as far as doctors go, but she's not a nice person."

"Meaning?"

"She's nice to her patients, but she treats the rest of us like shit."

"Hmmm..."

"What is it?"

"Some vampires look down on humans."

"Why?"

"My family never has, but there are older families who consider vampires a superior species to humans, though if we were truly superior, humans wouldn't outnumber us a million to one. My late wife came from one of those lines, though she was very grounded and never looked down on humans. We call them vampire elitists."

"Do you recognize the name Bonneville? Or Le Sang?"

He shook his head. "I don't. But names can be changed."

"Easily enough," I said. "Plus there's the further enigma that both doctors, who apparently look enough alike to be twins save for hair color, don't seem to exist anywhere on paper."

"Which makes it all the more likely that your doctor is a vampire. She could easily glamour her way into any position."

"I'm sure she's an actual doctor," I said. "Like I said, she's brilliant in the ER. I've watched her perform some pretty miraculous feats."

"Vampires can't glamour up medical miracles, so at least we know she's qualified for the position she holds. That's a good thing. You said she's in Barbados now?"

"That's what she told me. A three-week vacation with her husband."

"Have you met her husband?"

I shook my head. "I didn't even know she was married. It surprised me, actually."

"Why?"

"Because she's such a mean person. I didn't think she could possibly be married. But there's always one glutton for punishment out there."

"Or she could be lying to you."

"True." I paused a few seconds. "She might be the one who

was feeding on me. If she's truly a vampire."

"Has Dante ever told you how rare female vampires are?"

"No."

"They are. For some reason, vampire pregnancies almost always produce a male. Plus, our females often don't survive childbirth. So if Dr. Bonneville is a vampire, she's one of only a few thousand left in existence. And if she's an elitist..."

"What?"

"Nothing. I'm just thinking out loud." His voice wavered a bit. "Tell me, Erin, because I'm a big believer in instinct. How strong is this feeling you have that she's involved in the disappearance of my daughter and the other women?"

Sadness hit my heart. Julian seemed alive in that moment—alive and distraught over the disappearance of his little girl, his daughter he loved so much, who was pregnant and alone. I wished I could give him more hope, something more to hold on to.

But I couldn't. My feeling came from the fact that she'd appeared in my dream and then morphed into Bea. And there was also the fact that no one besides Dante had fed on me since Dr. Bonneville had left for vacation.

Before I could answer, Julian spoke again. "Erin, I must find my brother. Time is of the essence now. If our priority is the women, and one of them is my daughter, we need to follow every lead. But you need to be sure. We don't have time to follow a false lead."

Talk about pressure. What could I say? I couldn't bear the thought of Julian following my "feeling," only to be led on a wild goose chase. If we followed my feeling and didn't find the women, and then time for Braedon ran out...

"You're asking me to be sure of a feeling, Julian."

"Yes, Erin, I am."

"I can't be. I'm not clairvoyant."

"I'm not asking you to be. I'm asking you to use your intuition. Do we find this Dr. Bonneville? Do we begin from scratch? Have your brother and River map out the clues?"

Go with my feeling? Or go with two experienced detectives?

Really, there was no choice. I'd never forgive myself if I led us to a dead end and we were too late for Dante's uncle.

"I'm not sure, Julian. I'm sorry. Let's forget Dr. Bonneville. For now, at least."

# SEVEN

# DANTE

"*I* give up!"

*The words I'd considered screaming since I'd been taken.*

*But I hadn't screamed them.*

*And now they were not coming from me.*

*They came from the man I'd thrown off me.*

*Red rage boiled inside me.*

Fight or die in the arena.

"Show him. Show me. Show the world what you're made of, Dante."

*A low growl emerged from my throat, and in a flash, I was back on my feet. My muscles flexed of their own accord, tearing the sleeves of the ragged shirt I wore.*

Fight or die.

Fight or die.

Fight or die.

*Many times I'd wished for death.*

*But never had I succumbed.*

*I would not succumb now.*

*I didn't know this person. This vampire. But if there could only be one victor...*

*It would not be him.*

❖

My eyes shot open.

Even now, I still felt the sharp pain of my broken nose. I'd never let anyone break it again.

*Fight or die in the arena.*

Had I killed?

No. I shook my head vehemently, trying to clear my head. I was not a killer.

*I am not a killer.*

Erin. Where was Erin?

Her place on the bed was still warm. She was here. She was fine.

I let out a breath I didn't realize I was holding. Then I got up abruptly, walked to the bathroom, turned on the faucet, and splashed some icy water on my face.

Then, in the mirror...

What I saw...

I curled my hand into a fist and punched the mirror, like I had that night at the restaurant when something was taunting me.

I regarded my reflection, in pieces like the shattered glass.

❖

My eyes shot open again.

I was still in bed, but I was far from relaxed. My hands

were curled into fists, my knuckles white.

A dream within a dream.

*And the darkness that was always with me. That was me.*

*Go back*, I begged myself. *Go back and remember what you did.*

*Fight or die in the arena.*

*Once bonded, never broken.*

"Get out of my head!" I pulled at two fistfuls of my hair.

Footsteps rushed up the stairs.

"Dante!" Erin rushed toward me. "What's wrong?"

Couldn't upset her. Couldn't put any of this on her. "Nothing, baby. Bad dream."

She sat down next to me and held me. "It's okay now. I'm here."

Yes. She was here. Everything would be fine as long as she was here.

As long as my darkness didn't drive her away.

As long as *I* didn't drive her away.

But I would. If I ever thought she was in harm's way, I'd drive her so far away I'd never find her.

It would kill me.

But better me than her.

Except...the blood bond.

Oh, God.

If what Bill had found out was true, neither of us could live without the other now.

So if the darkness came for Erin...

"Hey."

Her voice broke into my thoughts, soothing me.

"Your dad's here. You'd better put some clothes on."

I nodded as we both got off the bed, and I pulled on some

jeans and a T-shirt. Had to compose myself. Couldn't let Erin see the darkness.

*Drive it out, Dante. Drive it fucking out.*

*Easy, son.*

My father's voice.

But not his voice.

Only in my head.

It wasn't him. Only me, thinking of him. Letting him help me.

So different from when I heard *her* in my head. Here, with my father, I knew it wasn't him. I was letting him help me, using his fatherly love for me.

When *she* showed up in my head, it was all *her.*

*If I'm here in your head, it's because you want me here.*

Her words.

*Not true. Not true.*

*Not true not true not true.*

"Dante?"

I turned to Erin. She was so beautiful. So soft and feminine. So mine.

"I'm okay, baby."

"Are you sure? I've had my share of bad dreams lately. I know they can screw with your mind."

God, she had no idea. I touched her cheek, her skin so soft against my fingertips. "I'm fine. Why is my dad here?"

"Let's go downstairs. He can tell you himself." The slight crack in her voice sounded a little off.

"You all right?" I asked.

She nodded.

I wasn't buying it. "Tell me."

"It's nothing. Seriously."

Then my father appeared. "It's me," he said. "I'm afraid I gave Erin a heavy burden that I shouldn't have."

"Julian..."

"No, Erin. I was wrong, and I can't keep this from my son."

My teeth reacted, prickling my gums. "Keep what from me?"

"It's your uncle," he said. "He doesn't have a lot of time left. I didn't want to burden you with it, but I told Erin. I needed to know how certain she was about Dr. Bonneville being involved in the disappearances. We can't afford to waste time, Dante."

Erin smoothed her palm over my forearm.

*Don't blame your father* were the words she didn't say. *Couldn't* say.

"I'm a ghost, Dante, but I still have the feelings I had as a living being. If I didn't, I wouldn't be here protecting you. I still feel my brother. We came from the same fertilized egg. That's a bond that will never be broken. He's in trouble, son. He's weakening."

"But—"

My father held up his hand. "Your sister is the priority. She and the others. Trust me. I never wavered from that. But we need to find them quickly so we can refocus on Braedon. If we want him to live."

"We need to confer with River and Jay," Erin said.

"Dad," I said. "You mentioned you went through Em's place after she disappeared. Do you still have your vampire senses? Acute vision?"

"I do, but I didn't see anything out of the ordinary."

"Still," I said. "River and Jay could dust for fingerprints."

"Yes," Erin agreed. "They know what to look for. That's where we should start."

"Except how do we get in?" my father asked. "The four of you are still flesh and blood."

"We get someone to pick the lock," Erin said. "Except it's a crime scene. It's probably taped off."

"Not a problem," my father said. "I can take care of anyone who's hanging around. All you need to do is get in. Did the cops find any evidence at the hospital after the other disappearances? After Lucy's disappearance?"

"Not that Jay or River ever mentioned," I said.

"It's unlikely that fingerprints would be left in a hospital," Erin said. "Things are always being wiped down, and medical personnel almost always wear gloves. Plus, there's the time lapse. These patients seemed to just disappear and no one remembers anything. The perpetrator could have easily wiped everything down himself." She cleared her throat. "Or herself."

"Erin," my father said. "You don't sound like you're ready to give up on your suspicion about Dr. Bonneville."

She nodded. "You're right. I'm not. But let's see what Jay and River can find at Emilia's place first. We can search Lucy's place too, though she disappeared from the hospital."

"Good enough," Julian said. "Now we just need to hope either Jay or River know how to pick a lock. Either that or we'll have to glamour a locksmith."

"We won't have to," I said, an image forming clearly in my mind. "I can do it."

❖

*The door was still locked.*

*All this time, I'd thought it was unlocked, that* she*'d left it unlocked so I could get out.*

*No. She'd left it locked.*
*But she'd left tools for me to pick the lock.*
*And pick the lock I had.*
*Insert. Twist. Turn up.*
*And I was free.*
*Unchained.*

# EIGHT

# *Erin*

I widened my eyes. "You can?"

He nodded.

"Dante, how..."

"I'm not sure. But I can. Someone taught me. Sometime."

"Who?"

"I'd tell you if I knew."

"When, son?" Julian asked.

"You know when."

"While you were there." He cleared his throat, as much as a ghost could clear his throat. "I see. Do you know *why*?"

"I have no idea. I had no idea I could do it until just now. But I can. I've done it before."

"If someone taught you how to pick locks, that person must have had a reason," I said.

"I'm sure there was a reason," Dante agreed. "I just don't know what it is. But I can help now. I can get into Em's place."

"What kind of locks can you pick?" Julian asked.

Dante paused a moment. "Any kind. Deadbolts. Padlocks. Combination locks. I can do it all."

"Em has a deadbolt," Julian said. "What do you need?"

He wrinkled his forehead. "One of those little screwdrivers used to fix eyeglasses. Or a bobby pin. Anything thin that I can insert into the mechanism to force tension."

"I've got you covered." I went upstairs, scanned my junk drawer in the bathroom, and found two stray bobby pins. I went back down and handed them to Dante.

"Good enough," Julian said. "Let's call River and Jay and have them meet us at Em's."

⚜

Dante's actions fascinated me. An odd mixture of pride and dread coiled in me. He didn't speak. He just bent one of the bobby pins into a right angle and inserted it into the keyhole. He inserted the other one above the first and moved it slightly. Within a minute, he unlocked the door.

River wiped the lock with a soft white cloth and then handed all of us—save Julian, of course—rubber gloves. "We don't want fingerprints at the crime scene."

He had already removed the crime scene tape. It was nighttime, so no one was there, but Julian stood outside just in case to glamour anyone who might come along.

The four of us entered Emilia's apartment. It was small, just a living area, a small kitchen, a bathroom, and one bedroom. Not much ground to cover.

"How do you dust for fingerprints?" I asked Jay.

"We're not here to do that, Sis," he said.

"Why not? I thought that was the purpose of breaking and entering here."

"If we see anything out of the ordinary, we'll take it to a lab where they'll check for fingerprints," my brother said. "But it probably won't do us any good."

"Why the heck not?"

"Finding fingerprints is a lot harder than detective shows make it look," River said. "Most of the prints here will belong to Em, so we'd need a set of elimination prints to rule her out. She's never been arrested, so her prints aren't on file anywhere. Even if we had them for comparison, finding a print other than hers here would be like finding a needle in a haystack."

"Oh." Talk about feeling stupid.

"Plus," Jay added, "no prints were found when the others were removed from the hospital. If the same perps are involved, they most likely wouldn't have left prints here."

"It was a legitimate question, love," Dante said. "You just asked it before I did."

"We're looking for clues other than prints, Sis," Jay said. "And I bet we find some now that we know what we're dealing with."

"Exactly what do we know?" I asked.

"We know that Em was taken by force," River said. "She can't be glamoured, so she was either taken out of here at gunpoint or she was drugged and removed. Whichever way, unless she was drugged while she was asleep—which is unlikely, given her acute hearing—we might find some evidence of a struggle, unless whoever took her cleared it away."

"Dad didn't see anything," Dante said, "other than that her bed was unmade. But Em never made her bed a day in her life."

"Uncle Jules didn't know what to look for. We do."

"What are we looking for, then?" I asked.

"Anything out of the ordinary," Jay said. "River's a great

detective and Dante's her brother. They'll know if they see something unusual. You and I are here just to get a feel for who she was. Shit. I mean *is*."

Luckily, neither Dante nor River noticed Jay's blunder. They were heading toward the bedroom already. A harsh reality whirled into my mind.

Emilia could be dead.

Lucy could be dead.

The others could all be dead.

A hard lump lodged in my throat.

"Easy, Sis," Jay said. "We'll figure this out."

"But they could be—"

"I know. But let's believe that they aren't. And if we find that they are, let's figure out who did it and why and make sure they never, *ever* do it to anyone again."

I gulped back the sobs that were threatening to pour out of me and nodded.

"You and I can take this room and the kitchen. Let Riv and Dante deal with the bedroom and bathroom."

I nodded again, feeling sick.

Really sick.

# NINE

# DANTE

River had a system. He eyed everything with scrutiny, looking for things I couldn't even imagine. He pulled the stray hairs from Em's hairbrush and put them in a plastic Ziploc. "DNA," he said.

"Why do we need Em's DNA?"

"In case we find something that's not from her, to contrast."

"How will we know whose DNA it is?"

"We won't, but at least we'll have a clue. Next step will be to find out whose DNA it is."

"That sounds more than complicated."

"It is. You didn't think being a detective was easy, did you?"

"Didn't the cops who checked this out already do all of this?"

"Yeah. But I want to do our own investigation. The department isn't invested like we are." He fingered all the items on the bathroom counter—toothpaste, a toothbrush, a hair clip, a bottle of mouthwash—putting them back as he found them. Then he opened the cabinet above the sink. "Prenatal vitamins,

Tylenol, the usual." He closed it. "Nothing out of the ordinary. Let's check the wastebasket."

"You want to go through my sister's trash?"

"Absolutely." He picked up the small trash can between the sink and the toilet. "That's why we're wearing gloves. Well, one of the reasons." He pulled out a wad of tissue and set it on the counter.

"She blew her nose. Interesting," I said sarcastically.

"Nothing out of the ordinary." River picked up another tissue, examining it closely. "No blood."

"Why would there be blood on a tissue?"

"She might have had a nosebleed. You never know."

"Why does that even matter?"

"Everything matters, cuz. Something that seems completely innocuous can end up being a huge clue." He lifted his brow and held up a white stick. "Something like this."

"What's that?"

"It's a home pregnancy test," he said. "And it's recent. Now why would Em use a home pregnancy test? The hospital confirmed she was pregnant when she went to the ER."

"Maybe she wanted to be sure."

"But that was weeks ago. This test is recent."

"How can you tell?"

"First of all, it hasn't turned yellowish. But there's something else."

"What?"

"Emilia probably emptied her trash more than once since she found out she was pregnant."

"Maybe she just wanted to make sure she hadn't miscarried or something?"

"Dante, a woman will know if she miscarried. There's lots

of blood and sometimes pain."

"How am I supposed to know that?"

"You would, if you'd been— Shit. Sorry."

My teeth ached to descend, but I buried my anger as best I could and said nothing. This was about Emilia, not me.

River pawed through the trash. "No box for the test. If Em had taken the test herself, most likely the box and wrapper would be in here. But it's just the stick, the part you pee on."

"Someone wanted to make sure she was pregnant," I said.

"Exactly. Now who, other than her family, would be interested in Em's pregnancy?"

"The father?"

"Shh," River warned.

"They don't know he's the father," I whispered.

"Right. And he doesn't know either. So *not* the father. Who else?"

"I don't know."

"I do. Vampires."

"Vampires other than us?"

"Sure. Vampire women are rare. Vampire pregnancy is even more so. Here we have a young vampire woman who's pregnant, and there's no father in the picture. She lives alone. An easy mark."

"So," I extrapolated, "if Em's disappearance is related to the others at the hospital, that makes it even more likely that vampires are involved."

"Exactly," River said. "Give the man a Milk Dud."

"What?"

"Never mind. Something stupid my sarge used to say. Anyway, there's something else good about this."

"What?" I asked again.

"If whoever took Em is interested in her pregnancy, she's most likely alive."

I nodded, smiling slightly. My sister was alive. Thank God. "But the others?"

River sighed. "I don't know. I just don't know, cuz." He bagged the pregnancy test. "We can check this for prints, though it's a long shot. I'll take Em's hairbrush to rule her out. But whoever handled the test, if it wasn't Em herself, probably used gloves if they have any sense."

"Sense? These are criminals."

"Not all criminals are stupid, Dante. So far, whoever is responsible for these disappearances has eluded us, so they're definitely not stupid." He held up the zipped bag holding the white stick. "But if my intuition is correct, whoever took Em made a serious mistake by leaving this here." He pawed through the rest of the wastebasket. "There's only a few days' worth of trash here. More evidence that this pregnancy test is new."

"Good. Are we done now?"

"Are you kidding? We haven't checked the bedroom yet."

Pawing through my sister's bedroom was only slightly less uncomfortable than pawing through her bathroom. As my father had said, her bed was unmade. River examined it carefully, pulling back the covers and then leaving them exactly as they were.

"How are you so meticulous?" I asked.

"I have to be. If the department took photos, this needs to stay as accurate as possible. No one can know we were here."

"I get that. I mean, how are you able to replace it so exactly?"

"I just remember where it was to begin with." He sighed. "No evidence of a struggle that I can see."

"Okay." Must be a detective thing.

I examined the contents of her dresser. Seeing my sister's underwear was more than a little disturbing. Thank God for the rubber gloves.

*You're on the right track. Keep looking.*

Dad?

Then a laugh. An evil laugh.

No. It was *her. She* was here, inside my head.

*Fuck you!* I said silently. *Not now!*

I managed to get *her* out, but I didn't know for how long. My fangs prickled, itching to descend. But I had to stay in my right mind, not allow the darkness to take hold.

Emilia needed me.

*Look to your left.*

Again not my father.

*Get the fuck out!*

Still, I couldn't help myself. I glanced to the left without moving my head. A piece of glass shone on the floor, nearly hidden in a dark corner.

I picked it up.

"Hey, Riv. Check this out." I held up the tiny glass bottle. "Vodka. It's empty."

"Good find." He grabbed it and bagged it. "Em's pregnant. She wouldn't be drinking."

"This could be from a while ago. We all know Em isn't the world's best housekeeper."

"True enough, but it's worth looking into further. We can see if there are any prints."

Why would *she* want me to find a tiny liquor bottle?

Unless it hadn't been *her* at all.

Perhaps it had been...

I shook my head to clear it. No. The darkness was not its own entity. It was part of me, and I *could* control it.

I threaded my fingers through my hair, sighing. Now what? A liquor bottle? A pregnancy test? What were we missing?

*Seek and ye shall find.*

*Yeah, yeah, yeah...*

The pregnancy test stick was a legitimate clue. What if more clues existed? Then, damn it, I would find them. My little sister's well-being depended on it. On *me*. I dropped down onto my hands and knees. The darkness in the room didn't affect my vision, and when I didn't see anything right away, I raked my fingers through the nap of the carpet. Nestled in the yarns of the carpeting was a tiny earring stud. So tiny it was nearly invisible. Probably belonged to Emilia. Not that I memorized every earing she every wore, but this looked like her style—understated.

I picked it up and then threaded my fingers through the carpet again. Had a jewelry box been knocked over? Not that I could see.

My fingers stopped on another object, a small metal pin deep in the carpet, so deep that a great weight must have ground it in. Like a man's foot, maybe. I pulled it out.

Etched in the gold was a symbol, something familiar yet different.

I'd seen this before.

⚜

*The bearded one was their leader. Erin was right. His eyes were dark blue, not brown.*

*And he wore a gold pin on the lapel of his black leather jacket.*

*A symbol I couldn't see, no matter how hard I squinted.*

*A symbol that I knew—and I didn't know how I knew—was important.*

❖

"River," I said.

"Yeah?"

"Come look at this."

He put down the book he was examining and knelt down next to me on the carpet in the corner of Em's bedroom. "What is it?"

"It's a lapel pin. I've seen it before."

River took it from me and examined it. "When?"

"In a dream. In Erin's dream, actually."

"What the hell are you talking about, man?"

I quickly explained how my father had given Erin a small glamour to remember the dream, and somehow, I'd been able to see the dream as well.

"I've never heard of anything like that," he said.

"Neither have I. Dad and I thought maybe it was part of the blood bond."

"Or...part of whatever's making you able to do some pretty extraordinary things." He eyed the small pin once more. "What do you make of this?"

And then it hit me. The symbol. Where I'd seen it the first time.

*Fight or die in the arena.*

Then on the bearded vamp—Decker—in Erin's dream.

I grabbed it back from River and looked at it closely, trying to will myself to interpret the tiny etching.

It was a fleur-de-lis—a typical symbol found in New Orleans, originally a symbol of the old French monarchy. This symbol was different, though. The two outside petals were oddly shaped. They came down into points.

They were fangs.

# TEN

# *Erin*

"I feel like we're beating a dead horse," I said to Jay.

Dante and River were still in the bedroom. Meanwhile, Jay and I had scoured the kitchen and living room twice, finding nothing.

"Hopefully they're having better luck," Jay said. "Let's go see."

I nodded, and we walked into Emilia's bedroom.

Dante and River were sitting on the floor examining something.

"Hey," Jay said. "I hope you guys have had better luck than we have. The kitchen and living room are clean."

"We found a few interesting things," River said, handing something to Jay. "Have you ever seen this before?"

Jay regarded a small gold piece of jewelry. "A fleur-de-lis. Though I've never seen one with sharp points like that before."

River bared his fangs. "Look familiar?"

"Fuck, man. Uncanny. Those are vampire teeth."

"Yup," River agreed.

"May I see it?" I asked.

Jay handed the small pin to me.

⚜

*A chill swept the back of my neck.*

*"I'm sorry, Erin."*

*Another man entered the nurses' computer station. Tall and burly. A leather jacket. Dark hair and beard.*

*And fangs.*

*I gasped, my heart hurtling in my chest. "Wh-Who are you?"*

*The vampire closed his eyes and inhaled. "Finally, we will taste you."*

*I eased backward until the back of my legs hit the computer table.*

*Nowhere to go. The vampire was between me and the door.*

*"Abe...please..."*

*"I'm sorry, Erin." His eyes were shadowed, glazed over.*

*"Are you glamoured?" I whispered.*

*"I'm sorry, Erin."*

*The vampire took one step forward slowly and then another, inhaling deeply again.*

*"I'm hungry." Another breath in. "Really fucking hungry."*

*"Really fucking hungry," another voice echoed.*

*A second vampire had entered.*

*Then another behind him.*

*And another.*

*"I'm sorry, Erin."*

*"Abe!" I screamed, furiously glancing around. "Dante!*

*Help me! Dante! Dante!"*

*"He's not coming for you," one of them said, his eyes dark and full of fury. "No one is coming for you."*

*"You belong to us now," said another.*

*"Us," they all echoed.*

*"I'm sorry, Erin." Abe moved away slowly, his lanky body shifting awkwardly, like an automaton.*

*"Help!" I cried with desperation. "Help me. Please!"*

*But no one was here. The ER was desolate. Where was everyone? Anyone?*

*Four vampires, their faces pale and their eyes smoking, stalked toward me slowly, their canines stark white.*

*Fangs. So many fangs. So many fangs that wanted to bite into my flesh. Suck my blood.*

*"I'm sorry, Erin."*

*"She's pretty, too," one said. "We can take more than her blood. Have fun with her hot body while we drain her."*

*I screamed once more, slinking against my computer table. Nothing I could do. Nowhere to run. They formed a wall between the door and me. I felt around for the knob to the drawer under my station and pulled it open slightly.*

*A few pens and a package of chocolate cupcakes. The pens could do a little damage, but I couldn't take on four of them.*

*The bearded one lunged toward me, his fangs dripping with saliva.*

*I closed my eyes and screamed once more.*

I'm sorry, Erin. I'm sorry, Erin. I'm sorry, Erin.

⚜

"Baby?"

*I'm sorry, Erin. I'm sorry, Erin. I'm sorry, Erin.*

"Baby?" A warming touch coursed through me.

"Are you okay?"

I opened my eyes.

"I... Something happened. This pin made me remember something. That dream I had about the vampires coming for me at the hospital."

"Have you seen this pin before?" Jay asked.

"I have," I said. "In a dream. One of the vampires was wearing it."

"Decker," Dante said. "The bearded one."

"How..." I held out the pin to him.

"I don't know. I got into your dream when my dad glamoured you into remembering it. I saw this pin on his lapel. At the time, I couldn't make out the symbol, but once I saw this, I knew it was the one."

"Crazy," Jay said. "What do you suppose it means?"

"A fleur-de-lis was a classic symbol of French royalty," Dante said.

"But those symbols didn't have fangs," I said.

"No," River said. "It's also a classic symbol in New Orleans. And history tells us that it has a jaded past. It was used to mark slaves."

I clamped my hand over my mouth, nearly dropping the small pin.

"Despite its troubled history," River continued, "it's still an emblem of our city. It's on our football helmets, for heaven's sake. Most people see it as a symbol of unity."

"But what if..." My mind raced.

"What if...what?" Jay asked.

"I don't know. Who would design a fleur-de-lis with fangs?

I mean, I guess a vampire would."

Dante cleared his throat. "A vampire, yes," he said slowly. "A vampire who considers herself royalty. A vampire who enslaves others, holds them captive."

# ELEVEN

# DANTE

Three figures surrounded me, moving in slow motion.

"DDDDaaannnnntttteee?"

Erin's voice. I think it was Erin's voice.

"CCCCCuuuuuzzzz?"

River.

River was here.

But I was not.

I was somewhere else, looking down upon Erin, River, and Jay.

Erin still held the gold pin.

The pin with the symbol of *her*.

How had I not remembered?

That symbol had been everywhere while I was held captive.

Everywhere except on me.

Her goons wore it.

The vampires I fought in the arena wore it.

And now...Decker wore it. In the dream. Had he worn it

when I was fighting him in the alley behind Joseph's magick shop? I hadn't noticed. Then again, I'd been wound up something fierce.

He—Decker—was working for *her*.

*She* had my sister.

*She* was interested in my sister's baby.

*She*

*She*

*She*

*All those questions you seek answers to? You already know, Dante. You already know.*

*Why?* I pleaded silently. *Why would you lead me to this clue?*

And it came to me as quick as a fox.

*She* wanted me to find her. *She* was luring me back to her.

*She*

*She*

*She*

The darkness—the darkness I'd felt first in Erin's apartment, the darkness I now knew was part of me. It descended over Emilia's bedroom like a black veil.

My gums prickled as my fangs descended.

"DDDDaaannnnttttteee?"

"DDDDaaannnnttttteee?"

"DDDDaaannnnttttteee?"

And then a soothing touch, the fragrance that was part of me.

Erin stood before me, her green eyes wide and frightened. "Dante?"

Warmth surged through me. Erin's blood gave her warmth, and she infused that warmth into me with her very touch.

"Dante?" she said again.

I nodded. Couldn't seem to form words.

"Does that mean you're okay?"

I nodded again and tried to clear the frog out of my throat, the fog out of my brain.

"You've seen the symbol before, cuz?"

Once more, I nodded. "Yes. I'm almost sure I have. Over and over again. When I was...gone."

"So you know the meaning of the symbol?"

"No one ever told me, but I'm sure it's a vampire-created symbol. It makes perfect sense."

"I have to agree," River said. "And if that's true, whoever held you captive is also involved with the disappearing women."

"Or wants us to believe they are," Jay added.

"Good point, partner."

"How did you find the pin, Dante?" Erin asked.

*Someone told me to look to the left.*

I couldn't say that. Just couldn't. Couldn't let them know that she still had hold of me.

"I found an empty bottle in the corner, and then I found an earring lodged in the carpet. I felt around in the carpet to see if anything else was there, and that's when I found the pin."

"Amazing," Erin said. "We could have easily missed it."

"Seems like it might have been planted," River said.

"Yeah," Jay said, "or it fell off a collar and got ground into the carpet when someone stepped on it."

"Just as plausible," River agreed.

"What else did you find?" Jay asked.

"This." River held up the bag holding the pregnancy test stick.

"What? Wait. That can't be." Erin wrinkled her forehead.

"I know," River said. "Yet here it is."

"May I see it?"

River handed it to her.

"Definitely a test. Pretty new too, and positive."

"No surprise there," River said.

"Wait." Jay whipped his hands to his hips. "Your sister is *pregnant*?"

# TWELVE

# *Erin*

Dante and River exchanged a glance I couldn't read.

"Yeah."

"Who's the father?"

"I don't know," I said. "Why do you care?"

"Just wondering," Jay said. "Her name's Emilia?"

"Shit," River said.

"Is there a photo of her around here?" Jay started walking around the bedroom. "Dark hair? Blue eyes, by any chance?"

"Fuck," River said.

"Partner," Jay said, "is there something you know that I *don't*?"

Dante pulled out his wallet. "Here's a photo, Jay. You already know her."

Jay grabbed the wallet from Dante. "Shit the fucking bed."

"You're lucky I'm not pulverizing you into little bits," Dante said to my brother. "If not for Erin, I would have beat the shit out of you long ago."

"Dante"—I grabbed his arm—"what in the world are you talking about?"

He sighed. "It's Emilia's story to tell."

"I don't care. You better start talking"—I balled my hands into fists, fighting to keep from using them—"or I will walk out of here and you'll never see me again!"

He rubbed his temple. "I wanted to tell you. I wanted to tell both of you, but it's her story."

"Do I have to ask again?" I stood with my hands on my hips.

"Your brother had sex with my sister. Once. And got her pregnant."

I turned to my brother. He was staring at the photo in Dante's wallet.

"You remember her now, huh?" Dante said angrily.

"She's beautiful. Of course I remember her. But it was a... onetime thing. I had no idea..." He shook his head.

Dante's fair face reddened, more than I'd ever seen it.

*Oh, shit.*

"Look, if I'd known, I'd have been there. For the pregnancy, I mean."

Dante growled.

I turned to River.

His fangs were out as well, though he wasn't snarling.

"I can't believe you kept this from me. And from Jay!" I rubbed at my forehead as anger rushed through me. "What happened to honesty between us? To the blood bond?"

Dante surged forward and grabbed me, his eyes fiery, the rims around his irises more apparent than ever.

"Hey," Jay said. "You watch it with her."

"This is between Erin and me," Dante said through

clenched teeth. "I'll deal with *you* later."

Jay wedged himself between us. "You'll deal with me *now*. This concerns me more than it does any of the rest of you."

My heart thundered as fear pulsed through me. Dante wouldn't hurt my brother. Would he? Jay was big and muscular and strong.

But so was Dante.

And Dante was a vampire. His teeth were as lethal as any wild animal's. He could tear my brother apart.

"Don't you go near my brother. I'll *never* forgive you."

"Stay out of this, Erin," Jay warned.

"I will *not* stay out of this. How long have you known about this, Dante, and *now* you're going all feral on us? How could you keep this from me? From Jay?"

Dante snarled.

"Don't pull your vamp shit with me," Jay warned. "If I'm the father of your niece or nephew, you owe me the truth. Especially with Emilia missing. Who has more invested at this point? My child is suddenly involved in this. My child who might be— Fuck." He stepped backward.

I took the chance to move slightly away myself and meet Dante's blazing gaze. "He's right, Dante. This involves him now. Don't even try to say it doesn't." I whipped my hand to my neck and then turned to River. "Those bite marks on Jay. It really *wasn't* you."

River shook his head. "No, it wasn't."

Jay touched his neck. "Bite marks?"

"Remember? When we were having breakfast several weeks ago and I thought they were bug bites?"

"Shit. She bit me?"

I nodded. "And then glamoured you into not remembering it."

"Why that little—"

"You better think real carefully before you finish that sentence," Dante gritted out.

Jay edged backward until his legs met Emilia's unmade bed, and he plunked down. He sat, staring at nothing in particular.

My heart was thumping with anger at Dante for not telling me, but he did have a point. Emilia should have been the one to tell Jay. On the other hand, screw his point. I was still mad as hell. I resisted the urge to hurl the amethyst geode on top of Em's dresser at his head.

I went to my brother. "Hey. You're going to be a father. I'm going to be an aunt."

"Maybe," he said. "She's gone. We don't know what they might be doing to her. To the baby."

I sat down next to him, ignoring the darting glares coming from Dante and River. I'd deal with them later.

"We'll find her. We'll find Lucy and the others."

"It's all coming together now, Sis. Look at all the connections. River hooked up with Lucy, and she disappeared. I hooked up—"

Dante opened his mouth, but I sent him daggers with my eyes.

"—with Emilia, and she disappeared. And now you're involved with Dante, and the vampire thugs are after you..."

I patted his knee. "I'm fine. I'm here. We'll find the others. We have to."

"We sure do," he said. "Especially now. Why didn't she tell me?"

"I don't know. Was it truly a onetime thing?"

"This is kind of embarrassing to discuss with my sister."

He glanced up. "And in front of her brother and cousin, who look like they want to rip my guts out."

River's stance softened. Dante's did not.

"No one's asking for details," I said. Big time TMI.

"Are you sure it's mine?" Jay looked up.

"It's yours, man," River said. "Your scent is all over her. I knew it right away."

"And she admitted it," Dante added. "Who the hell do you think you are, fucking my sister?"

I shot him another glare.

"Hey, it was consensual." Jay stood. "Are you going to tell me you've never met a pretty girl and had a one-night stand?"

"As a matter of fact, I haven't," Dante said, snarling.

"Jay..." I tugged on his arm. "He hasn't been...around."

"Right." He turned to River. "What about you, partner?"

River's cheeks pinked a little. "A few times. But I always used a condom."

"So did I," Jay said. "I always do. Apparently condoms aren't foolproof."

"Or idiot proof," Dante said, seething.

"Stop that!" I advanced on the man I loved. "My brother is *not* an idiot. You've known about his role in this pregnancy for how long, and *now* you're pissed off about it? Frankly, Jay and I are the ones who have the right to be angry right about now."

Dante's eyes softened. Just a little, but they softened. "River and I kept quiet out of respect for Em."

I inhaled and let it out slowly, trying to get hold of my anger. "Emilia asked you not to say anything?"

"That's right."

"Why?"

"How the hell should I know? I hated keeping this from

you. Hated every minute of it. I felt so strongly the need to tell you the truth I wondered if our blood bond required it. But she's my sister. My sister!"

"And he's my brother! So stop all the growling, and let's figure out how we can work together. Nothing has changed. You were willing to work with Jay before. Now everything's out in the open."

River stepped forward then. "She's right, cuz." Though his fangs were still out.

I drew in a deep breath once more. I had to make something right. "I'm sorry," I said to River. "I'm sorry I accused you of feeding on Jay."

He nodded. "Accepted."

I eyed my brother.

"And I'm sorry," he said. "Oh, hell. I'm not sorry. We had a good time. If I'm sorry about anything, it's that she's had to carry this burden alone."

"Are you going to marry my sister?" Dante asked, his eyes dark.

"No."

"You fucking—"

I grabbed Dante. "Stop it. If Emilia wanted to get married, she would have gone to Jay."

"Right," River agreed.

"I'm willing to get to know her if she wants to, and we'll see where it leads. But I'll always be there for my kid." He raked his fingers through his hair. "If we ever find her, that is. God, I'm so fucking scared right now."

"I get you, partner. The woman I love is out there too," River said.

"You're in love with her?" Jay asked.

River nodded solemnly. "It happened fast. Too fast, really. I can't say it's forever love yet, but I want her back and I want her safe."

We all had personal stakes in this now. Every single one of us. I grabbed Dante's hand, trying to calm him.

But—

Julian appeared before us, and I gasped.

"We need to get the four of you out of here. Now."

## THIRTEEN

# DANTE

"What's wrong?" I asked, my teeth still long.

"The Claiborne vampires are on their way here. Another ghost sent me a warning through Bea."

Dark energy welled within me as the anger arrowed at Jay found a new target. "Bring them on. I'm ready to have this out once and for all."

"Dante, we can't let them know we're onto them." River inhaled and turned to Jay and Erin. "I don't smell either of you. Are you wearing that potion?"

They both nodded.

"Okay, then they're not coming here for us," Erin said. "If that's the case, why are they coming here?"

"They must be involved in Em's disappearance." River bared his teeth. "Why else would they come here?"

Jay stood. "Fuck it. Let them come."

"Jay," River said. "These are thugs. Drug runners. *Vampire* thug drug runners. If they find us here, it won't be pretty."

"I'm armed. Aren't you?"

"Of course, but I'd bet they are too."

My blood boiled hot. Jay was with me now. If River went along, we'd fuck them up good.

"There are four of them," Erin said as the voice of reason. "Maybe six. In my dream I thought I saw six, but then only four."

"The four of you are no match for four vampires, let alone six," Julian said. "Let's go."

"I took out two of them by myself," I growled. "They weren't armed then."

"It's the middle of the night, son. Get the hell out of here. I'll stay and see what I can find out."

"He's right, Dante," River said. "If they figure out we're onto them, they'll make it more difficult in the long run. Let's go. Uncle Jules will stay here and report back."

*Attack. Fight.*

*Fight or die in the arena.*

Every instinct in my body demanded that I fight. To beat those fuckers to a pulp and force them to lead us to Emilia and the others.

A low snarl vibrated from me.

Then Erin. Erin's soft and soothing touch. Oh, she was still pissed as hell, but her touch...

Erin was still here. Em and Lucy were gone, but Erin was still here, and no way in hell were the thugs getting their hands on her.

"All right. Let's go."

❖

Erin and I returned to our place alone. Dawn was breaking, and I was hungry.

Hungry for Erin's blood.

I was still on edge from dealing with telling Jay the truth, finally, and then knowing the Claiborne vamps were on their way to my sister's home. As if they hadn't done enough already.

But Erin.

She was here.

And she was angry.

She'd given me the silent treatment the whole drive home.

Now, all I wanted was to sink my teeth into her flesh and draw the elixir of life from her. Then fuck her into oblivion.

The look on her face said that wasn't going to happen.

At least not yet.

"All this time," she said, her voice low. "All this time you knew my brother was the father of Emilia's baby."

She was playing with fire, whether she knew it or not. I wasn't about to back down. My hunger was consuming me.

"Yes."

"You lied to me."

"I didn't lie. I just didn't tell you."

"Semantics, Dante. You know it as well as I do."

"Look. I told you I wanted to tell you. That wasn't a lie. It wasn't my place. You said you understood."

"I do." She balled her hands into fists. "It doesn't matter. I'm just so damned angry at you!"

Oh, God. A pink sheen covered her from head to toe. Yes, she was clothed, but I could imagine. I'd seen it before, when I'd told her she was descended from a vampire.

Something else I'd kept from her.

The high-pitched hiss of her blood flowing from her heart out through her arteries slowly drove me insane. Her blood was rushing rapidly, and her adrenaline spiked, giving it a more pungent aroma. Her anger brought forth testosterone, which, mixed with her already abundant estrogen, turned her scent into a fragrant melody.

I inhaled, taking it in, letting it infuse me with desire, hunger, need.

*Thu-thump.*

*Thu-thump.*

*Thu-thump.*

Her heart sucked the red nectar from her veins and then pumped the oxygenated liquid back out through her, reaching every cell of her body, turning even the tips of her fingers pink with her essence.

I grabbed her arm, hauling her against me. Then I bared my fangs with a snarl.

Her eyes widened for an instant—only an instant, and then she narrowed them, issuing me a challenge.

I did *not* back down from a challenge.

Did she think I wouldn't take her blood while she was angry with me? Upset with me?

*Think again.*

I grabbed her ponytail and yanked her head to the side, salivating.

The carotid. The rapid thud of her pulse. I'd always avoided the carotid, going instead for the slower flow of the jugular.

Not today.

I snarled so low I barely heard it escape my throat.

I slackened my hold on her just a little, enough so she could pull away if she so desired.

She did not.

In a flash, my teeth sank into her creamy flesh, and the red gold of her body flowed into me from the swift geyser of her carotid.

I sucked and swallowed from her, taking, taking, taking. Soothing the rage inside me as only she could.

And as her blood flowed over my tongue and down my throat, I calmed. The rage fell from a boil to a simmer.

The darkness within me would always produce a simmer, but I could control a simmer.

I removed my teeth and licked the two puncture marks on her smooth skin, helping the blood coagulate.

She pulled away, regarding me, her eyes smoldering.

She was staring.

I cocked my head, silently asking her if anything was wrong.

Still she stared. Anger no longer laced her eyes. Desire did. "Something about you, Dante. When your lips and chin are smeared with my blood. It...does something to me."

Indeed it did. Her musky arousal wafted in the air.

I smiled, my cuspids still long and sharp.

She placed her hand at my neck and drew me toward her, our lips meeting.

This was not the first time she had kissed me after I'd fed. It would not be the last.

Our lips slid together and our tongues twirled. My cock responded instantly, and when she pressed her hand to the bulge in my jeans, I nearly began to contract.

I broke the kiss and met her green gaze. "Fall to your knees, Erin."

She widened her eyes.

"Fall to your knees. Unbuckle my jeans, and suck my cock."

Like lightning she knelt, freed my erection, and her lips, now stained with her own blood from our kiss, encircled it.

I closed my eyes, groaning, my gums tingling.

She took me nearly to the base, farther than she ever had before. I clenched my teeth, bearing down, determined not to ejaculate prematurely. No, she would suck my cock until I was good and done.

"That's good, baby. Take me all the way."

She slid her full and swollen lips up and down my shaft, her saliva providing warm lubrication.

Her head bobbed as she sucked back and forth, and I grabbed her ponytail and began moving her head at the rhythm I preferred.

She didn't resist me. In fact, a groan vibrated against my cockhead from her throat. Though I ached for her tight little pussy, this time I would come down her hot throat. I needed this control.

"I want to come in your mouth, baby."

She nodded slightly, as much as she could with her mouth full of my big cock.

I unclenched my teeth and let go, baring my fangs with a low growl. My balls scrunched up, and tiny convulsions began within them, growing harder, harder, harder, through my cock as I emptied myself into Erin's mouth.

She took all of me. And as I watched the motion in her throat as she swallowed my semen, I growled in victory.

Victory.

*Fight or die in the arena.*

No. I wasn't going there yet.

I would not allow thoughts of the past to take this pleasure away from me. I looked down at her. Her lips were now smeared with the mixture of her blood and my semen. They'd never looked more luscious. I pulled her toward me and crushed them to my own. She moaned into my mouth, making me even more crazy, as we kissed, harder and harder, a raw kiss full of so much passion that I never wanted to stop.

As much as I never wanted it to end, I had to eventually pull backward to take a breath. As I inhaled swiftly, she touched her hand to my cheek. Her fingertips warm from the blood flowing beneath them.

I gazed into her beautiful green eyes. "Upstairs. Now."

# FOURTEEN

# *Erin*

I was so wet. Still so angry...but so fucking wet.

As angry as I was, pulsing need overpowered it. I regarded Dante, meeting his gaze, and then I turned and obeyed him, walking up the stairs.

Though I wanted to rush, run and get to the bedroom as quickly as possible, I forced myself to walk slowly. I wanted to make him wait. My anger hadn't abated. Not at all. So he could fucking wait. He'd already had his orgasm, and he'd already had his blood. Now he just wanted to control me, and while I was okay with that, I couldn't help giving him some torment after keeping such a vast secret from me.

"Faster," he growled from behind me.

His palm came down on the cheeks of my ass. Oh, it was covered in a pair of jeans, but still I felt the sting.

"I said *faster.*"

I smiled again. My body throbbed with desire, and I wanted to go faster. Wanted to obey him. But I forced myself not to.

"You're walking a thin line, Erin." His voice had lowered even further.

*Slap!* His hand came down on my ass once more, nearly knocking me forward. I climbed the last step.

"Run."

I continued walking.

"Damn it, Erin. I said run."

I turned to face him, his eyes as dark as I'd ever seen them, the amber around his irises like twin wheels of flame.

"You're playing with fire, Erin."

I smiled, heat flashing through me. "Then let me get burned."

He said no more. He simply pushed me into the bedroom.

I had never given a thought to spanking as a part of sex, but I had to admit that the couple of slaps Dante gave me on the stairs had my juices flowing.

"Do it. Spank me."

He growled. "I will *not*."

Disappointment surged through me. This was his punishment. Getting me all hot and bothered for spanking and then refusing to deliver.

"Get those clothes off before I rip them off you with my teeth."

He meant it. He'd done it before. Would he be able to rip through thick denim?

I had no doubt.

I'd already lost enough clothes to Dante's aroused frenzy. I flipped open the snap of my jeans and then brought down the short zipper.

Slowly.

He seethed above me, his eyes full of the sexual rage I'd

come to know so well. The sexual rage I'd come to love, come to need, come to ache for.

Everything about Dante made me quiver, made me want him, made me yearn to give him all of me.

What more could I give?

"Get those fucking jeans off, Erin."

I swiftly rolled them over my hips and wriggled out of them, toeing off my shoes and socks as I went. Then, before he demanded it, I took off my shirt and bra. Only my cotton panties—Dante had destroyed all my thongs—stood between me and total pleasure.

He closed his eyes and inhaled. "Something's different. Something's different about you."

Different? About my scent? "It's probably the potion. In fact, I should reapply it."

"No. Not yet. Let me savor whatever this is." He inhaled again. "It's something tangy. Citrusy." He inhaled again. "Almost...eggy. God, Erin. You're fertile."

"Impossible," I said. "I'm on the pill, remember? The pill suppresses ovulation."

He inhaled again.

"I've never smelled a fertile human woman since I came of age, but every instinct I have is telling me you're ripe. If I fuck you right now, you will get pregnant."

"Dante, I won't."

"No wonder you're so irresistible to me. No wonder your blood had a special pungent tang to it. You're ready, Erin. You're ready to take my seed and make our baby."

My heart was already thundering, but now it seemed to drop into my belly. "Dante..."

"I've never wanted you so much." He pulled down his jeans

and his cock sprang forward. "I just came, and look. I'm ready again. Ready to shove my dick inside you and make a baby with you."

Talk about a mood killer. As much as I loved Dante and wanted his baby, now was not the time. Forget the fact that I was mad as hell at this man. We had to find Emilia and Lucy, River's dad, figure out the secrets of the *Texts*. No room for a kid right now.

"Dante, we can't."

His eyes shot wide. "We *can*. We *will*."

"No, Dante." I reached toward him tentatively. "I'll be fertile again. It happens once a month for me. Right now isn't the time."

My nipples were hard and tight, and my pussy wet and ready. I sniffed, and he was right. Something new was in the air. No birth control was one hundred percent effective. Had I taken my pill every day? Had I missed a day? With everything else going on, it wasn't out of the realm of reality. Missing one pill could throw the whole thing off. Still...I never missed a pill.

Never.

"Please, Erin. Please. The ache is overwhelming me. I need to put a baby inside you."

"Dante, I want it as much as you do. But we have other responsibilities right now. You know that."

He growled, showing me his fangs.

Dear God, he was magnificent.

Quickly I reached for the potion on my nightstand and poured a few drops onto my fingertips. I rubbed it onto my vulva, hoping to mask the scent that was driving Dante mad, taking care not to let it touch the goods.

God, his baby.

A beautiful baby.

But not now. Not the right time.

"Yes," he said, his voice snarly and low. "Now."

*Please work. Please work.* If he didn't back off, I knew I wouldn't be able to deny him.

Not when he was looking at me that way.

In the meantime, I could suck his cock again. As much as my pussy throbbed, as much as I wanted his tongue inside me, I couldn't let him near that part of me if what he said was true.

I couldn't get pregnant. Not until we found the women and solved the mysteries.

He advanced toward me slowly, his eyes glowing with yearning need, his cock ready and willing.

Then—

I cocked my head. "Was that a knock on the door?"

"Let them wait," he said, snarling.

"No. What if it's about Emilia and Lucy?" I hastily pulled on my jeans and shirt. "We have to see who it is."

Before he could grab me and trap me on the bed, I raced out the door.

I gasped when I saw Julian in the living room.

"Sorry," he said. "I can't open the door. It's River and Jay. I have news about Emilia's apartment."

# FIFTEEN

# DANTE

*C*ontrol.

Not grabbing her and forcing my cock into her had taken the most control I'd ever had to muster.

I'd done it. For Erin.

I would *not* be able to do it again.

The urge to mate with her overwhelmed every part of me.

To unleash my sperm inside her, feeding from her neck at the same time, would create a new life. I felt it in my very soul.

Control.

I'd proved I possessed it.

But that scent. That fertile scent, like moist, dark soil smelling of chocolate and truffles, creating the perfect environment for a seed.

Only it was Erin's womb. The perfect environment for *my* seed.

The fragrance still clung to the air, but already it had faded to a lesser scent.

That damned potion.

But she was right. We couldn't fit a child into our lives right now.

Strange though.

I'd been with Erin nearly every night for the past month, and she took her pill at the same time. I didn't recall her missing it.

Ever.

But she *was* fertile.

Not a doubt in my mind.

"Dante!"

River's voice. The antidote for my hard-on. Still it took nearly a minute more before I could fit back into my jeans. I left the room and walked down the stairs.

"There you are," River said. "We have news."

My fangs were still descended. At least my cock had gone down to semi-hard.

"What?" I said, trying not to sound too growly.

"It's Uncle Jules's news, really," River said.

Jay and Erin were sitting at her small kitchen table. My father stood, as usual.

"What is it, Dad?"

"Two vampires returned to Emilia's apartment. One had a bandage over his nose, so I assume he's one of the two you had a run-in with, Dante."

"A beard?" I asked.

"Yeah. Big dark-brown one."

"That's Decker. He seems to be their leader."

"I got that feeling as well," my father went on. "Anyway, they were definitely looking for something. Something they didn't find."

I pulled the gold pin with the vampire fleur-de-lis engraved on it out of my pocket. "This?"

"I can't think of what else it might be," my father said. "Which means they didn't leave it on purpose."

"Did the other vamp have a similar pin anywhere on him?" I asked.

"Not that I saw."

"How long were they there?"

"A little over an hour. They scoured the entire place, and when they left, they weren't happy."

"Did they talk about anything?" Jay asked.

"A lot of cursing," my father said. "The bearded one said, 'Are you sure you had it when we came here?' The other didn't answer but nodded. The last thing the bearded one said before they left was, 'She can't ever know about this.'"

*She.*

Bea had said the vampires worked for a female boss.

Erin was sure the ER doctor, Bonneville, was involved.

Could she be the female boss?

Or could *she* be the female boss?

I'd seen the symbol.

In the arena.

*Fight or die in the arena.*

I sighed.

"What is it, son?"

"I've had some memories. New ones. I don't know how significant they are, but I can tell you one thing. I've seen that symbol before. On the humans who tortured me. On a vampire. A vampire I fought sometime while I was gone. A vampire I might have..."

God, I couldn't think it.

"What is it, Dante?"

Erin. Sweet Erin. Would she run from me and never look back? If I'd committed such a heinous act, I wouldn't blame her.

"*She* made me fight."

"Fight whom?" my father asked.

"Other vampires. Male vampires. At least I think they were all vampires. They didn't have any scent to me, and they were always masked."

"And one of them wore the symbol?"

I nodded. "Probably more than one. Most of the memories are blurry."

Erin stood and walked to me slowly, taking my hand.

"A vampire you might have...what, Dante?"

*Fight or die in the arena.*

I closed my eyes, squeezing her hand. "Please don't leave me."

She cupped my cheek. "Never."

I opened my eyes to find four pairs, including a ghostly set, staring back at me.

*Fight or die in the arena.*

"A vampire I might have...killed."

# SIXTEEN

# *Erin*

He was shivering.

My big strong man, who, only moments ago, had been willing to forcefully impregnate me, was now shivering.

He was still large, still magnificent, still even a bit ferocious. Anyone else might have missed the slight shudders. But I didn't. I knew him that well.

Dante was afraid he might have killed a person. Perhaps more than one person.

I grabbed his hand. "You're not responsible for anything you might've done while you were held captive. You didn't ask to be there."

"Son," Julian said, "Erin's right."

"I honestly just don't remember. She made me fight. Someone taught me how to fight."

"Bill, Brae, and I taught you when you were a teenager."

"I know. I remembered what Bill said about always going for the nose. But Dad, I remember doing things that no one taught me. At least not anyone I recall."

"Do you remember all of your life before you were taken?" River asked.

"Yes," Dante said. "It's during the last ten years that my memory is very fuzzy. There are giant gaps in it, but sometimes memories come to the surface."

"We will get to the bottom of this," Julian said. "I promise you."

Dante seemed to relax a bit. I didn't for a moment believe he'd killed anyone. No. He was too good a man. He wouldn't kill unless his life was truly threatened, and I doubted it had been. He wouldn't have been kept alive for ten years if his captor wanted him dead.

I didn't want to say as much in front of everyone else in the room. I held on to Dante's hand, trying to comfort him, trying to assure him that I knew he could never do anything so horrible.

"Well," Jay said. "Now we're pretty sure we know that the pin was left accidentally, and we know whoever they're working for is a female, though your vagabond voodoo lady already corroborated that. River and I are going to drop off the pregnancy test, the little vodka bottle, and Emilia's hairbrush at the lab to test for fingerprints. It's a long shot, but maybe something will come up in the system."

"How?" I asked. "You guys voluntarily quit the force. You don't have access."

"Sis, don't underestimate River's capabilities."

Of course. Glamouring. "Sorry. Lost my head for a minute."

"If you and Jay will excuse us, River," Julian said, "I'd like to talk to Dante and Erin alone."

"Yeah. Sure."

River and Jay left quickly.

More quickly than I expected.

"Son," Julian said, once they'd left, "I know what you're thinking, and I know what you're afraid of. I want you to look at the control you have now. And you know exactly what I'm talking about."

"Elaborate," I said. "*I* don't know what you're talking about."

Julian attempted to clear his throat, as much as a ghost could who didn't actually have a throat to clear. But that was what it sounded like. "The control he has with you, among other things. He's learning to control his newfound powers."

"Oh, okay." I got the distinct feeling that Julian was hiding something from me. I'd ask Dante about it later. Right now I didn't want to add to his distress.

"My point is," Julian continued, "that I truly believe that you never took the life of another."

"What if I did, Dad? What if I was forced to?"

"But you don't remember killing anyone."

"I don't. But new memories surface all the time."

"Dante"—I caressed his hand—"you know in your heart that you did not kill anyone. You don't have it in you. Trust in that."

"I'm trying, baby."

"If you can't trust in that, trust in me." I traced circles in his palm. "I know you didn't kill anyone. I *know* it."

That got a faint smile out of him.

"I agree with Erin," Julian said. "Besides, if there were any ghosts running around whose bodies had been killed by you, I would know it."

"Would you?" Dante asked.

"I feel certain I would."

"But you can't say for sure."

"Son, I haven't talked to every ghost out there. Some choose to leave this plane forever, but if a ghost had been wrongfully killed, he'd probably stick around to try to do something about it."

Julian's words comforted me, but I wasn't sure they were having any effect on Dante. "What can I do for you?"

He sighed. "I don't know. I think I just need some time alone, honestly."

I nodded. "I understand. I need to run an errand anyway."

"I don't want you going out alone."

I smiled. "I'll be fine. I have the potion, remember?"

"Where are you going?"

"Just to the pharmacy. I won't be long. You can have your dad tag along if you're worried."

"She'll be fine, Dante. It's morning now," Julian said.

Dante nodded.

"Are you sure you're okay? I can stay."

"I need to think, Erin," he said. "I need to try to... Shit. I have no idea what I need. Except for you. I need you."

"You have me."

"I know." He smiled. Sort of. "Go ahead and run your errand."

⚜

I stood in line behind a woman with two screaming toddlers, waiting to consult with the pharmacist at my pharmacy. In my hand were my birth control pills.

Seconds seemed like hours, until finally—

"May I help you?"

I walked to the desk to talk to the woman clad in a blue scrub shirt. "Are you the pharmacist?"

"She's in the back. May I help you?"

I pushed my container of pills toward her. "I need to find out if these are defective in some way."

"Are you having any issues?"

"Apparently I'm ovulating, and these are supposed to suppress ovulation."

She cocked her head. "How do you know you're ovulating?"

*My vampire boyfriend smelled my egg.* No, couldn't say that. "Could I just speak to the pharmacist please?"

She rolled her eyes. "Sure. Wait here, please."

I didn't mean to be short with her, but I needed to find out if my pills had been tampered with. I was religious about taking them at the same time each day, so a failure was highly unlikely.

A few seconds later, a gray-haired woman in a white lab coat appeared at the counter. "I'm the pharmacist on duty. What can I do for you?"

I handed her my pills. "Is there any way you can tell if these are truly the medication they purport to be?"

She took the container. "They look authentic to me. Why do you ask?"

"I understand that they *look* fine. But I'm ovulating, apparently, and I take them the same time each day."

"No contraceptive is a hundred percent effective."

"I know that. I'm a nurse. But I'm ovulating, and—"

"How do you know you're ovulating?"

"I took one of those ovulation tests." Better answer than the truth.

"Why would you do that if you're on the pill?"

*None of your damned business!* "I understand this sounds

a little on the ridiculous side. All I really want to know is if these pills contain the ingredients they're supposed to contain. Is there any way you can find out?"

"All right. Let me take a closer look. Wait here please." She returned a minute later. "They are identical to the other medication of this brand that I have in stock. Beyond that, I can't help you. You'd have to have the chemicals analyzed at a lab to make sure they contain the requisite hormones."

So much for that. "All right. I appreciate your help. Thanks."

As soon as I got back to my car, I called Jay.

"Yeah, Sis?"

"Have you guys made it to the lab yet?"

"We're here now. What do you need?"

"The address. I have something else for you to analyze."

## SEVENTEEN

# DANTE

*F*ight or die in the arena.

Those words.

I had fought.

I hadn't died.

I tossed fitfully in bed, trying to relax, trying to free my mind to remember.

Remember...

*Seek and ye shall find.*

*I am seeking! I don't need your help.*

*Then why am I here?*

I squeezed my eyes shut, forcing *her* from my mind.

I would remember, and I would remember on my own terms. I did not need her help.

❖

"*Who* are *you?*" I asked the masked vampire.

"*Who are* you?" *he said back to me.*

*We eyed each other, sized each other up. I was taller. He was broader. His eyes were dark blue or brown, almost black. Everything else about him was covered.*

*I didn't remember getting there. I didn't remember putting on clothes or a mask, but clearly I had. Or someone had dressed me.*

*How many times had I been here?*

*This could be the second or the thirty-second. All lines were blurred.*

*I didn't feel like fighting, didn't think I wanted to, but still my fangs descended and my adrenaline spiked as a low growl escaped my throat.*

*What was happening to me?*

Fight or die in the arena.

*I snarled at my opponent, baring my cuspids and circling him, my muscles flexed and ready to strike.*

Fight or die in the arena.

*I struck, an uppercut to his jaw.*

*No pain. If I hit with more force than the resistance he gave me, I wouldn't feel it.*

*Where had I learned that? I didn't know. Didn't care. Just wanted to pummel this man who'd done me no wrong.*

Fight or die in the arena.

*Darkness.*

*Evil.*

*All around me.*

*I growled, my canine nerve throbbing and my teeth sharpening.*

*I struck again, this time with ten times the force.*

❧

I shot up in bed, my eyes wide.

Still nothing.

I'd beaten my opponent. Beat him and beat him and beat him.

But then my memory ended.

I could never see the outcome.

"Damn it!" I said aloud.

I'd sent Erin and my father away so I could be alone with my thoughts, to try to remember.

Remember...

Remember...

To no avail.

I got up and went downstairs. I heated up a cup of coffee and took a sip, hoping to stave off the bloodlust that accompanied my becoming unglued. Erin wasn't here, and I'd already fed from her today anyway. We didn't keep any bagged blood in the house. Maybe I should remedy that. Now.

I texted River to find out where he got his blood, and when I had an address and the name of the discreet butcher, I realized Erin had taken the car.

Shit. Time to get a car of my own.

I texted River again, asking him to get some blood for me and bring it over.

He responded right away.

*Jay and I are on our way over. I'll get some on the way. We have news.*

News.

The fingerprints.

Could they get them that quickly?

Of course they could. River glamoured the techs into doing it.

I took two more gulps of my coffee, and then Erin arrived.

Along with her fertile scent. My groin tightened and my fangs descended. I closed my eyes.

*Control. Must have control.*

"Hey," she said. "Are you feeling better?"

"Not really. I could use some..." I nodded to her neck.

"More today?"

"Yeah. I won't take much. I just need to relax a little. It's kind of like a glass of wine at the end of a hard day, you know?"

*Control. Take her blood. That's it.*

She nodded, walking into my arms.

We held each other for a few moments, and I let her nearness warm me, soothe me. Surprisingly, I found I no longer needed her blood.

When she turned her head, baring her creamy neck, I simply pressed my lips against her smooth skin.

She giggled. "That feels nice. Go ahead."

"I'm okay, baby. I guess I just needed *you*." I cupped her cheeks and brought my lips to hers in a soft kiss. My cock began to harden, and I pulled away, forcing myself not to breathe in the scent of her womb. "River and Jay are on their way over."

"I know. I was just with them."

"How long were you gone?" I asked. I hadn't bothered to look at the time.

"A couple of hours. Have you been asleep?"

"Off and on. I was trying to get more memories. It was just more of the same. Where did you go?"

"To the pharmacy, and then I went to meet River and Jay at the lab. I wanted to get my pills checked. I think they might have been tampered with. I'm religious about taking my pill on time. I shouldn't be ovulating."

I inhaled deeply. "You are. You definitely are." My gums began to itch once more. The scent was still there, though less intense with her potion.

"I believe you. I know pills aren't perfect, but when used correctly they almost never fail. I just want to make sure I didn't get a bad batch or something."

"Sounds reasonable."

"The pharmacist couldn't tell anything, so I took them to Jay and River to have them analyzed at their lab."

"And?"

"It'll take a few hours."

"Oh? River just texted me that they have news."

"They do. On the fingerprints. They found—"

A knock sounded on the door.

I opened it, and Jay and River walked in.

"Hey, cuz."

"What did you find out?" I asked.

"Nothing definite yet. But there is something odd. We used Em's hairbrush to get her fingerprints for comparison, but there were two distinct sets on the brush."

I turned to Erin. "Do women usually share hairbrushes?"

"Not usually," she said. "It's kind of like a toothbrush."

"Just because someone else picked it up doesn't mean they used it," Jay said. "That's not even the weirdest thing."

"Okay..." I said.

River cleared his throat. "The pregnancy test stick has three distinct sets of prints, and the little vodka bottle has four."

"How could you possibly find four distinct prints on such a small bottle?" Erin asked.

"The techs at the lab are wizzes," Jay said. "They can lift a print off of almost anything. But here's the strange part. These idiots didn't wear gloves. It's almost as if they wanted to get caught."

"Or they planted someone else's prints to throw us off," River said.

"Now what do we do?" I asked.

"Jay and I have the print files." He held up a thumb drive. "We just have to break into the databases and see if we can find a match. Problem is, if the person hasn't ever been arrested, their files won't be in the database."

"I don't think we're dealing with very nice people," Erin said. "If the prints aren't counterfeit, chances are we'll find them."

"We're definitely not dealing with very nice people, Sis," Jay said, "but if they're vampires, they could have easily glamoured whoever was taking their prints, or glamoured their way out of it before it even got that far."

Erin sighed. "True."

"We'll do our best," River said. "For the time being, we can assume that one of the sets on the hairbrush belongs to Em."

"In the meantime, I've been thinking," I said, even though the thought had only occurred to me while River was speaking.

"What?" Erin asked.

"I'm going to take another stab at the *Texts*. We no longer have the Nocturnal Truth site, and Bill refuses to use his knowledge of the council to help."

"You said a couple online French lessons were no help," Erin said.

"They weren't, but I have to try. There are some similarities to modern French. It's not like we have another choice at this point. Something has to explain what's going on with me."

"He's right," Jay said. "We have to try."

I turned to regard the coffee table where the book sat.

# EIGHTEEN

# Erin

Dante went rigid and bared his fangs.

I followed his gaze.

The *Vampyre Texts* were gone.

"Did anyone move that book?" Dante said through clenched teeth.

"Of course not," River said.

"Ditto." From Jay.

Dante turned to me.

"Why would *I* move it?"

"I don't know. Where the hell is my Dad?"

Julian appeared. I didn't jump this time.

"The fucking book is gone," Dante said.

"I can see that."

"Bill had someone break in here and move it."

"Not possible," Julian said. "The shield wasn't just for your grandfather. It covered anyone working on his behalf."

"Then who took it?"

"I wish I could tell you," Julian said. "I have no idea."

"You mean you weren't hovering around here when it was taken?" River said.

"I actually do have other things to do than just 'hover around,'" Julian said. "I'm working hard to figure out what's going on here. I've been following Decker and his gang."

"Any leads?"

"No. They haven't met up with any female. They *have* been running some illegal substances, and something else, which is a little strange."

"What's that?"

"Blood. Bagged human blood."

I shot my gaze toward the ghost. "Let me guess. B positive blood, right?"

"Not a surprise to you," Julian said.

"Not even close. We've been low on B pos at the hospital forever. Dr. Bonneville—" I stopped, my mind churning. "She sent me to Tulane to get more B pos weeks ago. As far as I know, it never showed up. Every time I went to the bank, we were out of it. It's not even a very common blood type. But Lucy and the others, except for Emilia, are all B positive."

"Are these vamps keeping their own personal supply of B positive blood, then?" Dante said. "Is that what you're thinking, Erin?"

"I have no idea. But I've had a hunch for a while that B positive blood has something to do with all of this."

"But as you said," River said, "Em doesn't have it."

"No, but her baby does."

"How do you know that?" Jay asked.

"Bea told me."

"When?" River asked.

"Well..." I hedged.

"What?"

"She told me...in a dream." A dream in which she'd morphed from Dr. Bonneville.

"For fuck's sake," River said.

"Hear her out," Julian said. "Since I passed over, I've learned that dreams mean a lot more than I always thought they did."

"Another premonition?" Dante asked.

Jay shook his head. "She doesn't need a premonition. I'm the father, and I have B positive blood."

"Which means the baby could have B or O blood," I said. "The Rh factor is a fifty-fifty proposition. That plus my dream is pretty good evidence the baby is B positive."

"Sorry, Sis," Jay said. "Dreams aren't evidence. But I'll agree with you on the pretty good chance that the baby is B positive."

I paced around the room. "You all must think I'm an idiot, putting stock in a dream."

"This is all fascinating," Dante said sarcastically. "But someone broke in here and stole the fucking book. If it wasn't Bill, who the hell was it?"

Right. The book. Shit! "I've been locking the door."

"Doesn't matter," Dante said. "Picking locks is easy. You all saw me do it."

"Where did you learn that?" Jay asked.

"I have no fucking idea."

"So the thugs are running blood. What other drugs, Uncle Jules?"

"I didn't get a good look. But from their conversation, they had oxy, Percocet, and, of all things, lithium."

"Pharmaceuticals." River shook his head. "This is high-end shit. They have a contact in the business, or they're getting it smuggled in."

"Dr. Bonneville," I said quietly.

"What, baby?" Dante asked.

"I'm telling you. Everything in me is telling me Bonneville is a part of this."

"Because of your dream?" Jay asked.

He wasn't being mean, not even facetious, but it irked the hell out of me anyway. "No, not just because of a dream."

"Then because of a feeling," he said.

"Damn it!" I punched his arm. Hard.

"Hey, Sis. Chill. Jesus."

"I know it sounds completely nuts. I just can't shake the feeling. Plus, there's the dream. Plus—" A thought speared into my mind. I grabbed my purse from the kitchen table and pulled out my packet of pills, two of which were missing. I'd given them to Jay and River for the lab. "She stopped by here personally to tell me that a patient of mine had been transferred. Why not just tell me at the hospital?"

"Because she was going on vacation," Dante said. "That's what you told me."

"Yeah. But since when does Bitchville care about keeping *me* informed? She came *here*." I paced again, tugging at my hair. "She fucking glamoured me. I know it. She came here and..."

"Baby." Dante pulled me into his arms. "What are you trying to say?"

"I shouldn't be ovulating. I never miss my pill. I swear to God, if that lab report comes back and I've been taking sugar pills, then I know for sure. Bonneville switched my pills."

"Why would she do that?" Julian asked.

The words tumbled off my tongue before I consciously thought them.

"She wanted me to get pregnant. With Dante's baby."

# NINETEEN

# DANTE

Erin pregnant. With my baby. Just the words had my teeth descending, my groin tightening. I inhaled. Her ripeness was still thick in the air.

But my cousin. My father. Her brother.

So fucking what? I pulled her to me and kissed her mouth. Hard.

*Mine. Mine. Mine.*

*Dante!*

My father's voice.

*Dante! Cool it, cuz.*

River.

Then a strong arm yanked Erin away from me.

I growled, baring my fangs at her brother. "I'm stronger than you'll ever be."

*Fight or die in the arena.*

"Dante, please." Erin touched her swollen lips.

"Why, you motherfu—"

River grabbed Jay and forced him backward. "Easy, man.

He'll take you out with a look right now. Don't push it."

"If he thinks it's okay to—"

"He doesn't. He's responding to something else." River turned to me. "You okay?"

Okay? I was fucking hard for the woman I loved. I wanted to impregnate her. I wanted the rest of these losers to leave my house.

"Control, son."

My father. Speaking in his "father" voice.

"Don't give in to it," he said again.

Erin pulled away, fear etched in her eyes. "Don't give in to what, Dante?"

The darkness. But the darkness wasn't making me want Erin. I wanted her anyway, especially while she was fertile. The darkness was, however, making me attack her in front of others.

*Control, son.*

"I'm sorry." I closed my eyes, summoning everything within me to help me control myself. I opened my eyes. "She's fertile. The blood bond. It's difficult."

"And I shouldn't *be* fertile," Erin said. "Someone wants me pregnant. It has to be Dr. Bonneville."

River rolled his eyes toward me so only I could see. *Here we go again*, he was saying.

"Look, baby," I said, still aching in my jeans for her, my fangs still out. "We don't know any of this for sure. We don't even know she's a vampire."

"Then who else was feeding from me? It wasn't Logan. And the feedings stopped once Bonneville left."

I snarled. Just the thought of someone sinking her teeth into flesh that was mine had me on high tension.

"Son."

Control.

Right. Control.

"Son. I need to speak to you alone."

Erin's eyes widened. "Julian? Is everything okay?"

"Everything's fine. Indulge me. Dante, I'll meet you in the bedroom." He vanished.

I squeezed Erin's hand. "I won't be long." I traipsed up the stairs and into our bedroom.

My father had materialized and was standing by the armchair in the corner. "Sit."

I sat.

"I know this will be difficult for you, Dante, but you must leave Erin alone for a few days. She can't get pregnant. If what she says is true—"

"It was a dream, Dad."

"I know that, but we can't take the chance. If someone wants her pregnant, there's a reason for it. As long as she's not pregnant, she's safer. If Emilia was taken because of her baby, we can't let the same thing happen to Erin."

My fangs throbbed again as anger rose within me. "I won't let anyone harm her," I snarled.

"I know. That's why she can't get pregnant. If she's as fertile as you say, she'll become pregnant if you two have sex. Vampire seed is very potent, and human women are so much more fertile than vampire women. It's part of why we've nearly become extinct."

"Can't you smell it? She's ready. Ripe and ready."

"Ghosts don't smell, Dante. You know that."

Of course. "What about River?"

"I see no indication that he's smelling anything unusual about her. Perhaps the potion is masking it. Or he's just behaving himself, which is more likely. He was taught to control his urges."

"And I wasn't." I growled. "Not my fucking fault."

"No one ever said it was." He held up his hand to keep me from interrupting. "The darkness that has taken root inside you is part of why you want to lose control. Fight it. Always fight it."

*Fight or die in the arena.*

"Keep fighting it. I promise you, Dante, that we will figure out what it is, what is going on within you, and when we do, we will know how to stop it."

"What if I don't want to stop it?" I snarled. "What if this is who I am now? Who I'm supposed to be?"

"Maybe it is. Maybe all vampires have this potential. Which is why we need that damned book!"

"You're sure Bill couldn't have had it stolen?"

"Positive. That shield was strong and reinforced with my ashes. You saw how it affected Bill when he tried to take the book. It would have affected anyone working on his behalf the same way. A shield can't be fooled."

I drew in a deep breath and let it out slowly, trying to calm my nerves. My body.

I succeeded. Sort of. Erin's scent was still thick in this room.

"Someone else took it. But who?"

"That, son, is what we need to find out."

# TWENTY

# *Erin*

"I wish he wouldn't get so possessive of you," Jay said to me once Dante and Julian had left the living room.

"I'm sure he wishes you hadn't fucked his sister," River shot back, his fangs bared.

"For God's sake," I said. "Would the two of you cool it? I know you're both all alpha and strong and big brother—or cousin—and all that other bullshit, but there's so much more at stake here. Lucy and Emilia, for example?"

Jay sighed. "Right. Sorry, Sis."

River nodded. "You're right."

"Good." I let out a huff. "Now. You guys are the detectives. Where do we look for the book? And where do we look for Dr. Bonneville?"

"In Barbados," River said. "That's where she said she was going. It'll be easy enough to see if she's registered anywhere on the island. Of course she could be traveling under an alias, or she could have lied to you about going on vacation and she's right here under our noses."

"If she were, wouldn't she still be feeding on me?" I asked.

"Not necessarily. Not if she has another source readily available," River said.

"And not if she's not a vampire," Jay added. "We still don't know for sure that she is."

I turned to River. "What is it about B positive blood?"

He shook his head. "Nothing that I know of. I don't feed from human beings, and I know nothing about blood types in cattle and sheep."

"Never?" Jay asked. "Not even once?"

"No. Not even once."

"Never even tempted?" I asked.

"Of course I'm tempted. I'm tempted every day. But we learn to control it. Think of it like a recovering alcoholic. He never stops wanting booze, but he knows if he has one drink, he'll slide right down the rabbit hole. It's not worth it."

"Okay. I get it. I'm sorry I asked. It must be hard for you."

"No harder than it is for you to deny yourself something you want. It's just a part of life. We get used to it." He cleared his throat. "Bill did tell me something once. In fact, I'm pretty sure he told Dante too, before he was taken."

"What?" Jay asked.

"Apparently some vampires can distinguish among blood types. It's some kind of genetic anomaly. But it doesn't really matter, because we don't feed on humans. Most of us, anyway."

"But some vampires can tell the difference between, say, O and B blood?"

"And A and AB. Yeah. If what Bill told me was true."

"Bill would have no reason to lie to you back then," I said.

"Probably not," River agreed.

"So it's possible that certain vampires might have a preference for B positive blood."

"Yeah."

"Which could explain why all the women, except one, who disappeared are B positive."

"Maybe."

"And why we were always out of B positive at the hospital," I went on.

"Sure. Maybe," he said again. "But why those particular women? Why not all women with B positive blood? And why were two of them returned unharmed? Not drained? Something isn't adding up yet."

I bit my lower lip. He was right. Something definitely wasn't adding up just yet. But we were on the right track. I felt sure of it. "Plus, someone got into my home. Dante's and my home. A vampire could have glamoured me to steal the book, but Dante is usually here with me."

"Which means it happened while you were out," Jay said.

"And it probably happened quickly," River added. "Whoever took it knew where to look. But Bill couldn't have told anyone, or the shield wouldn't have worked."

"Yeah." Jay cleared his throat. "According to a *ghost*."

"I trust Uncle Jules," River said.

"So do I," I added.

"Whatever," Jay said, clearly holding back an eye roll. "If it was sitting right here on the coffee table, the thief didn't have to look far, whether he had inside information or not."

"Good point," River said. "It never occurred to me that anyone else would even know we had the book, let alone want to take it from us. Most vampires have a copy of the *Texts*. It's like having that big family bible on the mantel. The one no one ever opens."

"What do you do when humans come to visit?" Jay asked.

This time River rolled his eyes. "We put it away, numbnuts."

"What if they show up and surprise you?"

River wiggled his fingers in Jay's face. "We glamour them. For fuck's sake, Jay."

"I thought you said you don't glamour. That it's immoral."

"For something as innocuous as hiding a book, we don't worry too much about it. When I say it's unethical, you know very well what I mean. Shit, partner."

"Okay, okay." Jay backed off. "Let's look around. Maybe we can find some clues that tell us something about who might have been here."

I left the two of them to their sleuthing. I wouldn't know what to look for anyway, and right now, I needed a drink of water. I walked into the kitchen, poured myself a glass, and took a long drink.

Someone had been in our home. Dante's and my home. I cringed. No one had touched me, but I felt violated—the same as I had when I'd dreamed about the vampires coming after me at work.

Dante would protect me. I knew that in my heart and in my mind. So would Jay, River, and Julian.

None of that was enough anymore.

Lucy, Emilia, and others were gone, were possibly in danger.

Somehow, B positive blood was involved.

Thug vampires were after me, thugs who ran drugs and blood for some elusive female boss.

Those same thugs had been at Emilia's apartment.

An ancient book held secrets we weren't allowed to know. In fact, someone was making damned sure we'd never know.

And now...that someone wasn't Bill.

Most of all...Dante was changing.

Little by little I saw it, felt it.

*Knew* it.

We had to find out where they were hiding the women and get them back.

And damn it, if we couldn't find them, I could do something.

I could bring the bad guys to us.

I marched up the stairs, my brother and River engrossed in their search and paying me no mind.

I stormed into the bedroom. "Dante!"

He sat in the wingback chair in the corner of the room, his father's ghost standing next to him.

"Yeah, baby?"

I drew in a breath, my heart pounding. "I want you to get me good and pregnant."

# THE QUEEN

Darkness becomes you, Dante.

Darkness will *always* become you.

I'd planned to come for you when you were ready, but your change is awakening swiftly, and your strength is more profound than even *I* could have imagined.

No. I will no longer come for you.

I no longer have to.

You will come to *me*.

# BLOOD BOND SAGA

PART 11

## PROLOGUE

# *Erin*

Someone had been in our home. Dante's and my home. I cringed. No one had touched me, but I felt violated—the same as I had when I'd dreamed about the vampires coming after me at work.

Dante would protect me. I knew that in my heart and in my mind. So would Jay, River, and Julian.

None of that was enough anymore.

Lucy, Emilia, and others were gone, were possibly in danger.

Somehow, B positive blood was involved.

Thug vampires were after me, thugs who ran drugs and blood for some elusive female boss.

Those same thugs had been at Emilia's apartment.

An ancient book held secrets we weren't allowed to know. In fact, someone was making damned sure we'd never know.

And now...that someone wasn't Bill.

Most of all...Dante was changing.

Little by little I saw it, felt it.

*Knew* it.

We had to find out where they were hiding the women and get them back.

And damn it, if we couldn't find them, I could do something.

I could bring the bad guys to us.

I marched up the stairs, my brother and River engrossed in their search and paying me no mind.

I stormed into the bedroom. "Dante!"

He sat in the wingback chair in the corner of the room, his father's ghost standing next to him.

"Yeah, baby?"

I drew in a breath, my heart pounding. "I want you to get me good and pregnant."

# ONE

# DANTE

My teeth sharpened and my cock grew granite solid.

Erin stood before me, her cheeks red, her blood hissing—that high-pitched sound only I could hear, the sound that drove me to the brink of insanity.

"Leave," I said to my father.

"Dante..."

"I said *leave*."

"Control, son." He vanished.

Control?

I didn't *need* control. Erin was giving me permission to do what I instinctively wanted more than anything in the world.

Fuck her. Mate with her.

Impregnate her.

When part of me was growing inside her, we'd be bonded in a wholly different way.

I inhaled.

Her scent had become stronger with her need, her desire. The dark chocolate and truffles were spiked with excess estrogen and progesterone, with the richness of her fertile womb.

*If someone wants her pregnant, there's a reason for it. As long as she's not pregnant, she's safer. If Emilia was taken because of her baby, we can't let the same thing happen to Erin.*

I closed my mind to my father's words.

Erin wanted this. I wanted this.

My fangs throbbed as my cock threatened to explode.

*She can't get pregnant. If she's as fertile as you say, she'll become pregnant if you two have sex.*

"Damn it!" I yelled.

"What is it?" Erin asked.

I paced, threading my fingers through my hair while my dick strained against my jeans.

"What is it?" Erin said again.

I faced her, her body warm and inviting, her fragrance irresistible, the whoosh of her blood beneath her skin a delicate and enticing sound.

In one swift movement, I could shred her clothes and have her lying on the bed, open and ripe, ready for me to take.

In one swift movement, I could be inside her wetness, sheathed by her, ready to explode into her fertile warmth.

In one swift movement...

"Dante..."

"Damn it! Damn it! I can't."

"You can't what?"

"I can't get you pregnant. I can't. Not now."

"Why the hell not?"

"Because it could put you in danger. I can't have that, Erin. I just can't."

She walked toward me with a seductive air. "Don't you see,

Dante? That's exactly why I must get pregnant."

"No. Just no."

"If I'm pregnant, they'll come for me. I can lead you to them."

I shook my head vehemently. "They can't have you. They will *not* take you. If I have to use every last shred of control inside me, I will use it to protect you."

Her beautiful lips parted on a sad frown. "You don't want me?"

Crazy words. I ached for her. Burned for her. I closed my eyes and exhaled, trying like hell to cool off.

Didn't work. I opened my eyes. "I want you more than I want life right now. More than the sweet taste of your blood, Erin. More than the air I breathe."

"Then what's—"

I clenched my teeth. "Stop it. Don't come any closer. I'm begging you, Erin. I won't be able to control myself."

She reached forward slowly and touched my cheek, making me burn even hotter. "Please, my love. *Please.*"

Perhaps just one kiss. One small caress of my fingertips to her soft skin. One taste of her lips, of her nipples protruding through her shirt.

I grabbed her wrist and yanked her hand away. "Don't."

She lifted her brow, her eyes wide. Her arm twitched, but she didn't try to touch me again. Instead, her gaze fell to the bulge in my jeans. "At least let me take care of *that* for you."

If only... To have her sweet ruby lips encircling my cock, licking and sucking me...

My eyes ached to close, but I forced them to stay open.

If I let her unzip my jeans, put her mouth all over my erection, I would lose control. I'd tear off her clothes and shove my cock deep inside her.

I'd fuck her.

Fertilize her.

And she'd be pregnant.

They'd come for her.

"No," I gritted out. "No, Erin."

She stretched her arm outward, aiming for my crotch, and I sent her a red glare.

She stopped mid-stretch.

"No," I said once more.

God, I deserved a medal for this.

If I ever doubted my control, I could put all doubts to rest now. This was taking everything I possessed.

"Dante, I—"

"Leave," I gritted out. "Now."

"But—"

"Damn it, Erin. Do you think I'm made of steel?"

Her eyes twinkled. "A certain part of you might be at the moment."

I bared my fangs on a snarl. "Get. The fuck. Out."

She flinched slightly, but she didn't move. "I'll never fear you, Dante. Never."

I didn't want her to fear me. I just wanted her to leave.

God, no. I didn't want her to leave. I wanted her to stay, *ached* for her to stay. Yearned for her to present her pussy to me, the sweet road to her fertile womb. Longed to free my hard cock and pound into her, making her mine, making a child with her.

*Do it! Do it!*

The urge was overpowering me, threatening to take control. If I didn't do something, anything, I'd succumb quickly.

*Control, son.*

Everything came down to control...and Erin was my control.

I growled, summoning the last bit of discipline I possessed.

With no motion on her part, Erin's feet glided backward toward the door, her eyes wide. Her jaw dropped, and she squealed. Once she was outside in the hallway, the bedroom door slammed shut.

I hadn't moved.

Neither had she.

# TWO

# *Erin*

I was frozen. Numb.

I'd been ousted from my own bedroom, yet I hadn't moved a muscle. Hadn't budged. Neither had Dante.

*I'll never fear you, Dante. Never.*

My own words, and I'd meant them. I *still* meant them, but I was a little freaked out.

Okay. A *lot* freaked out.

He'd moved me. How? Telekinesis. Another new power. First ultra-glamouring. Then levitating.

And now?

I shivered. What was going on with him? We needed answers now more than ever. Without the book, and without any leads to the women, how would we get them? Only one way existed that I could think of—me getting pregnant.

But Dante wouldn't cooperate.

He'd wanted me. He couldn't hide it. His determination and control had taken over. He was protecting me. I got that.

I did. But for once, just once, I wanted to protect *him*. Do something that could help *him*.

"Dante!" I turned the knob on our bedroom door. It didn't open. "Dante! What the hell *was* that?"

No response, not that I expected one.

"Dante, this is my bedroom too."

Again, no response.

"Let me in!"

"Erin."

I gasped when I turned to see Julian.

"Leave him be, Erin. Please."

"But I want to—"

"I know. You're a brave woman. You're willing to put yourself in harm's way to lead us to the others. I know what you're doing."

"Then let me do it."

"I can't."

"It's the only way."

"It's not an option. Not for Dante, and not for me either."

"Why not?"

"You mean too much to him. He can't have you in danger. You need each other."

"I know that, but—"

"This isn't up for debate, Erin. Dante needs you. He needs you *here*, so he can feed."

I swallowed. "We don't know for sure."

"Does it even matter? He loves you. He won't let you put yourself in danger for this. And neither will I."

"Why in the world—"

"Don't even think about questioning me."

I huffed. "Excuse me? You're not *my* father, Julian."

"You're right. I'm not. But I care about you as if you were my own, and Dante is my son. Any child he makes with you is my grandchild. I'd give my life all over again to see that you're protected."

I bit my lower lip.

"Do you think it was easy for him to cast you out of the bedroom? He's bonded to you, and you're fertile. I have the utmost faith in my son, but even I am surprised he was able to resist you."

"Julian, he moved me out of the room."

"He didn't have a choice, Erin."

"No, you don't understand. He *moved* me from the room. Literally. Without touching me."

Julian lifted his brow. "He...what? Literally?"

"Yes, *literally*. Psychically. Telekinetically. Whatever word you want to use. He growled, and then I slid across the floor and out the door, and the door shut. But neither Dante nor I actually moved. I didn't budge a muscle, and he didn't touch me, yet somehow he got me out of the room and locked the door."

"I see."

"Do you? Can ghosts make sense of something that the living can't?"

"I didn't mean I understand. What's going on with Dante is something new to all of us. We need that damned book more than ever."

"I know. Bill's copies aren't the only ones out there. Can't we get another one?"

"Only vampires will have them, and we can't get in to take one without the ability to glamour. Vampires can't be glamoured."

"What about the vampire doctor? Jack Hebert? Does he have one? Wouldn't he help us?"

"I already had River check with him. His older brother has the only family copy, and he's on the council. The council has already proven to be less than helpful, through my father and the elder ghost."

I sighed. "What do we do, then?"

"I wish I knew."

I gestured toward the bedroom door. "Is he...okay?"

"He'll be fine. You'll need to steer clear of him for the next twelve hours or so, though."

"Where am I supposed to go?"

"You can stay with River and Jay. I've already explained the situation to them."

"But..." I bit my lips again.

"What is it?"

"Well...it's River. If I'm fertile—"

"For goodness' sake, Erin. River is a grown man. He's smelled a fertile woman before. He's perfectly capable of controlling himself. Besides, he can't smell you anyway. You're wearing your potion."

"But Dante—"

"Dante loves you. He's bonded to you. He requires your blood for sustenance. Plus, he never had the chance to learn to control his instincts the way River has."

I nodded, feeling like a world-class jerk. Here I was ready to assume River might do something criminal. "I'm sorry."

"It's all right. It was a valid question."

I paused for a few seconds. Then, "I don't want to leave him, Julian. I love him. He needs me."

"He does, which is why you need to stay away. If he loses

control and gets you pregnant, he won't be able to protect you. That, more than anything else, will kill him, Erin."

"Will you stay here? Keep an eye on him?"

"Of course. That was always my intention."

I breathed a sigh of relief. "He needs you too."

"I know. My son has endured more than any person should have to. I will be with him here on this plane for as long as I can be. He and I have a lot to learn from each other."

I smiled. "You're a good dad, Ju—" I jumped at a pounding on the door downstairs. "What the heck?"

Julian vanished while I walked quietly down the stairs. River had opened the door, and Bill entered.

"What do you want?" River demanded.

"I want my other copy of the *Texts* returned."

"I don't know what you're talking about."

"It's missing. The one I had stolen from here and replaced with the fake. You took the second copy from my office. Now you've taken the first as well."

River rolled his eyes. "We haven't gone near your place since we took the copy out of your office."

Bill eyed the coffee table. "Where is it?"

"Maybe you should tell us?"

Julian appeared. "He doesn't know. He had nothing to do with its disappearance. Trust me."

"My son is right," Bill agreed. "Now where is the other one?"

"We have no idea," Jay piped in. "Someone stole the one we had, and we didn't take your other one."

"It's true, Dad," Julian said. "Whoever took our copy most likely took yours as well."

Bill sighed and rubbed his forehead. "Those books cannot

fall into the wrong hands."

"Seems you think *our* hands are the wrong hands, Gramps," River said.

"You have no idea." Bill stared at River with an evil glare. "No idea at all what you're dealing with. This isn't a game, River."

River advanced toward Bill, his fangs descending as he walked. "You really think this is a *game* to us? Emilia is missing. My girlfriend is missing. Not to mention my father. This is no game, Bill."

"I'm sorry." Bill relented. "Bad choice of words. But what's inside the boo—"

River's hands curled into fists. "All we want is to find the women, damn it. Find the women and figure out what's going on with Dante and Erin. Find my dad. Is that too much to ask?"

Bill shook his head. "No. It's not."

"Then either help us or get the fuck out."

"I can't—"

"Don't start that shit again," River said. "You *can* help us. You choose not to. If that is still your choice, get the fuck out."

"But I—"

"I'm not kidding, Bill. Em and Lucy are out there. For God's sake, my father—your own son—is out there. You're willing to forsake all of them just for some secrets in a stupid book?"

Bill didn't speak.

"He's right, Dad," Julian said. "What's more important at this point? Secrets? Or people?"

"If you knew the secrets," Bill said, "you wouldn't be asking that question."

"Then tell us," River said. "Fucking tell us."

I shivered. Not from fear, but from all the alpha vibes in

the room. And Dante, the most alpha of all of them, wasn't even here.

"He's right again, Dad," Julian said. "Tell us what you know. Let us weigh the importance of it."

"I...can't. Please try to under—"

"We will *never* understand," Julian said. "I'll make the offer one more time. Tell me. Just me. Let *me* decide what to do once I know."

"Julian—"

"I'm no longer slave to a body, brain, or hormones. I can be objective."

"Not where your brother and your daughter are concerned."

"Why do you say that? *You're* doing it. Your son, granddaughter, and grandson are all involved here."

"I have the wisdom of an elder."

"Your wisdom hasn't done you a lot of good, has it?" Jay offered with a chuckle. "You've allowed not one but two books to be stolen from your home, books you *claim* contain secrets no one should ever know."

"This isn't any of your business," Bill said. "Stay out of it."

"The hell I will. What concerns my sister concerns me."

I sent my brother a pleading look, which he ignored.

"Look," Jay continued. "I don't know where you get off barging into my sister's home and making accusations and demands, but you can get the fuck ou—"

Jay's eyes glazed over and he stared into space.

"You glamoured my brother?" I edged toward Bill. "*Get out.*"

Bill held up a hand. "Erin, this is for your own good, for Dante's own—"

"Enough!" Julian's voice emerged with a roar that seemed to come from every corner of the room.

Everyone stopped, even Bill. Jay came back to life. I rubbed my arms against the shivers that erupted.

"You speak of your wisdom," Julian said. "For God's sake, Dad. I'm dead! I have the wisdom of the noncorporeal plane. You have no idea the amount of knowledge I possess. This has gone far enough. You can't trust your grandsons with the secrets. You can't trust your son. You can only trust yourself, and you're willing to sacrifice your other son and granddaughter to protect whatever is hiding in that damned book. I've. Had. *Enough*. It's all bullshit. Fuck you. Fuck you!"

I dropped my mouth open. Had I ever heard Julian curse? Not that I could recall. I moved toward my brother. He plunked down on the couch to watch, and I joined him.

Bill bared his fangs. "You will not speak to me in that tone, Julian."

Julian guffawed. "You think your teeth can do anything to me? Please, Dad, your lack of control is beneath you."

"How many times—"

"Don't." Julian's voice carried throughout the room. "Just *don't*. I'm not interested in how the book will lead to darkness. I'm not interested in how you're doing what you have to do. We've heard it all before. And if you *ever* bare your teeth to me again, it will be the last time you have teeth."

"Trying to scare me, son?" Bill laughed. "You're *air*. You can't do anything to me."

"Think again!"

Energy crackled through the air, and Bill stumbled, falling to the floor, his eyes wide.

My skin went icy. Julian was pure energy. I knew that,

but I'd never seen him actually use that energy in the material world. River and Jay stared at Julian, their eyes as wide as Bill's.

"All right, Julian," Bill said, standing. "You win. I will speak to you. *Only* to you."

"It's about time," River said. "No secret is worth all these lives."

"Your uncle will be the judge of that," Bill said.

"Yeah. I get it." River turned to Julian. "Talk fast, will you?"

"River," Julian said, his voice grave. "Know this. If I agree with my father's assessment, I will not divulge the secrets of the *Texts*."

"Are you fucking kidding me, Uncle Jules? What about my dad? Lucy? Em? Dante, for God's sake?"

Dante appeared at the top of the stairs. "Don't talk about me like I'm not here."

"Well, you weren't here," River said. "Now you are. You missed some major shit."

"Yeah, I heard it all." He descended. "Good for you, Dad."

Julian eyed me, motioning toward the door.

"I guess that's my cue to exit," I said to Jay. "I'm staying with you guys tonight. Let's go."

"Now?" Jay said. "This is just getting good."

"Now," I whispered, knowing full well the vampires in the room could most likely hear me, "unless you want to watch something a big brother should never see." I grabbed my purse and walked out the front door.

# THREE

# DANTE

Bill.

Just the man I *didn't* want to see.

My teeth were in their full glory, sharpened to painful points. Erin's scent hung in the air, so fertile and moist.

She was gone, and I ached for her. Even the anger toward my grandfather couldn't overpower the ache. The need.

"What are you doing here?" I snarled.

"Put those teeth away, Dante," Bill said. "They won't do any good against me."

I snarled again.

"Son." My father's voice was stern.

"This is my home," I said to Bill. "You chased out the other person who lives here. Now you can get out as well."

"Son." My father again.

"I can't do anything to a ghost with these teeth, but I sure as hell can rip *him* apart." I gestured toward Bill.

Bill lifted one corner of his mouth in a half smile.

Damned shithead was goading me.

*Fight or die in the arena.*

If Bill wanted to fight, I could fight. I'd bested every vampire I'd come across, and my grandfather would be no exception. I snarled once more.

"Son." This time my father's voice took on a tone I'd never heard. It was more than commanding, more than demanding obedience.

It was deeper. Darker. Menacing.

I turned toward him.

His teeth were bared. I hadn't seen his cuspids elongate since he'd appeared as a ghost. I wasn't sure he had that power anymore.

But then it dawned on me. I wasn't seeing *him*. I was seeing a manifestation, and he could make himself appear however he wanted...or not at all. Of course he could make his teeth descend. He could probably also make his head explode.

"Easy, Dante," River said. "Your dad just knocked Bill off his feet. Apparently he has power we didn't know about."

I regarded the apparition that was my father, lifting my brow in query.

"Pure energy can be harnessed to do just about anything," he said. "I only recently discovered this, though I haven't heard any other ghost speak of it."

"And you needed it to put Bill in his place," River said. "Good call, Uncle Jules."

So my dad could do other ghostly things. Strange things that other ghosts couldn't, or at least didn't talk about. Great. We'd deal with that later. Right now, I was so full of adrenaline and testosterone and unsated lust that I could take down anyone. Even a ghost with unharnessed energy and imaginary fangs. My father, however, was not my target. My grandfather was. The jerk still goaded me. He might be a vampire elder, but I was young, and strong, and mad as hell. Without Erin here, I had no control.

Perfect.

"What the fuck are you doing here?" I grabbed him by his shirt collar and slammed him against the front wall.

"I'm going to talk to your father. Tell him what I know. Now let go of me."

"Free yourself." This time I did the goading, my fangs long and sharp. "Show us how strong you are, elder. Show *me*."

"Dante." My father.

"Cuz." River.

I ignored them.

This time, Bill and I would have it out.

*Fight or die in the arena.*

As always, I would be victorious.

"Do what you want to me, Dante," Bill said, his voice strained from my hold. "You're strong. You've bested me. I cannot release myself."

I squeezed his throat tightly. "That's right, asshole. Don't forget it. I'm ten times the vampire you'll ever be. I can *destroy* you."

"Dante." Again, my father.

I expected him to throw his energy toward me and force me to release his father. I braced myself, ready to hurl back whatever hit me.

Nothing did.

"Let him go." My father again, his voice no longer commanding. "Let him go, Dante, not because I'm telling you to, and not because he deserves your mercy. He doesn't. Let him go because it's the right thing to do. Not for him, but for yourself."

*Control, son.*

The words he didn't say.

*Erin. Be worthy of Erin.*

I loosened my grip. "So you're going to tell my dad what you read in the *Texts*, huh? Then you might as well tell me. My father and I have no secrets."

"No, Dante," my father said. "I've agreed to speak with my father alone."

"Bullshit." I turned to River. "You agreed to this?"

"We don't have a choice," he said. "Bill refuses to tell us."

"Why the fuck not?"

"You're young and hormonal," Bill said. "And you, Dante... You're exhibiting abilities that are unheard of in a vampire your age."

He was talking about the glamouring. He didn't know about the levitation or the telekinesis.

God.

I'd moved Erin without so much as lifting a finger.

Moved the woman I loved right out of our bedroom.

Could she ever forgive me?

I'd had no choice. I would have fucked her if she hadn't left, and I had to protect her. With my life if it came down to that.

"I don't trust you," I said through clenched teeth.

"Dante, a word," my father said.

"Not now."

"Yes. Now. The bedroom."

Getting sent to my room by my father was getting old, but I wanted to hear him out. Perhaps he had every intention of telling the rest of us what Bill ultimately told him. "Not while he's here." I nodded toward Bill.

Without a word, Bill left my home. I stalked up the stairs.

My father had already materialized in the room. "Listen, son, I need to do this. It's the only way to find out the secrets your grandfather is hiding."

"There are other ways," I said.

"What other ways? The website we were banking on has shut down, and we have no idea how to get in touch with the owner. The book is gone, and now Bill's other copy is gone."

"What?"

"Yes. That's why he came here today. Someone stole the other copy from his place. He came here to get the one we had, but it's gone too."

My mind raced. "Then someone other than Bill wants to keep us from deciphering that book."

"So it would seem."

"Why?"

"That's what I'm trying to find out."

"Do you truly trust him to tell you what he knows?"

My father shook his head. "I don't trust him for anything anymore. But I have to try."

"He could be feeding you a load of bullshit."

"He could. Yes. But I do think he truly cares about the missing women. I know he cares about Brae and Emilia."

Did he? I wasn't so sure. If he did, he'd help us find them.

"What about the information he said he'd give us at Napoleon House? He said he had avenues, as an elder, that we didn't have. Then the elder ghost stopped him. What makes you think that same ghost won't stop him from divulging the secrets of the *Texts*?"

"That ghost doesn't *know* the secrets of the *Texts*. Bill read them without the council's knowledge."

Right. That was true. Still...

"The ghost is probably stalking Bill, watching his every move."

"Oddly, he's not. I'd know if he were. He can't get into the house, thanks to Bea's shield, but he's never around when Bill leaves the house."

I raised my eyebrows. "That hardly makes sense."

"I agree. It's not the book that worries the elder ghost. It's something else. Some council secret."

"What could it be?"

"I don't know. I'll never be an elder. You will be one day."

"Great, but we need their help *now*."

"We do. Let me deal with my father. I'm his son. His *dead* son. When he looks at me, he sees what could become of the rest of you. That will get to him."

"It hasn't so far."

"Don't let him fool you. He's old and strong and adept at hiding his feelings. This *is* getting to him. I'm sure of it."

"All right." I nodded. "Fair enough. Where's Erin?"

"I sent her over to River's."

"Why?"

"You know why. In twelve to twenty-four hours, her ovulation cycle will be complete. You need to stay here. Away from her."

"She came to *me*."

"I know that. I've convinced her not to try that again."

"Why would she voluntarily put herself in the position to get taken?"

"Because she loves you. She loves Lucy, and she cares deeply about the others. We seem to be out of leads, and she figured if they came for her, she could lead us to them."

"But why—"

"Because she wants to help, Dante. She's at the end of her rope, just like the rest of us are."

"We still have the fingerprints River took to the lab. We're not completely out of leads."

"River said those are a long shot, son."

I raked my fingers through my hair. "I know. Damn!" I sat down on the bed. "She's trying. She went to see Cynthia North, the patient who was returned to University. She's putting herself out there. Trying so hard..."

"She loves you. She wants to help."

"I want to protect her. I *need* to protect her. I feel like protecting her is the most important thing I'll ever do."

"I understand. Truly. Now I want you to try to understand something."

"Yeah?"

"Your grandfather is trying to protect *you*. You and River. He thinks whatever is in the book will harm you."

My teeth descended quickly with a snap of pain. "Don't try to make me feel for Bill."

"I'm not trying to make you do anything."

"I don't buy it. What about Em and Uncle Brae? Em's baby, for God's sake. Isn't he concerned about protecting them?"

My father sighed, an interesting sound coming from a ghost, kind of like the air being forced out of a basketball. "He claims to care, but on the other hand, he seems to have forsaken them. As a parent myself, I cannot understand that, which is why I need to learn what he knows."

"Did you mean it when you told River that you won't tell us if you feel it's in our best interests not to know?"

He was silent for a few moments before he spoke. Then, "I

hate lying to my father, but I will tell you. I can't *not* tell you. I want my brother and my daughter returned safely, and I need you to help with that."

Thank God! My father wouldn't let me down. I hated that I'd actually thought he'd keep me in the dark.

"But I'm warning you, Dante. You need to keep hold of your control. No matter what secrets are revealed, remember what the *Texts* truly are."

"Our history?"

He smiled, even chuckling a bit. "Yes, our history. Perhaps some philosophy and dogma, and definitely something that has your grandfather spooked. But in the end, the *Texts* are only words. Mere words. And words cannot harm anyone."

# FOUR

# *Erin*

"Exactly where am I supposed to sleep?" I asked, looking around River's small apartment. "He takes the bedroom, you take the couch. And that leaves...?"

"The floor?" Jay smiled.

"Great."

"Ease up, Sis. I'm just kidding. You can have the couch. I'll take the floor."

"That just means you'll be uncomfortable instead of me."

"I won't. I'll run over to my place and get my air bed."

"Do you think it's safe?"

"It's broad daylight, Sis. Plus I'm wearing that minty stuff you gave me."

"Then I'm going with you. I want to make a stop along the way, if you can get an address."

"Where?"

"To see Bella Lundy, the woman who was taken from the free clinic and then returned."

❧

Bella Lundy lived in Desire Area, one of the seedier neighborhoods in New Orleans.

"Is this safe?" I asked timidly as we drove through the narrow streets.

"It's safer than hanging around Claiborne Bridge at night," he said, "which you've been known to do."

"Actually, I haven't. That was Dante and River. He wouldn't let me go at night."

"Smart man. Don't worry, Sis. I'm armed. We'll be fine. It's the middle of the day, anyway."

"Which means Bella might not be home."

"True. But unemployment is high in this area, so she just might be, after all."

Jay stopped at a small house painted light green. The porch railing was broken, but otherwise it looked well kept. The lawn was mowed, anyway, with only a smattering of dandelions. A few lawn chairs sat on the porch, and a dented Ford Ranger was parked under the adjacent carport.

"Okay," I said. "Now what?"

"We knock on the door."

"Show your badge," I said. "That way they'll talk to us for sure."

"Can't."

"Why not?"

"I no longer have a badge, remember? Because of Grandpa Bill's stunt, Riv and I had to quit the force. They don't actually let us keep our badges."

"Crap." I rolled my eyes.

"I'll take the lead," he said.

"Why you?"

"Because I know how to ask the questions. But hey, if you want to, go for it."

"No, you're probably right." He was a trained detective, after all.

"This isn't anything official," he said. "Just chime in when you want to. The main thing is not to scare her off."

"Right." I nodded. Clearly I'd scared Cynthia North off at the spa and salon, so much so that she'd gotten another esthetician to fill in for her, and I hadn't even asked her anything yet. I had a strange foreboding that we were about to face the same kind of thing.

Jay and I left the car and walked over the spalling concrete walkway to the front door. A sad-looking wood wreath hung upon it.

Jay knocked.

Nothing.

Jay knocked again. I was about to give up when a little boy answered the door.

"Hi there," Jay said. "Is your mom home?"

He nodded his towhead but didn't move.

"Could you get her for me?" Jay asked.

"I'm not supposed to talk to strangers," the boy said.

"Hey, Jean-Claude, what are you doing?" A larger boy appeared. "What do y'all want?"

"We're looking for your mom. Bella Lundy."

"She ain't our mom. She's our auntie."

"Oh. My mistake, then. Is she here?"

"Yeah. Just a minute." He turned his head. "Auntie Belle, there's some people here to see you."

"Coming," a voice echoed.

Bella Lundy, presumably, appeared, wearing a pair of old jeans and a faded Iron Maiden T-shirt. She was blond like the little boys, though hers was clearly a dye job. Her inch of roots was dark brown. She held a dish towel. "Yeah. Can I help you?"

"I'm Detective Jay Hamilton," Jay said, "and this is my sister, Erin. She's a nurse at University."

"And I should care about that because..."

"We'd like to talk to you about your disappearance from the free clinic," he said.

"Shit." She turned to the boys. "Luc, you and Jean-Claude get out of here. Go out back and help your mom."

I figured she'd ask to see Jay's badge, but she didn't.

Once the little boys were gone, she stepped outside onto the porch. "I got nothing to say to y'all."

"Ms. Lundy," Jay said, "we need your help. More women are missing, and they haven't been returned. If you can tell us anything—"

"I can't."

Was it time for me to chime in? I had no idea, but maybe she'd react better to another woman. "My best friend is missing. So is my boyfriend's sister. Please. We need your help."

"I've already spoken to the police. I don't know anything. I'm trying to get through this, and I can't afford therapy, so if you don't mind, I'd prefer to just forget it. Now if you'll excuse me—"

I stopped the door she was shutting with my hand. "Please," I said again. "This is a matter of life or death."

She sighed. "I know I'll regret this, but come on in." She held the door open.

Jay and I walked into a tiny living room decorated with olive-green furniture and mud-brown carpeting. But it was clean. These were obviously proud people. Good people. I hoped that would work in our favor.

"I live here with my sister, Lorna. The boys are hers. Her husband walked out on her after the little one was born."

"I'm sorry to hear that," I said.

"Don't be. He was a gutter rat. She's better off. The poor thing is disabled. MS. Just got diagnosed last year. That's when I moved in to help. We get a stipend from the state, but it don't go real far. I'd work, but then who would take care of Lorna and the boys? It's a no-win." She gestured to the sofa. "Have a seat. You want anything? Some cold water?"

"Sure," Jay said. "Thank you."

She nodded. Shortly she returned with two glasses of water and handed one to each of us. I took a long sip, trying to ease my dry throat.

She sat down in a chair across from us. "I wasn't gone for long, and I don't remember any of it. Luc is only ten years old, but he took care of his mom and little brother for the two days I was missing. Bless him."

"How was he able to do that?"

"Lorna can move around. She's just really shaky and sometimes needs help on her bad days. Luc made them peanut butter and jelly sandwiches and made sure Jean-Claude got washed and went to bed on time. He's a good boy."

"Sounds like he is," I agreed.

"Sad to have to be the man of the house at ten years old," Bella said.

I wasn't sure what to say to that.

Luckily, Jay piped in. "It's great that he's so mature for his age."

"He hasn't had a choice. Ain't it sad when a kid can't just be a kid?"

"It is," Jay said. "I'm sure you and his mother are very proud of him."

"Oh, yeah. We definitely are."

"Can you tell us what you remember about your time at the clinic?" he asked.

"I'm not supposed to talk about it."

"Why?"

"I..." She tilted her head. "Huh. I'm not sure why. I just know I'm not supposed to."

Jay and I exchanged a glance.

"Why did you go to the clinic in the first place?" I asked.

"This is kind of embarrassing," she hedged.

"I'm a nurse. Trust me. I've heard it all."

"I thought I had VD."

"Oh?" I hadn't heard anyone refer to sexually transmitted diseases as "VD" in a long time. Maybe not since nursing school, and that was in a textbook.

"Yeah. I had some fierce itching and a tiny little sore. They took my blood, and... You know what? I never did find out the results, but the symptoms went away."

"Your results must have been negative, or they would have treated you. You probably just had a topical irritation of some sort. But they took blood? Usually it's just a urine test for chlamydia or gonorrhea or a finger prick for others like herpes and HIV."

"No, ma'am. They took a little tube of blood from right here." She motioned to the crease in her elbow.

"That's strange." I turned to Jay. "Especially at the free clinic. They'd go the easier, cheaper route and do the finger prick."

"Maybe they were out of those little finger prick thingies," Jay said.

"I suppose that's possible. Did they explain why they were taking blood from a vein?" I asked Bella.

"No, ma'am. I just assumed that's how they always did it."

"How old are you, Bella?" I asked.

"Twenty-three, ma'am."

Only three years younger than I was. How could I politely tell her to stop calling me ma'am? Made me feel like a granny.

Then something else occurred to me.

Twenty-three was prime childbearing age.

Lucy was twenty-five. Emilia twenty-five. Cynthia North couldn't be more than twenty-five either. What about the others?

I cleared my throat. "Bella, do you remember who the doctor was that you saw when you went to the clinic?"

"He was tall, thin build, kind of nerdy but cute. Dr. King, maybe?"

My heart sped up. "Dr. Crown?"

FIVE

# DANTE

*W*ords cannot harm anyone.

"What if they can?" I asked my father. "What about... spells? Dark spells." Enchantments.

"The words of the spell don't produce results," he said. "The energy behind the words does. Since when do you believe in spells anyway? I had to convince you that Bea's shields would work."

Enchantments. I'd been convinced, while I was held captive, that my bindings were enchanted. Otherwise I should have been able to break through them. I had the strength. I'd proven that.

In the arena.

*Fight or die in the arena.*

"I've learned to believe in a lot of things lately." No truer words.

"I know, son. So have I."

I smiled. "I guess we both believe in ghosts now, huh?"

"We do."

Ghosts... Something hit me like lightning. "Can you contact other ghosts on this plane?"

"I can try."

"What about that ghost from Napoleon House, the elder? What did you say his name was?"

"Levi Gaston."

"Right. He wanted to stop Bill from letting the council help us. Can you find out why?"

"I'd like to. In fact, I already had that idea, but I haven't seen him."

"How? If he's here, and you can see all the ghosts—"

"Dante, I can't see him if he's not in the same place I am. I've already been to his earthly home and to his grave. I didn't see him at either place."

"What about Bill's?"

"Bea shielded Bill's house from all ghosts but me, and I haven't seen him around that neighborhood."

"Yeah. That's right." I urged my mind to work. "Does he have any relatives that are still living?"

"I looked into that through some ghostly connections. He has a living son, two granddaughters, and two great-grandsons. But they aren't elders. They won't know what he knows. They aren't even vampires, and the boys are minors."

"He didn't marry a vampire?"

"No. Most of us don't. Vampire women are rare, son. I've already told you that. Brae and I were lucky to find Simone and your mother."

"We should visit Levi Gaston's son."

"He won't know anything."

"Still, what can it hurt?"

My father stayed silent for a moment. Then another.

"Are you going to say anything?"

"We will visit his son, Dante. But not to get information on what Gaston knows."

"Then why?"

"Because we might find Gaston there."

# SIX

# *Erin*

"Yes!" Bella said. "That's it. Dr. Crown."

"Dr. Logan Crown," I said.

"I don't think he actually said his first name."

"Did you happen to see his badge?" Jay asked.

"No." She rolled her eyes. "I was too consumed with crotch itch."

So much TMI there. Bella was a pretty young woman, much too young to have the gray bags under her eyes that made her look twenty years older. She shouldn't have to hang out with people who she thought might give her STDs.

More to the point, though, what had Logan been doing at the clinic? He was a resident. How did he have the time to volunteer at the clinic? The University residents kept ridiculous schedules.

I cleared my throat. Time to get onto something other than crotch itch. "Ms. Lundy—"

"Bella. Or Belle. Please."

"Okay. Bella, can you recall anything that happened to you while you were gone?"

"No." She looked down.

Jay nodded slightly at me. He thought she was lying.

"Anything at all?" I asked, trying to sound as sweet and nonthreatening as I could. "Others' lives depend on it."

"No. I don't remember anything. I really don't. Except..."

"Except what?" I prodded gently.

She sighed. "I have dreams sometimes."

"About what?"

"About...blood mostly. Blurs hovering over me, I assume they're doctors, taking my blood. They said they were testing it, that I was a perfect specimen, and I had all the characteristics they were looking for."

My stomach lurched. "What kind of characteristics?"

"My hair. They wanted to know what color my hair was." She let out a nervous laugh. "I'm not a real blonde."

I choked back a chuckle.

Then a thought speared into my head. Dr. Bonneville had asked me to research blood types and physical characteristics.

"Your blood type is B positive," I said more to myself than to Bella.

"Yes. I don't know what that means, really, but they mention it a lot. In my dreams, that is." She looked down again, folding her hands in her lap, and then up to meet my gaze. "Y'all will protect me, won't you? I mean, you said you're a cop and all."

Jay cleared his throat. "I'm not currently—"

I nudged his knee with my own.

"We'll do what we can," he said. "Why? Do you feel you might be in danger?"

"I'm not sure. I just know I'm not supposed to talk about any of this."

"How do you know that if you don't remember anything?" he asked.

"I don't know. It's just a...feeling, I guess."

Jay nodded. "I understand."

Did he? I couldn't tell. I for sure did *not* understand. "Is there anything else you can tell us?"

"Nothing other than the dreams. I honestly didn't even know I was gone. I woke up in the clinic, and I felt like no time had passed."

"Did they do any blood work on you?"

"Yeah. They took more blood. Said there weren't any drugs in my system."

Vampires. She didn't need drugs. She'd been glamoured.

I needed a minute. This was a lot to digest. I stood. "May I use your bathroom?"

"Yeah, sure." She pointed to a hallway. "First door on the right."

I ambled over the worn carpeting to the door. The hallway was at an angle, so I was no longer in Bella's line of vision. The bathroom door was closed, so I knocked, just in case someone was in there.

"Just a minute!" said a small voice.

One of the boys.

I looked around. Photos of the boys graced the yellowing walls. They were handsome little things, both blond and blue-eyed. Then a photo of a striking woman with dark hair and eyes. She looked like Bella but more dazzling. She was holding a newborn.

Must be her sister.

The littler boy, Jean-Claude, ambled out of the room. "Sorry. I'm done now."

"Thank you, sweetie." I smiled.

He ran into the room across from the bathroom. I followed him with my gaze.

"Is this your room?" I asked.

"No. This is Mommy's room. I share a room with Luc, and Auntie Belle sleeps in the basement."

The basement? Poor Bella. Though perhaps it was a full-sized basement and was finished, in which case she was most likely quite happy. I doubted it, though. This house was in need of some major updates.

A hospital bed sat in the room.

"Mommy asked me to bring out her book." He grabbed a dog-eared paperback sitting on a night table, and again I followed him with my gaze. "She likes to read."

"Do you like to read?" I asked.

He nodded. "I'm not as good as Luc, though."

"Well, Luc is older."

"That's what Mommy says." He pointed to a shelf alongside the far wall. "Luc can read some of these books. They're long, without any pictures."

"Oh?"

"Yeah. I still like pictures in my books, so I don't like these. Luc does. He likes the one called *Treasure Island*. That's his favorite."

"That's one of my favorites too. When you're older, I'll bet it'll be one of yours."

"Yeah. Luc has read a lot of these. Except for that one." He pointed. "We're not allowed to touch that big one."

# SEVEN

# DANTE

Andrew Gaston was a sixty-two-year-old man living in a smaller home in the Garden District. Erin had left her car—she drove to River's with Jay—so I grabbed her keys and left. I didn't have a number, so I didn't call first. I probably wouldn't have anyway. No reason to give Andrew a chance to leave.

"I'll meet you there," my father said, vanishing.

❧

I knocked on the front door. It was white with peeling paint.

Was he home? I didn't know anything about him. At sixty-two he could very well still be working full time. He wasn't a vampire, as my father said Levi had married a human woman. Did he even know about his father?

When I got no response, I knocked again.

This time the door cracked open. "Who's there?"

"I'm looking for Andrew Gaston?" I said.

"What do you want with him?"

"I just want to talk."

"Who the hell are you?"

"Dante Gabriel."

"Gabriel. Are you related to Bill Gabriel?"

*Should I admit to that?*

"Go ahead, son," my father's voice said, making me jerk. "Be honest."

His voice was clear as a bell, but Andrew made no indication that he heard.

"Yeah. He's my grandfather."

The door opened another inch. "Did he send you?"

My father had said to be honest. "No."

The door moved another inch. "Are you one of them?"

"One of who?"

"You know what I'm talking about."

"I'm afraid I don't, sir. If you'd just let me in, all I want is a few minutes of your time. It's about your father, Levi Gaston."

"He's dead."

"I know that. I just have a few questions."

"Why?"

"If you open the door, I'll be happy to tell you why."

The door opened, finally, and before me stood a tall man with graying hair and a goatee. He looked me over. "You're a Gabriel, all right."

"Yes, I am."

"You've got the build, the hair, the eyes. Damn. You look a lot like Bill when he was younger. Which twin was your father?"

"Go ahead," my father said, still invisible and, apparently, inaudible to Andrew.

"Julian. Do you know him?"

He shook his head. "I've seen photos, though. My father

was kind of... How should I say it? Obsessed with your father and his twin. Held them up to me as the standard I should try to reach."

How much did this guy know? "Why would he do that?"

"Hell if I know. The Gabriel twins were, in his mind, the perfect specimens of manhood." He scoffed. "I fell quite short of that."

Andrew Gaston was hardly a bad specimen. He had a full head of silvery dark hair, a strong jawline, and a muscular build. He could easily pass for ten years younger.

Why would any father want more from a son?

*Because he wasn't a vampire.*

I couldn't say the words. I had no idea if Andrew even knew his father was a vampire. Why would he hold his own son up to a vampire standard when he knew damned well he wouldn't produce vampire children with a human woman?

Unless he thought maybe he could...

We were here to find Levi Gaston. My father hadn't indicated he was anywhere on the premises, but I felt compelled to speak to Andrew. I couldn't talk to my father telepathically, even though sometimes I felt he could read my mind. My only choice was to continue, and he'd tell me to stop if he thought best.

"How much do you know about your father, Andrew?"

"I know he was an asshole."

"I can see why you'd feel that way. No father should admire another man's son over his own. I'm sorry you went through that. What else do you know about him?"

"I know why you're here," he said frankly.

"Yeah?"

"You're looking for something. I don't have it."

"I'm only looking for information," I said.

"I don't have the book," Andrew said. "Why else would you come here?"

"What book?"

"That piece of supernatural garbage. It's unreadable, anyway. We were never allowed to touch the damned thing. He only said it was a valuable antique, a piece of fiction. He left it to my sister. She was his golden child."

"He doesn't know," my father said. "I can't believe it."

He was still here. Thank God.

"Are you talking about a book called the *Vampyre Texts*?"

"Yeah. It's old and yellowed and smells like mold. She can have the damned thing."

"Where might I find your sister?"

He guffawed. "Good luck with that. She's dead."

"Oh. I'm sorry."

"I'm not. She was a loony bitch. So are her two kids." He shook his head. "My esteemed father left her all his money too, but she blew it all on plastic surgery. She was always broke before that. She spent all her money on beauty pageants for her older daughter."

"How can you spend that much money on plastic surgery?"

"It wasn't a huge amount of money. We didn't have Gabriel money."

Bill was very well off, but most of my father's money had come from my mother's side of the family. "Gabriel money" must refer to Bill's estate.

"Anyway," Andrew continued, "the beauty of the family ended up getting knocked up and had to get out of pageantry. They're all broke now."

"I see."

"Yeah. They live somewhere in Desire Area. We don't keep in touch."

"What about your sister's husband, the girls' father? Is he around?"

"Dead too. They died together in a car accident four years ago."

"Oh. I'm sorry."

"Good riddance. By then all the money was gone, and she went to hell with fat lips and a plastic face." He shook his head. "If my father had given me my share, I wouldn't have squandered it. I'd sure as hell be living better than this."

His house was fine. I wasn't sure why he didn't think he was living well. "What do you do for a living?"

"I'm a plumber."

"Do you have kids?"

"Nope. My partner and I split up five years ago, and we didn't have the equipment to make kids together."

Ah. Andrew Gaston was gay. Another reason he probably wasn't a perfect specimen according to his father. All I'd learned so far was that Levi Gaston was a supreme prick.

"I'm sorry."

"Don't be. We grew apart. It happens."

I nodded. "I get that. I mean I'm sorry your father was such a jerk."

"Water under the bridge. I'm long over it. Anyway," Andrew went on, "neither one of us was interested in adoption. Besides, I didn't have the best parental role model, you know? I'm not sure I would have made a very good father."

"I think you probably would have been a hundred times better than your own father was."

"Dante, watch what you say about a man's dead father."

My father's voice.

"What?" I said aloud. "He *was* a jerk."

Andrew looked around. "Uh...exactly who are you talking to?"

My father appeared instantly. "He's talking to *me*."

# EIGHT

# *Erin*

My heart dropped into my stomach.

*Vampyre Texts.*

Right in front of me, in this room, on this shelf, sat the book we needed.

"Where did this come from?" I asked Jean-Claude.

"It was my grandma's," he said. "She died."

"I'm so sorry to hear that."

He shrugged. "It's okay. I didn't know her. I was only one when she died. Luc says she was a mean old bag anyway."

A grandmother who was mean? Granted, I never knew my mother's mother, but my father's mother had doted on Jay and me.

"I'm sorry to hear that."

Was this little boy's grandmother a vampire, and if so, did Bella know?

And how could I get my hands on that book?

I looked around.

Money.

Money should do the trick. Lorna had MS. Medical bills. Bella wasn't working. They were probably on welfare and Medicaid. This house needed work.

As much as I hated to do it, I was going to pledge some of Dante's newfound money to Bella to get my hands on this book. Guilt nabbed me. I shouldn't. But he'd said what was his was mine, right?

Just as quickly, I changed my mind. I couldn't do it. If Dante and I were to have any relationship at all, we had to have honesty between us. I couldn't spend a large amount of money without talking to him first.

I had my own savings account. It wasn't a lot, but it was probably more than Bella had.

I quickly used the bathroom—why I was here in the first place—and then went back into the living area.

Jay was looking awkward on the couch.

He smiled when he saw me. "Sis, is everything okay?"

"Yeah, fine. I was talking to little Jean-Claude. He's very sweet."

"They both are," Bella agreed. "No thanks to their no-good father."

I ignored the father remark. I needed to get to the book. "He says both he and his brother like to read."

"Oh, yeah. All the time. But that's Lorna too. Always has her nose in a book." Bella shook her head. "She was the pretty one and the smart one. Ma always said so. Made me feel like a dumb and ugly piece of shit."

"I don't know why she would say that. You're very pretty."

"Not like Lorna. She was beautiful. Could have had quite the social life, but always had her head stuck in a book. Even when Ma dragged her to all those pageants."

"Pageants?"

"Yeah. I was just a little girl and had to tag along. Lorna hated the pageants. Still hates them. She blames our life today on that. Ma blew all her money taking Lorna here and there, all over the country. Lorna didn't do well. Still Ma wouldn't stop. She spent more money on classes and workshops for Lorna. She never even finished high school because she missed so much."

"I'm sorry to hear that."

"I keep telling her to get her GED. Heck, she loves to read so much. But since her diagnosis, she's lost interest in getting her education."

"Maybe I can help you."

Jay turned to me, his brows lifted. "Sis?"

"There's a book on your sister's shelf. Jean-Claude showed me. Would you be willing to sell it? My brother and I would pay well." I nudged Jay.

"Which one?"

"The antique copy of the *Vampyre Texts*."

Jay stiffened next to me.

Bella gestured with her hand. "Oh, that. It was our grandfather's. He used to collect old books. At least that's what Ma told us."

"Do you have any need for it? I'd be willing to pay you, let's say, five hundred dollars?"

"Gee. I don't know."

"How about a thousand?" Jay piped in.

I nudged him sharply. Who made an offer when the first one hadn't been turned down yet? But we were desperate. That was for certain.

"We could use the money." She sighed and stood. "Let me go ask Lorna. She's out back in her chair."

Once Bella left, I turned to my brother. "Why did you offer more money?"

"Because if she truly has a copy of that book, we need it."

"I know."

"Dante will be willing to pay loads for it. A thousand is nothing to him."

"I know," I said again. "But we can't spend his money. All we have is ours. And I only have a few thousand in savings."

"I've got about fifteen thousand. We can make this work." Jay rubbed his chin. "Let's hope she goes for it. Are you sure it's the same book?"

"I honestly didn't get a good look at it, but it was old and big, with a leather binding."

"We could be offering to pay for a phony."

"Well...yeah. I guess. Maybe I didn't think this through. Of course, I wasn't the one who doubled our offer." I poked him.

A few minutes later, Bella returned. "Lorna says we're supposed to keep the book in the family."

"Shit," I muttered. "Why?"

"I don't know. That's what Ma told her. But"—she smiled—"I convinced her to let it go. For five thousand."

My eyes shot wide. "Five grand?"

Jay cleared his throat. "I think we can swing that."

"Cash," Bella said.

I checked my watch. "There's no time to get to the bank before it closes, and we can only get three hundred at a time from the ATM. We can get you six hundred and bring the rest tomorrow. Will that work?"

"Sure. I guess," Bella said.

"Good." I stood. "Let's go get the book."

"No. You can't take the book until we get all the money."

"All right," I said. "I understand. Can we at least look at the book? See what we're buying?"

"I suppose so. Wait here."

She returned, lugging the large volume. She plunked it on my lap.

"It looks real," I said.

"So did the phony that Bill planted," Jay warned.

"Wait. Phony?" Bella said. "What are you talking about?"

"Nothing. We found a counterfeit copy of this book. Is there any way to know this is the real thing?"

"My mother said it's been in our family for centuries," Bella said. "Other than that, I have no idea."

"Since we can't get the money until tomorrow," I said to Jay, "we can talk to Dante and River first."

"Wait. What? You're not going to go get me the six hundred?"

"Well"—Jay cleared his throat—"no. Not if we can't take the book. That doesn't make any sense."

"Crap. I was hoping to get to Walmart and get some food. All we have right now is a loaf of bread and some boxed mac and cheese. Those little boys need milk."

"That's really all you have?"

"Well...some flour and canned stuff. Green beans and peas. Corn. SpaghettiOs."

"But no milk?" I asked.

"No." She shook her head. "We ran out this morning."

I had no idea whether Bella was telling the truth. I looked to Jay. He shook his head at me slightly.

He thought she was lying.

"We'll get you the six hundred," he said, "if you let us take the book."

Bella sighed. "Lorna said—"

"What have you got to lose?" Jay said. "But if we find out it's counterfeit, we return it, and you don't get the rest of the money."

"But I—er...we—can keep the six hundred bucks?"

"Sure," he said. "No problem."

"All right. Deal. But the book stays here until you come back with the money."

"Fair enough," Jay said, standing. "Come on, Sis."

# NINE

# DANTE

Andrew jerked backward. "What the fuck?"

"Dad..."

"It's okay. I'm Julian Gabriel, Dante's father."

"Are you some kind of magician?"

"Not exactly," he said. "I'm a ghost."

Andrew's eyes nearly shot out of his head. "I think I need to sit down."

"Yeah. That's a good idea," I said. "Let's sit. Except my dad doesn't really sit."

Andrew led us into a nicely decorated living room. At least I assumed it was nicely decorated. I didn't know shit about that kind of stuff. All the furniture was boxy, which looked out of place in the older house. Too modern. The art on the walls was also modern. At least I assumed it was, since I couldn't pick out anything I understood in any of it.

"I'm not feeling too good," Andrew said, sitting down.

"You want something? Water?"

"Yeah." He gestured to the kitchen. "Bottles in the fridge."

I quickly retrieved a bottle, returned, and handed it to Andrew.

He took a quick drink. "I'm thinking bourbon might be better."

"I'll even join you," I said. "Just tell me where."

"Bar in the family room." He pointed. "Get the good stuff."

I wasn't sure what the good stuff was, so I grabbed the most ornate-looking bottle and two glasses.

I returned and poured two fingers for each of us.

"What about your dad?" Andrew asked.

"Ghosts don't drink. Or eat. Or sleep. Or...whatever," my father said.

I took a sip of the bourbon and let its warmth slide over my tongue. "Dad, I'm not sure where to start."

"Have you seen your father lately, Andrew?" he asked.

"So you're Julian Gabriel." Andrew eyed my father's ghost.

"I am. Or *was*. However you choose to look at it."

"You're one of the two I never lived up to." He scoffed. "You're handsome, good build. Better looking than I am? Maybe. Depends on personal taste. Of course you're dead. At least I'm alive. I guess."

"You are," my father said, clearly choosing wisely to ignore Andrew's snide comments on his looks, "and so is my brother. He's missing. I'm hoping you can help us find him. So I'll ask you again. Have you seen your father?"

"My father is dead. How could I see him?"

"The same way Dante sees me," my father said. "Your father is on this plane."

"Damn. I thought for sure he was burning in hell." Andrew smacked his lips after taking a drink. "Somehow this flies in the face of all I believe in."

"There is no he—"

"Dad. Maybe not the time?" I swirled the brown liquid in my glass.

My father nodded. A thought occurred to me. Andrew could see my father. Why the hell could everyone else see him for the first time, and I couldn't?

I tamped down my emotion. Now wasn't the time to dwell on that. If I did, I'd get angry. Dark things happened when I got angry. I was a modern-day Bruce Banner.

"Have you had any indication that your father might have been around here lately?" I asked.

"Sorry to disappoint you, but if you're looking for my dead father, this is the last place he'd come. The bastard hated me."

Gratitude overwhelmed me in that moment. First chance I had, I was going to tell my father how much I loved him and was grateful for his support all my life. I couldn't imagine feeling the way Andrew did.

"I'm sorry you didn't have a better relationship with him," I said.

He took a drink. "Water under the bridge. I never could live up to his standards. He wanted a college boy, even though he never went to college himself. I was more interested in plumbing. So I did what I wanted. To hell with him. I have my own business, and I make damned good money. Bought this house myself." He took another drink, emptying his glass. "Of course he'd rather I wasn't gay, but that wasn't a choice I made to spite him, despite what he thought. I was born this way. It is what it is."

"I know." In fact, I knew far more than Andrew could conceive. The elder Gaston had kept a lot from his only son. I held up the bottle. "Another?"

"Absolutely." He slid his glass across the coffee table.

I waited for my father to intervene. How much could we tell Andrew? He clearly had no idea his father had been a vampire, and my guess was that the real reason Levi never approved of Andrew had little to do with his sexual orientation or his choice of profession. He coveted Bill's twin sons not for their strength, intelligence, or dark beauty, not even for their rarity as vampire identical twins.

He coveted them because they were born vampires.

Why was I feeling that so strongly? It didn't make any sense. Gaston had married a human woman, so how could he expect anything but human offspring?

And then it hit me.

First a spark, and then a jolt.

Bill said he could help us find the missing women, that he had council secrets that could help. The ghost of Levi Gaston threatened him if he gave away such council secrets.

Bill knew something.

Gaston knew something.

And it had everything to do with the missing women.

I regarded my father's ghost. He nodded slightly at me. Was he thinking the same thing?

In an instant, my father disappeared.

"Fuck," Andrew said. "I haven't had that much bourbon yet. What just happened?"

"He comes and goes," I said. "You get used to it after a while."

He shook his head. "Damn."

I stood. "Do you mind if I use your bathroom?"

"Yeah, no problem." He gestured toward a hallway. "Right on the corner, there."

I walked to the bathroom and shut the door. "Dad?" I whispered.

"Yeah. I'm here. He can't hear me, but he *can* hear you, so keep whispering."

I nodded.

"You looked like you wanted to talk to me alone. What is it?"

"I get the feeling that Levi Gaston was hoping he'd get a vampire son, even though his wife was human."

"I get the same feeling."

"But why? He had to know the biology. A human and a vampire always produce a human. It's part of why we're dying out."

"True. But perhaps he thought he could circumvent genetics. I need to confer with Jack."

"Good idea," I whispered. "But until then, what do we do? Bill seemed to think he could help us find the missing women, and Gaston stopped him. Bill knows something, Dad. I've felt it since I returned. He's different, and this could be why."

"Or he could be different because of what he saw in the *Texts* that has him spooked."

"True. Or maybe both. Why else would he think he could help us find the missing women?"

My father sighed. "I can't imagine he'd allow his own granddaughter to be taken."

"I'm not as convinced," I whispered. "Since I came back, he's been odd. He's been weird, even, refusing to teach me what I need to know, refusing to tell us what's in the *Texts* even though we need the information to figure out what's going on with Erin and me. All for what he feels is the greater good."

"You think he'd allow Emilia to be taken if he thought it

was for the greater good?"

I nodded. "I'm sure of it."

"Dad, where did you go wrong?" my father's voice lamented.

"What about Andrew? How much do we tell him?"

"There's no need to rattle his world any more than it already is. Just finish your drink, thank him, and leave. If he hasn't seen his father, he can't help us. We've already shown him ghosts exist. No need to tell him about vampires as well."

I nodded again, flushing the toilet for show. Then I ran the water to simulate washing my hands and returned to the living room.

"I took the liberty of pouring you another drink," Andrew said, raising his own glass.

I opened my mouth to object, but then decided I wouldn't mind another. "Great. Thanks."

# TEN

# *Erin*

"Look what we got." Jay plunked the large tome down on the small kitchen table in River's apartment.

River put down the glass of blood he was drinking.

"Partner," Jay said, "I don't know how I'll ever get used to that."

"Just be glad I'm not taking it from a vein," River said. "Where did you find that?"

"Bella Lundy's house. We went over to question her about her disappearance, and lo and behold, there it was on her bookshelf. Erin found it."

"You just took it?"

"No. We made a deal with her. She offered to sell it to us for five thousand dollars."

"Holy shit!"

"I know. In fact, we already gave her six hundred. All we could get once the banks closed. If it turns out to be a phony, Erin and I are out some bucks. But if it's real, we owe her another four grand and change."

"How are we supposed to find out whether it's real?" River said. "I can't read Old French."

"I don't know," I said. "There has to be a way. Isn't there a... vampire museum or something?"

"We try to stay *under* the radar, Erin, not advertise our history in a museum." River rolled his eyes.

"Don't be a dickhead," Jay said.

"What about Bill?" I asked. "He would know."

"Yeah. Bill's been so helpful so far." From River, again with the eye roll.

"Well, we need to find out one way or the other, because Bella Lundy is expecting the rest of the money tomorrow."

"No pressure or anything," River said.

"Look," I said. "We did the right thing. You would have done the same."

River sighed. "You're right. I would have."

"Then let's figure this out," Jay said.

"Any idea how?"

Jay rubbed his temple. "Not a one."

"Maybe Dante would know. He spent the most time with the other one," I said. "I'm not supposed to go near him until my ovulation cycle is over tomorrow, but you guys could take it over to our place."

"I'll take it," River said. "You stay here with Erin, Jay. Dante would have my ass if anything happened to her."

"Good call," Jay agreed. "I won't be any help with this anyway."

River picked up the book. "Don't wait up."

# ELEVEN

# DANTE

I left Andrew's place after I'd finished my second drink. My father hadn't returned after our chat in the bathroom, and though I called for him several times while driving home, he didn't reappear.

Ghost's prerogative, I guessed. Too bad, because I truly did want to let him know how grateful I was to him, thankful that I'd had a loving father and not a father who constantly compared me to someone else.

I pulled in to the townhome complex just in time to see River drive up and get out of his car, lugging a large book.

Had he found another copy of the *Texts*?

I motioned for him to meet me at the door.

"Jay and Erin got it," he said when we were inside, sitting at the table. "Bella Lundy had it. Said it had belonged to her grandfather."

"Only a vampire would have a copy," I said.

"Right, son."

My father had appeared.

"Uncle Jules," River said. "Can't you warn us when you're going to do that?"

"Sorry. If there's a way to do that, I haven't figured it out."

"Why'd you leave me alone with Andrew Gaston?" I asked.

"I wanted to confer with some ghosts who knew the Gastons. Turns out that Bella Lundy is the daughter of Andrew's sister, Cecily Gaston Lundy. Which means—"

"Bella is Levi Gaston's granddaughter."

"Then this is Levi Gaston's copy of the *Texts*," River said. "It must be genuine."

"There's a good chance it is," my father said, "but we can't be sure. We need someone to verify it, and Bill won't."

"Well, we need to do it quickly, because Erin and Jay promised Bella Lundy five grand if it was real."

I twisted my neck. "Say what?"

"You heard me. Your girlfriend and my partner bought this thing from Bella. Apparently she drove a hard bargain. They already paid her six bills up front."

"Was Bella Lundy the beauty queen?" I asked my father.

"No. That was her older sister, Lorna. The two great-grandsons are hers."

"I don't get it," River said. "Why wouldn't Levi Gaston want Bill to help us? His granddaughter is involved here."

"A couple things," my father said. "First of all, his granddaughter was returned and is no longer in danger. Second, he may not give a rat's ass. Dante and I learned this evening what he thought of his only son. Suffice it to say they weren't close. We can assume he thought a little more highly of his daughter, as he left her all his assets, but he may not have held her in very high regard either."

I quickly filled River in on the conversation with Andrew.

"We're just going to have to ask Bill again," I said. "But first we need to shield this book, not just from him but from *anyone* who wants to take it."

"I'm on it." My father vanished.

"He's off to see Bea, no doubt," I said.

"She's nuts, but she's proved to be pretty damned helpful," River said.

"I'm no longer sure she's nuts," I pointed out. "Pretty much everything she's told us so far has been accurate. Maybe she truly does have the sight."

"At this point, cuz, anything is possible."

✤

*Again I woke on the dank floor of the fighting pit.*

*How many times had I found myself here? I'd lost count.*

*I never remembered getting here, never remembered dressing or putting on a mask.*

*And I never remembered the end of the fight, striking the final blow.*

*I rose, letting my vision adjust to the blackness. Sometimes my opponent hid in the shadows. Sometimes he came at me with a vengeance, refusing to hide.*

*This time, he'd chosen to remain unseen, unheard. My acute senses were on high alert. I could actually feel his presence, perceive him, even though I couldn't see or hear him.*

*He was here.*

*He was waiting.*

*Soon he would strike.*

✣

"Hey, you all right?" River waved a hand in front of me.

I jolted back to the here and now. "Yeah. I'm good."

"You seemed a million miles away for a minute."

"Sometimes I see things. Things that happened to me. I'm remembering more and more. I want to remember, because it might help us. But..."

"What?"

The words formed in the back of my throat. *I don't want to remember just as much. I don't want to know what I did, what I might be capable of.*

I cleared my throat. "Nothing."

"We're going to figure this out, Dante," he said. "I promise you. We'll find Lucy and Em. We'll find my dad."

"Thank him," I said.

"Sorry. What?"

"Your dad. When you see him again—and you will—thank him."

"For what?"

"For being a good dad. He was. He *is*."

"I know he is. He's the greatest. I've missed him so much."

"I'm sorry I took him away from you," I said gravely.

"Don't go there, man. We both went out that night. I could have just as easily met your fate, and our dads would have gone after me. We both know that." His cell phone buzzed, and he glanced at it. "It's the lab. I need to take this."

I nodded.

"Hey, Joey," he said into the phone. "Got any news for me?"—pause—"Yeah, not surprising. Now we just need to figure out who switched them."—pause—"Not yet, no."—

pause—"Right. Thanks a bunch, Joey. You're the best." He ended the call.

"So?"

"Erin was right. Her pills were placebos. Simple sugar pills designed to look exactly like her birth control. Someone wanted her fertile and took the time and effort not only to duplicate the look of the pills but also to plant them here."

I shook my head. "Damn."

"You're surprised?"

"Not surprised so much as confused. Staying away from her was the hardest thing I've ever done, and to put that in perspective, I was held against my will for ten years."

"I get it."

He didn't, but he thought he did. Not his fault. "You still have full use of your nose. Do you smell anything weird in here? Someone who's not supposed to be here?"

He shook his head. "I already thought of that. There's a tiny residual scent of both Erin and Jay, from before they started wearing the mint potion, but that's it."

"Vampires," I said. "They've fucking been here. In my house."

"Erin thinks that ER doctor, Bonneville, made the switch weeks ago when she stopped by."

"Maybe. But what if it was the thugs?"

"If the thugs had been here, they'd have found Erin."

"Not if she wasn't here and they couldn't pick up her scent."

"They haven't been here, Dante. Trust me. I'd have picked up on it. I've learned to listen to my intuition where criminals are concerned."

"Who took the *Texts* then?"

"I wish I knew. No one who left a scent. That's for cer—"

Someone pounded on the door.
Now what? I opened the door.
My grandfather stood there.
He didn't look happy.

# TWELVE

# Erin

J ay's phone buzzed. He lifted his brow. "It's Mom."

My heart bumped. "Really? Shouldn't she be asleep?"

"Maybe it's her night off." He put the phone to his ear. "Hey, Mom. What's up?" His eyebrows shot up even farther. "You're *what*?"

"Is anything wrong?" I asked.

He shook his head. "I'm staying at a friend's for a while." He quickly rattled off River's address. "See you in a few."

"What was that about?"

"Mom's in town."

"What for? Is Dad with her?"

"I have no idea, and I didn't ask. She said she has to talk to us."

"Okay." This couldn't be anything good.

"You want a drink?" Jay opened the refrigerator and winced. "I'll never get used to seeing those butcher bags full of blood in here."

Blood. Dante. He'd need to feed.

I sighed. He'd have to wait until tomorrow evening. I promised Julian I'd stay away until my cycle had completed. On the way back from Bella's, after we'd picked up Jay's air bed, we stopped at a pharmacy so I could get an ovulation predictor test. I needed to make sure I was no longer fertile before I went back to Dante's. I also called my gynecologist and had her fill a new prescription for birth control. I didn't love the idea of using a backup method, so I wouldn't. Dante would know when I was fertile. He would be our backup method.

We'd rely on his control.

Jay grabbed a beer out of the fridge and gestured to me. I shook my head. I didn't want to drink.

I wanted to know what the hell was going on.

About a half hour later, the doorbell rang.

Jay opened it, and there stood my mother, looking as young as she always did, her dark hair cut in a stylish pixie, and her green eyes, so like my own except darker, as beautiful as ever.

"Hey, Mom." Jay gave her a hug and grabbed her suitcase. "Planning to stay awhile?"

"No. Not long. I told your father I'd be home as soon as I could." She turned to me and gave me a hug. "I've missed you two. Why you both decided to stay down here in this place is beyond me."

"It's a great city, Mom," Jay said. "Lots of history and... other stuff."

"You both do seem to be drawn here." She let out a sigh. "I think I finally know why."

"Oh?" I lifted my brow.

"This is going to come as quite a shock. I haven't quite accepted it yet."

"What?" Jay and I both asked in unison.

"I never knew my mother."

"We know that," I said.

"She died in childbirth. I always felt horrible about that, but your grandfather never blamed me. He was the most loving father ever."

"Grandpa was great. We know that as well," I said.

She walked to the couch and sat down. "Is anyone else here?"

"No. My partner lives here. He's out."

"Good. This is just too bizarre. I can't even—" She sighed and rubbed her chin.

My heart thumped. She knew. She fucking knew. I drew in a deep breath and let it out slowly. "We know, Mom."

Her eyes shot wide. "You couldn't possibly."

Should I just say it? I looked to Jay for reassurance, but he shook his head slightly at me.

He was right. What if Mom was here for a different reason and I spouted out that her mother was a vampire? She'd freak.

"Maybe not," Jay said. "Tell us what you need to tell us. I assure you. We'll be okay."

My mother cleared her throat. "I had a dream two nights ago. A very disturbing one."

I sure could understand that. I'd had my share of disturbing dreams. "Oh?" was all I said.

"I'm not sure how to say this, so I'm just going to say it." She inhaled. "My mother came to me in a dream. She looked the same as she did in old photos I've seen. And besides, I knew it was her. I can't explain it, but I just knew."

"I understand," I said.

"Do you?"

"I do. I've had odd dreams myself lately."

"Did anyone come to you?"

"No. But I know someone else who had a dream where a dead person came to him. And Mom, what he found out in his dream turned out to be true."

"I have no idea whether what my mother said in my dream is true or will be true. But I awoke knowing I had to do what she told me. I felt it very strongly."

"Like I said, I understand," I repeated.

"I do too," Jay agreed.

"My mother didn't say why, but she told me I had to find something that had belonged to her and give it to the two of you." She patted her suitcase. "I have it. It's in here."

"What is it?"

"I'll get to that. She instructed me to go dig up a safe she had buried before I was born. It was under a large oak tree on the property where she'd grown up in southern Ohio."

"You trespassed?" Jay said.

"I did. But the property is vast, and she assured me that no one would be the wiser."

"Are you sure you weren't seen?"

"I am. I'm not sure how, but I am." She cleared her throat. "Anyway, I got the small safe. It was heavy but I managed, and I got away as quickly as I could. When I returned home, I opened it using the combination she'd given me in the dream."

I gulped. "And?"

"Inside the safe were two things. One was a small jewelry box. Diamonds. A box of loose diamonds. My mother had buried diamonds!"

"Are you sure?" Jay asked. "They could be fake."

"They're not." She twisted her lips. "Well, they could be,

but why would my mother put fake jewels in a safe? All those years, we could have been living well. You could have gone to medical school, Erin."

Medical school. A jolt of sadness hit my heart.

"Are you sure she's the one who buried them?" Jay asked.

"I assume she's the one who buried them. How else would she know?"

Now probably wasn't the best time to tell our mother that her mother's ghost could have gotten that information from pretty much anyone else who was dead.

"I'm not sure you can assume that," Jay said. "First thing we do is get them appraised. Why didn't you do that already?"

"My mother said I should come straight here as quickly as I could."

"We should have them appraised as soon as possible," Jay said again.

She nodded. "Everything's in the bag."

"You didn't check that bag, did you?" I asked.

"Of course not. I couldn't check it or take it on a plane and risk the TSA confiscating it. I drove here."

My eyebrows nearly flew off my forehead. "You *drove*? All the way from Ohio? Alone?"

"For goodness' sake, Erin. I'm fifty-five. I'm not an invalid."

"And Dad was okay with this?" Jay asked.

"He couldn't get the time off, or he would have come along. He doesn't dictate what I do."

I couldn't help a smile. My mom was still as bullheaded and strong as ever. "Why didn't you tell us you were coming?"

"Because you would have asked a bunch of questions, and I wanted to talk to you both in person before I told you any of this."

"Fair enough," Jay said. "You said two things, Mom. What else was in the safe?"

# THIRTEEN

# DANTE

"**B**ill," I said, baring my fangs.

"Knock it off, Dante." He walked in, uninvited. "You don't scare me."

His demeanor said otherwise. His gait was decidedly stiff. I *did* scare him.

"Come on in," River said with sarcasm.

"You boys are in deep," Bill said. "I won't be able to help you if you don't knock it off right now."

"Because you've been so helpful up until now." I echoed River's sarcasm.

"I see you got your hands on another copy." He motioned to the book on the kitchen table.

"It might be a phony," I said. "We don't know yet."

"Oh, it's real," Bill said.

"And exactly how do you know that?"

"I'm an elder. We know most of what goes on in the vampire community."

River's fangs dropped. "You also know how to find the

missing women, including your own granddaughter. But you're not helping us."

"You're consigning your granddaughter and great-grandchild to death." Anger poured through me, but I held back. I could break him in half so easily, but he had information we needed. "It's time for you to come clean, Bill. Past time, actually."

Bill sighed. "You got anything to drink around here?"

"No," I said harshly. "Either talk or get the fuck out."

River ignored me, heading to the fridge. "I'm with Dante. You'll get nothing from us, but I need something." He peered into the refrigerator. "No blood?"

"I feed from Erin. We don't keep blood here."

"I guess it's"—he looked around until he found the two bottles Erin had bought—"either vodka or bourbon."

"Bourbon," Bill said.

"I wasn't offering you anything. Dante?" River raised his eyebrows.

"Nothing for me." I'd had two bourbons at Andrew's, and I wasn't gunning for any more right now. I wanted my full faculties dealing with my grandfather.

River poured two bourbons.

I arched my eyebrows. "I think you're forgetting whose home this is, cuz."

"What makes you think they aren't both for me?" River downed one, set the glass down, and brought the other back to the living room. "Look, Dante. Whether you like it or not, we need his help. I, for one, would like to try to convince him of that."

I huffed. "So would I. But we haven't had any luck so far."

"I'll tell you everything I know in exchange for this." Bill reached toward the book but jolted backward. "Damn it!"

"Bea works fast," I said. "Good for her."

"Why?" he said. "I've already assured you I'll tell your father what I read."

"Simple." I bared my teeth, holding back the snarl that threatened to erupt from my throat. "We don't trust you. You clearly don't give two fucks about Em and Uncle Brae. Or any of us, for that matter."

He walked into the living area and sat down limply. "I never wanted it to come to this. You boys mean everything to me."

"Bullshit." I said. "Actions speak a hell of a lot louder than words, and your actions are screaming that you don't give a fuck about any of us or the other innocent women who've disappeared."

"That's not true," Bill lamented.

"Then what gives?" River said. "If you have a way to help us find her, Lucy, and the others, you need to tell us."

"I know. You boys aren't the only ones struggling here."

"Yeah, yeah, yeah. Being held captive against my will for ten years and what you're going through right now—that's the same thing."

"Easy, son."

My father appeared again.

"Christ, Dad. Where the hell have you been?"

"You know where I've been. Taking care of that." He pointed to the *Texts* on the table.

"Oh, yeah. Thanks. It works."

"It does, Julian," Bill said. "I hope you know what you're doing, getting involved with voodoo."

"I'm hardly involved."

"Do you think I don't know you've given that woman your ashes?"

"I really don't care what you know, Dad. I'm doing what I have to do, just as you say you are."

"I told you I'd tell you what I read in the *Texts*."

"I'll hold you to that. But first we need your help finding Emilia and the others. What do you know about Levi Gaston?"

"He was a member of the council. An elder. He's dead."

"Yes, and his ghost showed up at Napoleon House that night. He spoke to you when you were about to tell us how you could help us find the missing women. I was there, Dad. I saw him. He didn't see me. At least I don't think he did. I stayed hidden. But I know you heard him. Erin heard him too. She seems very in tune with the noncorporeal plane."

"Gaston and I weren't friends. We both sat on the council and had to deal with each other, but I thought he was an asshole, frankly. He had ideas I didn't agree with."

"From what I know about him, I share your assessment," my father said. "What ideas are you talking about?"

"He was a supremacist."

"What?" River asked. "You mean an elitist?"

"He was far more than an elitist. He thought vampires were a superior species and was intent on finding a way to increase our numbers so we could exercise dominion over humans and other sentient beings. He studied the ancient art of alchemy for most of his life, even though he made his living as a genetic researcher at Tulane. He was sure he could find a way to increase the number of vampires in the population. He actually tried to court your grandmother, but Marcheline wanted nothing to do with him. Thought he was crazy. In some ways, I think he was."

"He wanted a vampire wife," I stated. Went right along with what I'd learned from Andrew.

"Of course he did, because he wanted vampire progeny. The fact that I married Marcheline also contributed to the bad blood between us."

"I met his son, Andrew," I said. "I got the feeling he thought Andrew might be a vampire and was angry that he wasn't."

"That is true."

"Why? Everyone knows a human and a vampire have human children."

"He was a geneticist and an alchemist. He thought he could find a way to produce a vampire child from a human-vampire mating. Obviously, he failed." Bill turned to my father's ghost. "He worshiped you and Braedon, and he hated me for fathering you. Not only did I have two strapping vampire sons, but identical twins, a true rarity. He thought he should have been the one to sire you. But how you came to be was truly simple. Your mother and I were both vampires."

"Why did we never know him, then?" my father asked. "If he was so infatuated with us."

Bill cleared his throat. "I wouldn't allow him near you. He was older than I was, but I was more powerful. Gaston let his emotions rule him his entire life. Emotions contribute to power, but only if they're properly channeled. He never learned to control his."

*Emotions contribute to power, but only if they're properly channeled.* Bill wasn't just talking about Gaston. He was talking about *me.*

I suppressed a growl.

"Do you think he's still trying to produce a vampire child from a human-vampire mating?" River asked.

"He's dead, River," Bill said.

"So? Uncle Jules is standing right here, helping us."

"That's the key word," Bill said. "He's *helping* you. He can't actually do anything physically."

"Seems to me Uncle Jules put you on the ground earlier," River observed.

My father remained eerily silent, and so did Bill, for a few seconds.

Then from Bill, "I'm not going to pretend to understand ghostly powers. But I do know that producing a vampire child would require physical action above an emotional outburst. Gaston can no longer pick up a petri dish or swirl metals together. He'd need help."

"He *has* help," I said. "The Claiborne vamps."

"They work for a female boss," River said. "Not a ghost."

"Maybe the female is helping him," I said. "Look. We know the Claiborne vamps were at Em's place, and we also know they stole your body, Dad, and buried it at St. Louis One. Somehow, this is all tied together."

"Maybe," my father said, "but we're only assuming that the elder Gaston had anything to do with this."

"True," River said. "It's all circumstantial."

"No need to assume." Bill sighed. "I can tell you. He is involved. To what extent? I don't know. But this has Levi Gaston written all over it. Why else would he want me to keep quiet?"

"Are you finally going to help us?" River asked. "Find the women?"

"I will. I will not sacrifice Emilia to whatever horrid thing Gaston is trying to do. But know this. If I help you, I will forfeit my seat on the council."

"So?" I said. "Who cares?"

"Dante," Bill said. "The council secrets are sacred. We take an oath."

"So you break an oath. Emilia is worth it. Lucy and the others are worth it," River said.

"You don't understand," Bill continued. "If I break the oath, my punishment is death."

# FOURTEEN

# *Erin*

"A book."

She pulled out a leather volume.

The *Texts*? It didn't look like those I'd seen. It was smaller, for one, and the leather binding was a lighter color. This was a newer book. In addition, there was no title on the cover or on the spine to identify its contents.

"What book is this?"

"I don't know," my mother said. "I can't open it."

"What?" I grabbed it from her and tried to open the book cover to reveal the first page. To no avail. It was glued shut somehow. "I don't get it."

"Your grandmother told me this book was one of a kind, and that it would give you answers when you needed them."

"How can it give us answers if we can't open it?" Jay asked.

"It's been shielded," I said, more to myself than to either of them. "A spell."

"Charmed, was how my mother put it," Mom said. "This

book is apparently around sixty years old."

"It looks brand-new," I said. "The page edges are yellow, but the cover isn't cracked at all. I wonder if it's ever been opened."

"My mother didn't say," Mom said. "She just said it was a family heirloom, and that the two of you needed it. It would open when necessary."

Jay, ever the skeptic, took the book from me. "This could just be a paperweight. Not a book at all."

"Your grandmother swears otherwise."

"Did she tell you anything about the diamonds? Why she hid them?" I asked.

Mom shook her head. "I'm not sure I'll ever forgive her for that. We could have had a much easier life."

"She probably didn't plan to die in childbirth," Jay said.

Mom closed her eyes, frowning.

"Geez, Jay," I said.

"It's okay. I'm okay." Mom shook her head. "But why would she keep something so valuable from your grandfather?"

"We don't know they're valuable yet," Jay said. "She seems to have been leading you to the book. That's what she said we needed, right?"

"Yes," Mom said. "That's true. She didn't mention the jewels."

"See?" Jay fingered the leather binding on the book. "They could be fake."

"Then why would she bury them in a safe along with an heirloom?" I said. "That doesn't make any sense."

"We'll get them appraised first thing tomorrow," Jay said. "If they *are* valuable, what do you want to do with them, Mom?"

"I can't even begin to think about that until we know for

sure. I don't want to get my hopes up."

I nodded. My mother was nothing if not sensible. This whole "mother coming to her in a dream" thing must have really tested her beliefs.

"You must be exhausted from all that driving," I said. "I'd give you the couch here and take the floor, but I think you could use a real bed. Why don't you and I check into a hotel for tonight?"

"Why aren't you sleeping at home, dear?" she asked.

*I'm ovulating, and my vampire boyfriend won't be able to control himself.*

Nope, couldn't say that.

Did she even know her mother had been a vampire?

She'd said she understood why we were drawn here, but that could be because her ghost mother came to her in a dream, and now she believed in ghosts.

"Varnish," I said, thinking quickly. "I just had my baseboards varnished, and the smell is really strong."

"A hotel, then," she said, "but not one of those haunted places. I've had enough ghostly interaction for a while."

"What did you tell Dad?" Jay asked.

"I told him the truth. Of course, he thought I was crazy, but when I shed a few tears, he told me to take a week off and come down here."

⚜

An hour later, my mother and I were in a hotel room with two queen beds. After she had fallen asleep, I grabbed my purse and went into the bathroom.

I sat down on the toilet seat and pulled the ovulation predictor test out of my purse.

I closed my eyes. What would it be like to have Dante's baby?

The familiar beautiful image popped into my mind.

Dante's and my baby. Our child.

Our vampire child.

# FIFTEEN

# DANTE

I couldn't believe what I was hearing. "The vampires on the council are murderers? They'll kill you if you divulge council secrets?"

Bill shook his head. "No. I will take my own life."

My stomach lurched. My father had taken his own life for me. As angry as I was at Bill, I did not want him to die.

"That's crazy," River said.

"I agree, Dad," my father said.

"Why would you say that, Julian? You took your own life."

"For my children. For River."

"And I'd be doing it for Emilia and the others. I don't see any difference."

I stayed silent. When Bill put it in those terms, I couldn't find fault with it. Still, I didn't want any more blood on my hands.

I'd had more than enough.

❖

*Sticky red blood covered my hands.*

*Vampire blood.*

*Only this hadn't come from her. It had come from the vampire I'd destroyed in the arena.*

*He lay in the corner, his chest heaving, blood spouting from his nose and mouth.*

Finish him.

Fight or die in the arena.

*I stalked forward. His eyes were shut, and one eyelid was swollen and bruised. The black mask he wore was soaked with blood and sweat, and his swollen lips were parted as he panted heavily.*

*I knelt next to him, curling my strong hand into a fist once more.*

*One more blow.*

*One more blow right in the heart. Better yet, right in the lungs. One or both would collapse. His ribs were already broken, most likely, and pushing in on his chest cavity. He was gasping for breath.*

*He turned his head toward me, his blue eyes both menacing and pleading.*

*"Do it," he rasped. "Finish it."*

Fight or die in the arena.

*I never remembered the kill. I always remembered going in for it, and then—*

*I'd be back in my dungeon, strapped down, waiting for the goons to come torture me.*

*Or waiting for her to come sink her teeth into me and drink my blood.*

*My vampire blood.*

*"Do it," he said again, his voice tarnished by the blow I'd given his throat earlier.*

*I raised my hand, ready to take him out.*

*Ready to deal the final blow.*

*But instead, my hand, seemingly of its own accord, swung gently to his head and unmasked him.*

*Then...before I could memorize his face...nothing.*

❦

"The council seems to be a lot more sadistic than any of us thought," River said.

What? Had something else been said?

"We keep secrets for very good reasons," Bill replied. "When one of us breaks our oath, we suffer the consequences."

"How did Levi Gaston die, Dad?" my father asked. "Was he forced to kill himself?"

"Gaston died of natural causes. A brain tumor."

"What kind of tumor?"

"He'd had it for most of his life. It was benign, but during the last couple years of his life, it began growing and eventually took out his brain. Brain death."

"Has a council member ever been forced to commit suicide?" River asked.

"Not for decades." Bill shook his head. "We take our oaths very seriously. In fact, I shouldn't even have told you that we're required to end our own lives. As council members, we refer to that as being 'off the council.'"

"When it really means 'off the planet,'" River said.

"Off the corporeal plane, anyway," my father said. "I'm still very much here on this planet."

*One more word, Gabriel, and you're off the council.*

Those were the words the ghost had said to Bill at Napoleon House. Erin had told me.

"Semantics, Uncle Jules," River said.

"What if you refuse?" I asked. "It's a free country. No one can force you to kill yourself."

"You're right, Dante," he said. "Only I can. And I *will*."

I rolled my eyes. "This is the most ridiculous thing I've ever heard. You're cheapening what I went through. What my father went through. Do you know how many times I wanted to end my life rather than submit to more torture? And what about you, Dad? I saw what those degenerates did to your body. How many times did you think about ending it all?"

"You're forgetting, son. I *did* end it all."

"But not while you were being tortured."

"True. I did not. And yes, there were times I thought about it."

"But we *didn't*," I said through gritted teeth. "We faced everything like men. Like the strong Gabriel vampires you raised us to be, Bill. And now you're telling us you'll kill yourself for nothing more than giving away a secret?"

"Don't you think I would've taken my own life already if I thought it would save all of you? Braedon and Emilia? Damn it, there's something far greater at stake here. Secrets I've been sworn never to reveal for the good of all. I can't allow my personal feelings to rule me. Yet I'm doing it. I've already told you I'd help you." Bill shook his head. "There are things you don't understand."

"Maybe Dante and River don't understand," my father said. "They're young. But I've seen things you haven't, Dad. I've been to other planes."

"Do you think that matters, Julian? An oath is an oath. We gave our blood."

"A blood oath?" I scoffed. "Like that shit Riv and I did in the fourth grade?"

"Gaston is watching me," Bill said. "He'll tell the council what I've done, and they'll make sure I end my life."

"Simple enough then," my father said. "We'll have this conversation at your home."

"How is that simple?" Bill asked.

"Your home is shielded from ghosts. Present company excluded, of course."

"My home is— What?"

"The voodoo priestess, Bea, cast a shield around your home."

"And you can get in because..."

"Because she used my ashes in the shield. They contain residual energy that recognizes me."

"God." Bill rubbed his cheek. "How has this all come to this? You've got some vagabond voodoo queen—"

"Not queen," my father said. "Priestess. And she's been very helpful. Hasn't she, Dante?"

I nodded. How could I not? Bea was the first person to tell me I'd been targeted by a dark energy. Of course, she hadn't told me it was coming from me.

My grandfather stood, wrenching his hands, looking, for the first time, weak. Not physically weak, but as if something had poked a hole in his mental strength.

Something had.

All of us. Our needs. Em's needs. He'd been putting the needs of the many over the needs of the few, and now he was facing losing what, to him, was sacred.

"Bill," I said as seriously as I could. "We've had our differences, and I've considered you more against me than with me since I returned. But I don't want you to die."

"Neither do I, Dad," my father said.

"Ditto for me," River added.

"Gaston could be listening in right now," Bill whispered.

"I would know if he were here," my father said. "Trust me. He's a ghost like I am. We cannot hide from each other. I had to be extremely careful that night at Napoleon House. I didn't come near your table until I was sure Gaston was gone."

"You're sure?" Bill said.

"Dad, I would never lie to you when your life is at stake."

Bill nodded. "No, you wouldn't. You're a good boy, Julian. All three of you are."

Thinking of my father as a "boy" was a little alarming, but Bill was coming around. Already I could see the fatherliness in him returning.

I was still pissed as hell at him, but I couldn't have his death on our hands.

"Then are we in?" I asked. "You're going to give us the tools we need to find Em and the others?"

"I will help you as best I can," Bill said quietly. "And then I will deal with whatever fate has in store for me."

# SIXTEEN

## *Erin*

I awoke with a start and sat up straight. Where was I?

Then I remembered, when I heard the soft snore of my mother in the next bed.

The hotel.

Mom. The book. The diamonds.

The sun had risen, and beams of gold shone through the window in our room. I yawned, stretching my arms above my head and then turning to the clock on the night table.

Seven a.m.

Dante would need to feed soon.

I should go to him, but not before I took another ovulation test. Last night I'd tested positive. Time to pee on a stick again. I headed to the bathroom.

Three minutes later, I was in the clear. My ovulation cycle had ended. I was safe to make love with Dante, and suddenly I wanted him more than ever.

Only one issue. My mother was still sleeping in the room. I

walked back over to my bed and picked up my cell phone.

A text from Dante from a few hours earlier.

*Was up most of the night with River,*
*Bill, and my dad at our place. Bill's*
*going to help us, but we all needed to*
*get some sleep. Home now. Call me*
*when you're awake.*

I readied to make the call but then decided against it. If he needed sleep, I didn't want to wake him. Besides, I couldn't go home to feed him with my mom asleep here.

He could wait a couple of hours to feed. He'd probably drunk blood during the night with River and Bill. I yawned. I'd been up late as well. Since my mother was still asleep, why not get a little more shut-eye myself?

I snuggled back into bed.

⚜

*"Erin! Help me! Please!"*

*I hurried along the hospital corridor. Was it a hospital corridor? It was dark and narrow, but the pungent scent of isopropyl alcohol lingered in the air. Wherever I was, it was clean and sterilized.*

*Then a wail.*

*A baby's wail.*

*"Erin! Please!"*

*Who was calling? Who was pleading for help? Was it the baby's mother?*

*Or was there no baby?*

*The squawk again.*

*Definitely a baby.*

*I lost perspective as the narrow corridor elongated before my eyes. I forced my legs into a run, but the faster I traveled, the longer the hallway seemed.*

*And still the screams.*

*"Help me! Please!"*

*I ran, and I ran, and I ra—*

*A door opened, nearly hitting me. I stopped suddenly, maneuvering around it. I looked inside.*

*A blood bank.*

*I rubbed my arms from the coldness while I scanned the shelves. They were all full.*

*Of B positive blood.*

❧

I jerked upward in bed.

Those screams had sounded familiar to me. I'd heard them before, in another time perhaps.

Or in another dream.

But what was foremost in my mind was the blood bank. My skin was still chilled from the refrigeration.

A blood bank full of B positive blood, when the bank at my hospital was always out, despite us borrowing from other hospitals.

There was no shortage of B positive blood in New Orleans. It was being hoarded.

I let out a soft huff. *A dream, Erin. It was just a dream. You don't have any evidence that anyone is hoarding B positive blood.*

Except I knew.

At least I thought I knew.

What I needed was someone who could substantiate what I'd seen in my dream.

Someone with the sight, as she put it.

I needed Bea.

So many times I'd laughed at her antics, at her claims. But she hadn't let us down. Perhaps she truly did have the sight.

My mother was just beginning to rustle a little. She would wake up soon. How could I tell her I needed to go under Claiborne Bridge and talk to a homeless voodoo priestess? I certainly couldn't take her with me. If she smelled as good as Jay and I did, those thugs would sniff her out in a minute. Yeah, I had the potion, but my mother... This would be too much for her. I wasn't even sure she knew her mother had been a vampire. All she'd said was that my grandmother had come to her as a ghost in a dream.

What to do?

I texted Dante quickly.

> *I'm texting because I didn't want to wake you. I need to see Bea. I'll come home to you when I'm done. Don't worry. I'm no longer fertile, and I have my potion.*

Then to Jay:

> *Meet me under Claiborne Bridge.*

I scurried over to the desk and grabbed the hotel stationery and pen. I scribbled a quick note to my mother that I'd be back before checkout time and told her to get some more rest.

Then I returned to the bathroom, washed the essentials, dressed in yesterday's clothes, and left.

❧

Jay's call came while I was driving to the bridge.

"What the hell, Erin?"

"I had a strange dream. I need Bea's help. Besides, you should meet her."

"I'm on my way, but you're crazy."

"Then why are you on the way?"

"Because my little sister is not going under the bridge alone."

"It's broad daylight."

"I don't give a shit. Your boyfriend would have my ass if he knew what you were doing."

"He does know. I texted him." Of course I neglected to tell Jay that Dante was most likely asleep.

"And he's okay with this?"

"I haven't heard otherwise."

"I'm almost there. Meet me at Ray's on the Avenue."

"Got it." I ended the call.

Ten minutes later, I parked the car. Jay stood outside, tense and rigid.

"I still think you're nuts," he said as I walked toward him.

"This whole situation is nuts."

"I can't believe you left Mom in that hotel room."

"Would you rather I brought her here? She'd freak out. I don't think she knows, Jay. I don't think she knows her mother was a vampire."

"I'm not sure she does either," he said. "We have to tell her."

"I agree. Especially considering I'm living with one and you've impregnated one."

"Fuck." He shook his head. "I never thought I'd be talking about this kind of stuff with you."

"Get over it. I'm a nurse. I've heard it all."

"Yeah, you're a nurse. You're also my baby sister."

I waved my hand dismissively and walked toward Bea's lair. The area was pretty desolate. A few people slept, but most people were already up and out begging for the day. At least that was what I figured.

Bea sat in her usual place, her eyes closed. Was she sleeping? I hated to disturb her, but I needed to know if my dream had any significance.

Her eyes popped open as we neared.

"All dreams have significance, dearie."

Had I said that out loud? Jay stood next to me. No, I hadn't, or he'd have reacted.

"'To die, to sleep—to sleep, perchance to dream—ay, there's the rub, for in this sleep of death what dreams may come...'"

Shakespeare again. "I'm not thinking of dying. I just have some questions about a dream. Oh." I gestured to my brother. "This is Jay. My brother."

"I know that already. 'We came into the world like brother and brother, and now let's go hand in hand, not one before another.'"

"Huh?" Jay said.

"She quotes Shakespeare," I said. "And Thoreau. And Aldous Huxley, but only once. That I know of, anyway."

"O...kay."

I turned back to Bea. "I'm here because you know. Because

you have the sight."

"I already know that."

Of course she did.

"Good to meet you, Bea," Jay said.

"I've seen you before," Bea said. "You and your vampire partner. You walk at night."

"We *work* nights, yeah. But we're no longer with the force."

"I know that. I have the sight."

"I've heard that, yeah."

"Bea," I began, "I've had a dream twice now about a baby cry—"

"Erin!"

I turned toward the voice. Abe Lincoln. Another person for Jay to meet.

"Here comes old Red Rover." Bea cackled.

"Hey, Erin," Abe said upon arrival. "I'm so glad to see you're okay."

"I'm fine. The vampires have left me alone lately."

"I know. They haven't been around for the past few days, and I'm starved. Can you buy me breakfast?"

"Now just a min—"

I nudged my brother. "Abe, this is my brother, Jay. Jay, Abe Lincoln. I told you about him."

"Yeah." Jay's expression was unreadable.

Or maybe it wasn't.

He thought all of this was loony.

"I'm real hungry, Erin."

"Dante just gave you money for meals. Did you spend it already?"

"No. I got jumped."

"Red Rover," Bea said, "if you'd get your meals honestly

instead of letting those vamps feed on you, you wouldn't be hungry right now."

"Honestly?" Jay said. "You mean by begging?"

"What's dishonest about begging?" Bea asked. "'Whiles I am a beggar, I will rail and say there is no sin but to be rich; and being rich, my virtue then shall be to say there is no vice but beggary.'"

"You've got to be kidding me." Jay shook his head. "If he's selling his blood for food, that's more honest than taking money for doing nothing."

"''Tis not enough to help the feeble up, but to support him after.'"

I sighed. Bea could clearly quote Shakespeare forever, but I needed to get home to Dante.

"Abe, fine. We'll buy you breakfast." I scrambled in my wallet and pulled out a ten-dollar bill. "This will cover it. Now if you'll excuse us, my brother and I have some business with Bea."

"But I wanted to have breakfast with you, Erin."

"Another time. Please?"

"Sure. Okay." He ambled off, ten dollars richer.

At least I knew he wouldn't try to buy drugs. His labs had come back clean at the hospital.

I turned back to Bea. "I need your help, and you know you'll be well compensated. So could you lay off the Shakespeare quotes and actually talk to me? Please?"

"'Talking isn't doing.'"

"Yeah. I know that, but I need to talk before we do anything."

"No, Sis," Jay said. "That's Shakespeare again. From *Henry VIII*."

I sighed. "For God's sake. Bea. Please."

She turned to me, her eyes wide. They seemed darker than usual. No, it wasn't her irises that were dark. Her pupils were dilated. Even under the bridge, it was pretty bright at this time of day. How could her pupils be dilated?

"The baby is real. The girl is real. They need you. But you cannot go to them. It is not safe for you."

Jay nudged me. "What's up with her eyes?" he whispered.

"You've been lied to," Bea continued. "The girl and the baby are not where you think they are."

Bea bowed her head for a moment and then lifted it. Her eyes were back to normal.

"The girl and the baby. I didn't tell you about my dream yet."

"You didn't have to. I already know why you came here today."

"So you're saying the girl and the baby are real and that they need my help, but I can't go to them without putting myself in danger?"

"That is correct."

"Then you've been no help at all." Jay grabbed my arm. "Let's get out of here."

"No." I yanked my arm away. "Tell me. Where are they? I don't care if it's dangerous. I have to know."

She closed her eyes. "I don't know. The location is well shielded. But they are with others you know. Your friend. And your vampire's sister."

# SEVENTEEN

# DANTE

I growled as I read the text from Erin.

What was she thinking, going to Claiborne Bridge alone? I'd slept for four hours. That would have to suffice. I called River and told him to pick me up. I badly needed a shower, but I pulled on jeans, a shirt, and shoes.

I had to get a damned car.

River showed up within ten minutes. I filled him in, and we were off.

"You look...off, cuz," River said as we headed down the road. "Did you drink this morning?"

"Of course I didn't. Erin wasn't home. She had to stay away from me, remember? But she's not fertile anymore. Said so in her fucking text. She should have come right home to feed me, but instead she's chasing the voodoo queen."

"Priestess. Your dad corrected Bill last night."

"Fuck off, Riv."

"Man. You need to feed. Let's stop and at least get you a cup of joe."

"We're not stopping until we get to Erin," I said through clenched teeth.

"All right, all right. Your call. Fuck." He stared ahead at the road.

We made good time and got the car parked, and then we raced to the tent city under the bridge.

Bea sat in her usual place.

Alone.

Where the hell was Erin?

My fangs descended with a sharp pain. Would I ever get used to the rapid descent?

I'd felt it before.

Not so long ago.

*Fight or die in the arena.*

It happened when rage threatened to consume me.

As it did now.

"Where the fuck is Erin?" I demanded.

"Been and gone," Bea said. "Said she had to get back to her mother."

"Her mother?" I raked my fingers through my hair. "What the fuck are you talking about?"

"Her mother. She's in town. She came to bring something to Erin and her brother. Something they need."

"What? How is it that you know this and I don't? Why wouldn't she tell me?"

"She didn't tell me. She told me her mother was here. She didn't tell me the rest. I have the sight."

"Yeah. The fucking sight. Right."

"Calm down, Dante," River said.

"He needs blood," said Bea.

"You think so, Sherlock?" River shook his head. "Jay didn't

tell me anything about their mom being here, but he was asleep when I got in this morning, and I didn't want to wake him. Then he was gone by the time you woke me up with your phone call."

"Why would their mother be here?" I asked.

"I already told you," Bea said. "She had something they needed."

"What?"

"That's for Erin to tell you."

"What if she doesn't?" I seethed.

"She will. Have some faith, vampire."

Faith. Fucking faith. I was so sick of that damned word.

"Go," Bea said. "Feed. You're not thinking straight right now. 'I would give all my fame for a pot of ale and safety.'"

"You want ale?" I raked my fingers through my already disheveled hair. "You'll get nothing."

"She's quoting again, Dante. Probably Shakespeare. Read between the lines. She's right. You need to feed."

"For God's sake. Take me the fuck home, Riv."

⚜

I was ravenous by the time I got home, and seeing Erin, scenting Erin, drove me nearly insane.

Jay was there.

I didn't fucking care.

A strange older woman was there. Her mother, no doubt.

Didn't fucking care.

"Bedroom," I growled.

"Dante, this is my—"

"*Bedroom*."

"Dante—" From Jay.

"Don't you dare try to stop me."

The woman's face went pale. Paler than she already was. She was a vampire descendent, though I couldn't smell her. She had the look. Her children both resembled her in different ways.

Didn't care about any of that right now.

Only wanted blood.

Erin's blood.

"Bedroom," I said once more. "I won't say it again."

If she didn't respond that time, I'd hoist her over my shoulder and take her there myself, her mother and brother's presence be damned.

Erin nodded and rose. She walked too slowly, and I garnered every bit of control I had to only follow her and not grab her and puncture her skin right in front of her mother and brother.

What seemed like an eternity later, we reached the bedroom.

I shut the door, not quietly.

"Dante—"

"Don't fucking talk." I advanced toward her and growled, showing my fangs. Then I pushed her head to the side, baring her milky white neck. Her carotid pulsed, hissing with every beat.

*Thump.*

*Thump.*

*Thump.*

She didn't struggle, simply stood waiting.

I sank my teeth into her rosy flesh.

Sweet red gold. As her blood flowed quickly from her artery, I didn't take the time to let it float across my tongue as

I usually did.

No. This time I sucked harshly, swallowed quickly, desperate for the drug I craved.

Desperate for the euphoria that came with a feeding from Erin's potent nectar.

I closed my eyes, sucking, swallowing, not taking any time to savor. Only intent on feeding my body what it required.

More. More. More.

*Dante.*

A voice from somewhere outside my bubble of contentment and nirvana.

A voice I ignored.

*Dante.*

More. More. More. Blood still flowed into me, nourishing me, filling me—

*Dante!*

Erin.

Erin was asking me to stop.

No. No. No.

Don't want to stop.

*Keep feeding,* the darkness coerced. *Take it all. Drain her, and you'll be what you're meant to be. All your questions will be answered.*

The words were persuasive. Tempting. To know all, finally. To finally understand what was happening to me and why...

*Dante!*

Then warmth. Overflowing of warmth from the woman I loved.

Erin.

Sweet beautiful Erin, who gave of herself so freely.

No. Never harm Erin.

Never.

With every ounce of strength I possessed, I removed my teeth from her succulent flesh, licking the wounds to help heal them.

Erin pulled away from me, her face paler than normal. Tiny quivers racked her body.

"Dante."

"I'm sorry."

The words meant so little. I'd been tempted. So tempted to take all of her, to glory in what I could become with the nourishment of draining her.

What *had* I become?

What was I capable of?

For the first time, the potential answers to those questions terrified me.

"I'm sorry," I said again softly. "So sorry."

She reached toward me, caressed my cheek. "You were hungry. That's all."

Oh, she was right. I'd been starving for her, but that was hardly *all*. Something dark had taken me over. Something sinister that lived within me.

Control.

I had it.

But I feared that one day my control wouldn't be enough.

## EIGHTEEN

# Erin

Dante was suffering. I could see it in his eyes. They were a strange mixture of hunger, desire, and regret.

"You won't harm me, Dante."

He didn't answer, just backed away from me.

I missed the warmth of his skin, the stubble beneath my fingertips.

Dante was always warm after he fed.

I began walking to the bed, when I stumbled under my shaky legs. He swooped toward me like a lightning bolt, taking me into his arms and depositing me gently on the mattress.

"My love." His voice was low, raspy.

"I'm all right."

"I'm so sorry."

"You were hungry. If Bonneville hadn't screwed with my pills, you could have fed yesterday."

"I fed yesterday. River had blood."

"But not *my* blood. You need my blood." The blood bond. I

believed it. I'd always believed it on some level, but now, having seen the effect of Dante being deprived of feeding, I knew it in my heart and my soul.

The blood bond was real.

And now my whole body was vibrating with a sexual hum.

I wanted Dante.

I wanted to make love.

He inhaled sharply. "I can smell your arousal, baby."

"Come here then."

He shook his head. "I want you. Always. But I took a little too much of your blood, and you need to save your energy for a few hours until you recover. Besides, your mother is probably wondering who this primeval man is who forced her daughter up the stairs."

Oh, God. Mom! And Jay!

I'd nearly forgotten they were downstairs.

"Shit," I said. "What am I going to tell them?"

"I'd suggest the truth," Dante said. "Your brother already knows."

We were both still dressed.

"Come on." He tugged my hand, helping me up from the bed. "You need hydration. This won't get any easier if we wait. When we're done, we'll finish what we started up here."

❧

My mother's pallor went white. Stark white. Whiter than the walls in my living room, even.

Wasn't every day you found out your daughter was in love with a vampire, your son was expecting a child with a vampire, and your mother had *been* a vampire.

My mother got all of this in a matter of twenty minutes.

"Are you going to say anything?" I asked timidly.

Nothing.

Just her lips in the shape of an O.

"Hey," Dante said, "Bea said your mom gave you guys something that you'd need. Is that true?"

"Oh, yeah!" I'd nearly forgotten. I grabbed my mother's tote bag that sat at her feet. "Mom? May I?"

Nothing.

I smiled at her. "It's all okay, Mom. I promise. I know it's a lot to take in. Jay and I have both been there. You'll get through this, and you'll accept your heritage."

Nothing. Then a slight nod, her jaw still dropped.

I opened her tote and pulled out the leather-bound volume. It was still sealed shut, as if glue had been glazed around the edges. I handed it to Dante.

"What is this?"

"We don't know. My grandmother hid it and some jewels in a safe on her parents' old property."

"Why?"

"Again, we have no idea. We're going to get the diamonds appraised, and they belong to Mom. It's the book we think we might need."

"It's not the *Texts*," he said.

"Well, no. At least it's not identical to the *Texts* we've seen so far. But it could be another printing."

"I suppose so." He fingered the leather binding. "No title. Nothing." He pulled at the cover. "And it won't open. It could just be a knickknack."

"It could, but why would my grandmother tell my mother that we needed a knickknack?"

He nodded, still running his fingers over the indentations in the leather. "It looks old, sort of. Yet new."

"I got that same impression," I said. "Like it's decades old but has never been opened. Apparently it's over sixty years old."

"If your mother's dream is accurate, and we need this book, why can't we open it?"

"She said we'd be able to open it when we needed to."

He raked his fingers through his hair. "For God's sake. It's just like the rest of this mystery. For every answer, there's a new question."

"That's kind of the way mysteries work," Jay said dryly.

The men's gazes met, and for an instant, a spark of anger surged between them. Then it dissipated. Thank God.

These were two of the three men in my life whom I loved most, and I didn't want bad blood between them.

I was still thirsty, even after two glasses of water, and my mother sure looked like she could use a drink, though she hated alcohol. "I'll get you some water, Mom."

I poured four glasses and came back to the living room, handing one to each person. Then I downed my entire glass, letting the cool liquid soothe my parched throat.

"I don't understand." Finally, my mother's voice.

"There's nothing to understand, Mom," Jay said. "It just *is*. Nothing has changed. You were always the daughter of a vampire. You just didn't know it."

"She died...because of me." My mom took a sip.

Dante set his glass down on the coffee table. "You can't look at it that way, Sharlene. May I call you Sharlene?"

She nodded. "It was *her* name. After she died, my father named me for her. Do you think he knew?"

"Whether he did or didn't doesn't really matter at this

point, Mom," I said. "He loved her. We know that, at least."

She nodded. "Still, but for me..."

"Sharlene," Dante began again, "don't blame yourself. Your mother knew the risks. Childbirth is difficult for vampire women. My own mother died giving birth to my younger sister."

"And she's now pregnant. With Jay's child?"

Dante nodded. "But she won't die. We won't allow that to happen."

"How can you prevent it?"

"I don't know, but we will. Count on that."

"I want to meet her." My mother took another drink. "Right away. This mother of my grandchild."

A weight dropped into my belly.

Jay cleared his throat. "That will be kind of difficult."

"Why? Are you two not together? I don't understand."

"We're not together, but that's not the issue." Jay took the last swallow of his drink. "She's missing."

My mother lost the grip on her glass, and it tumbled onto her lap, spilling what was left of the water. She didn't seem to notice.

"That's the mystery we're dealing with," Jay continued. "Well, one of them, and the more we uncover, the more everything seems to be related."

My mother's face went even paler, if that was possible. "I sure could use a smoke right now."

"Don't undo twenty years of being nicotine-free," I said.

"But a woman is missing. Aren't you all beside yourselves?"

"We are," I said, my nerves jumping. "We have been. Not only is Dante's sister missing, but my best friend and a few other women. Plus Dante's uncle."

"My God..." She picked up her glass, still not seeming to

notice the water she'd spilled. "How in the world did the two of you get involved in all of this?"

"That's a long story," I said. "I promise we'll tell you everything, but you should probably call Dad and fill him in."

"Your father?" She shook her head vehemently. "Oh, no. Never."

"What?" Jay asked.

"Tell him I'm the daughter of a vampire? Some mutant human being?"

Dante snarled, baring his fangs. "Do I look like a mutant to you?"

My mother jerked backward.

*Good move, Dante. Yeah, right now, you look like a mutant to her.* I touched his forearm. "Babe, please."

"We're not mutants," he said in a low voice. "We're a closely related species. Our DNA is nearly indistinguishable. In some ways, we're superior."

I turned to regard Dante. He was serious. Completely serious. I'd never heard him say anything about being superior before.

"We have more acute senses, and our bodies move more quickly. We have the ability to adapt to nearly any situation by glamouring."

"And you need blood," Jay reminded him.

"Our one weakness. Our *only* one."

My blood ran cold. This didn't sound like Dante. And my mother was here, for goodness' sake.

Something wasn't right.

He stood, pacing around the room. "We're tired of hiding in the shadows, being forced to pretend we're merely human. We are vampire. *Vampire.*"

"Jay." I stood. "You need to take Mom back to her hotel. Please. And then call River."

"I'm on it. Come on, Mom."

"I'm not leaving her here with a monster," my mother said.

"He's not a monster," Jay said. "He's... Hell, I don't know. Erin can handle him. Right, Sis?"

"Yes," I said, willing my voice to sound as reassuring as it could. More reassuring than I felt.

Jay didn't want to go. I saw it in his face. But he knew as well as I did that Mom needed to get out of there.

Once they had left, I focused on Dante, the man—the vampire—I loved.

"Dante, I love you." I reached toward him, my hands shaking. "I love you. But this isn't you."

# NINETEEN

# DANTE

*D*ante, *I love you. I love you. But this isn't you.*

Her voice. Her sweet melodic voice. How I wanted to listen, to melt into the soft sound that enveloped me in warmth.

*This isn't you.*

*This isn't you.*

*This isn't you.*

But it *was* me. The dark energy had taken hold, showing me what could be for vampires. We were stronger. We were able to see more clearly, smell more acutely, move more quickly. We *were* superior.

How had I never seen it before?

If we could increase our numbers, we could take over, have warm blood fresh from a human whenever we craved it. Fuck stored animal blood.

Fuck humans.

Fuck all of it.

Vampires would rule, and I would be the strongest vampire of all.

How many had I defeated? Destroyed?

*Fight or die in the arena.*

Death. Darkness.

The end.

All was coming, darkness driving out the light.

But the light...

I could see it, like the sun's rays shining on the horizon.

Light...edging out the darkness. Darkness rising.

*Control, son. Control.*

*Dante, please. Talk to me.*

*Control, son. You're better than this. This isn't you. Grab hold of something, anything, to bring you back.*

*This isn't you.*

*Julian, what's happening?*

*Show him the light. Show him your love.*

Strong arms gripped me.

Stronger than I'd imagined, but the strength didn't come from the body they were attached to. It came from sheer will.

Sheer love.

Erin.

*This isn't you.*

*This isn't you.*

*This isn't you.*

Erin. How I loved her. Though my eyes weren't closed, now I saw her, holding me. Embracing me with strength and light and love.

Once again, she had saved me.

I kissed the top of her head. "Thank you, baby. Thank you, my love."

"Remember this, Dante." My father's voice. "Remember this feeling. Love will conquer the darkness. Never forget that."

Erin pulled away slightly. "What darkness?"

A slight pause. Then, my father's voice. "You haven't told her."

A statement, not a question.

His ghostly eyebrows drew in as I regarded his form. He was not happy with me.

Erin pulled away farther, our bodies no longer touching. "Haven't told me what?"

I'd intended to. Truly. But when? We'd hardly had time to catch our breath, and then she turned up fertile and had to stay away.

I inhaled. Her sweet non-fertile scent filled the room. Filled me with light and hope.

"That's it, son. There's something inside that it can't get to, that it can't touch. Hold on to that. Hold on."

"Dante, what is he talking about?"

"Tell her."

*Tell her.*

*Tell her.*

*Tell her.*

My lips trembled. "She'll leave."

"Trust. Have faith."

Faith. I was so sick of that word! But if I could have faith in anything, I could have faith in Erin. My true love. My blood bond.

"I won't leave," she said softly. "I love you. Whatever this is, we will get through it. Together."

# TWENTY

# *Erin*

I meant the words with all my heart.

Had the darkness returned? Had it taken control of Dante?

When I couldn't get through to him, I'd yelled for his father. He'd appeared instantly, as if he'd already known what was happening.

Dante didn't speak, so I turned to the ghost.

"Julian?"

"It is for him to tell." Then he vanished.

I reached toward Dante tentatively. His eyes were filled with love, and his teeth had finally retracted. If I had any chance of getting through to him, now was the time. "Dante? Talk to me. Please. I won't leave. Trust in that. We need each other now."

He sighed. "You have no idea how much."

"You think I don't? You think I'd put up with everything if I didn't need you?"

He shook his head. "You don't understand. The blood bond. It's..."

"It's what?"

"It's *part* of us now. Part of our physiology. We both need it."

"Of course we do."

"No. You don't understand."

"Then help me. Help me understand, Dante."

"How can I help you understand what I don't understand myself?"

"At least be honest, then. You haven't told me something, and though I should be mad as hell at you, I can't be. Not after what I just saw you go through. It was like you had two ropes tied around your waist, each forcing you in different directions. It scared me, Dante."

"Erin, I love you."

"I know that."

"Believe in that. Trust in that. Have faith in that."

"I do." I cupped his cheek, letting my fingertips slide over his rough stubble.

He sighed and then inhaled, holding his breath for a few seconds before letting it out. "I don't want any secrets between us."

"Neither do I. I'm an open book as far as you're concerned, Dante. You know that."

"There are a few things I haven't told you." He stroked his forehead. "Three things, actually."

I lifted my brow, trying to hold back the anger that threatened. "Oh? *Three* things?"

"You're mad."

I scoffed. "A little, yeah. And only because I know you're

going through something. Fuck. The hell with that. I'm fucking mad as hell." I took a few steps backward.

"The first two are really little things. Things I was waiting for the right time to tell you."

"I'd say now's the time."

He inhaled again. "The night I escaped, I glamoured a homeless man and stole his clothes."

Abe. He'd said that when we stopped at Café Amelie to have lunch. "You told me he was mistaken."

"I know. I'm sorry."

"I took your word over Abe's, and he was right!" I shook my head.

"I'm sorry, Erin."

I willed myself not to slap him across his gorgeous cheek.

"That's one. Give me the next one."

"My father glamoured you one other time. It was a subtle glamour, when you found me in the kitchen after I'd spilled the glass of blood. He just gave you a little push to accept the dog bite story."

"The story Bill glamoured me into forgetting. Perfect. I was violated twice that day."

"Erin, I didn't even know my father was there that day. It was before I could see him. Before he had shown himself to River and me. I found out about it later."

"And just conveniently forgot to tell me."

"He hasn't told you either."

"He's not the one I'm in love with! Christ, Dante."

"You're right. But believe me, those two things are tiny and insignificant compared to what I must tell you now."

I opened my mouth to bitch at him, but he held up his hand to stop me.

"Please, baby. I've only known about this third thing for a short time. I was trying to find the right time to tell you."

I tapped my foot on the floor. "Get on with it, then."

"This isn't easy."

"Get over yourself, Dante. This isn't easy for me, either."

"You can't leave me, Erin. You just can't. We're bonded."

"You haven't told me anything yet," I said through clenched teeth.

His teeth snapped down in an instant. "God, not now!"

"What is it?" I inched forward, my blood boiling. "Another reason not to tell me, right? Well, I have news for you. You're going to spit it out right now. Right fucking now!"

He closed his eyes and inhaled. "Fuck, Erin, your scent when you're angry—the adrenaline and testosterone—it's irresistible. Dark, so dark. Dark coffee, dark chocolate, the richest, darkest blackberry, the richest, darkest Merlot. The dark red of your blood racing through your veins. Dark everything. Darkness. You smell like darkness. All consuming darkness mixed with your soft love and light." He opened his eyes, baring his fangs and growling. "Now. Need you. Now."

I held up my hand. "Oh, hell, no. Not until you—"

In a flash I was against his hard body, his lips crushing to mine.

*No. Fight it. Don't open.*

My lips parted anyway, and he swooped his tongue into my mouth.

Anger and passion were a lethal combination—a combination that produced in me a desire and lust for this vampire like nothing I'd ever known.

This was the basic essence of life.

*This.*

*Us.*

He lifted me against him, and I wrapped my legs around his firm waist, our mouths still fused. He carried me swiftly up the stairs to our bedroom.

Our sanctuary.

Already the scent of arousal was thick around us, encapsulating us in a vibrant warmth.

Still we kissed, our tongues devouring each other's mouths, low hums vibrating from both our throats. More than once, I nicked my tongue and lips on his sharp fangs and tasted the tang of my blood.

My blood.

He'd already fed today, and he'd taken more than usual. But I had enough. Like a mother nursing a baby always had enough milk, I would always have enough blood for Dante. The knowledge was embedded deep in my heart. Deep in my soul.

I pushed away, breaking the kiss with a loud smack. Dante's eyes were blazing, the amber around his irises alight with fire. His lips were swollen and dark from our passionate kissing, and tiny smudges of my blood laced them.

More.

It was *my* need this time. Not his. I needed him to feed. Take from me. Consume me.

I tilted my head to the side, offering my neck. "Drink from me, Dante. Please."

His lips parted on a snarl. Oh, God, his teeth. Those pointed cuspids I could never fear. They caused no terror in me—only arousal, only deep, aching need.

"Your artery is pulsing, Erin. I can hear each thump. The most beautiful sound. It's a rhythm, like a soft drumbeat. The most perfect cadence." Then he sank those beautiful teeth into my flesh.

My whole body quivered as he tugged on my skin, sucking the sustenance from my body.

My nipples were already hard, ready, but they jutted out even farther with those sweet tugs as he fed. And my pussy... God, my pussy. I was so ready for his mouth, his fingers, his cock.

God, his cock.

It had been so long. Only a matter of days, but I felt like we'd been separated for eternity.

When he released me, I whimpered at the loss of his mouth upon me, but then his gaze met mine.

"Undress," he growled. "Now."

I was only too willing. Though tempted to go slowly, to tease him, I was too turned on to wait. In an instant my clothes lay on the floor in a mass of fabric. I stood before him, naked, squeezing my thighs together to ease the ache between them.

"Turn around," he demanded.

I obeyed, facing the bed.

Then the zip of his jeans. Slowly yet quickly. A few more seconds...

Then I was forced down onto the bed, my knees bent, and he stuffed his hard cock inside me.

A sound came from him—an exotic mixture of a sigh and a growl.

I got only wetter.

A lot wetter.

"Mine," he said, thrusting into me. "Always mine."

I clutched at the comforter, buried my cheek in it as he forced me closer and closer to climax, until—

"Dante! God, Dante, I'm coming!"

"That's right, baby. You come. Come. For me. Again and again and again."

My body responded to his commands. The orgasm twisted into another and then another, every nerve in my body pulsating and throbbing, all the energy arrowing straight to my pussy, which, for now, was the center of the universe.

"More," he said, still pounding me. "More. Again."

The orgasms rocketed through me. As one ended, another began, and still he plunged in and out of me, stretching me, burning me, making me quake with one climax after another.

I continued coming, my screams muffled by the bedding, my heart racing.

And my blood.

For the first time, I felt my blood flowing through my veins to my heart and then out again through the arteries. Tiny racing rivers embedded in my body.

He pulled one last climax out of me before he thrust in so deep I knew we'd become one. He grunted and groaned, snarled and growled, falling onto me, his chest sticky with sweat. His fangs scraped against my shoulder.

"I love you, Erin."

"I love you too," I said into the covers, my whole body limp.

But I had no time to rest. He pulled out, flipped me over, and spread my legs. "You're going to come again."

"Dante, no. I can't. Enough."

He growled. "Never enough." He slithered his tongue over my slit. "I'm inside you. The part of me that would make a baby. Do you know what a fucking turn-on that is?" He licked me again.

My body was so limp and sated, I couldn't come again. Just couldn't.

"But you will." Dante sucked on my clit and pushed two fingers inside me.

Had I said that out loud?

"So tight after you come, baby. You're clamping around my fingers like a vise. So sexy."

"No, can't."

A snarl vibrated against the lips of my pussy as he sucked, sucked, sucked, his fingers rubbing at that spot...that spot...

"Oh, fuck!" The orgasm hit me from behind this time, from my gut, and sparks traveled through my vessels along with the blood, taking me higher, higher, higher...

And then—

He punctured my thigh, drawing more blood from my willing body as my climax continued, and I shattered into a million sparks of energy.

I floated in euphoria, a light-blue cloud of rapture.

Floating, floating, floating...

Until I opened my eyes and met Dante's fiery gaze. His chin was slick with my blood and my juices. His eyes were on fire, his teeth long and sexy.

And I wanted something. Something more.

Oh, yes, we were bonded. Perhaps it was my desire. Perhaps it was my love. Perhaps it was my vampire heritage.

He'd taken my blood many times.

Now...I would take *his*.

"Show me, Dante. Show me what it feels like to drink blood from someone you love."

He bared his fangs on a sensual growl, bringing his wrist to his lips. I gasped when he punctured his own skin.

I gasped again as two crimson rivers glided down the pale skin of his inner forearm.

Then once more as he brought his wrist to my lips.

# THE QUEEN

You are strong, Dante. So strong.
You're fighting the darkness, fighting your destiny.
But what you fight is growing, maturing, evolving...
One day soon, you will no longer win the battle.

# BLOOD BOND SAGA

## SAGA

---

### PART 12

# PROLOGUE

# *Erin*

A snarl vibrated against the lips of my pussy as he sucked, sucked, sucked, his fingers rubbing at that spot...that spot...

"Oh, fuck!" The orgasm hit me from behind this time, from my gut, and sparks traveled through my vessels along with the blood, taking me higher, higher, higher...

And then—

He punctured my thigh, drawing more blood from my willing body as my climax continued, and I shattered into a million sparks of energy.

I floated in euphoria, a light-blue cloud of rapture.

Floating, floating, floating...

Until I opened my eyes and met Dante's fiery gaze. His chin was slick with my blood and my juices. His eyes were on fire, his teeth long and sexy.

And I wanted something. Something more.

Oh, yes, we were bonded. Perhaps it was my desire.

Perhaps it was my love. Perhaps it was my vampire heritage.

He'd taken my blood many times.

Now...I would take *his*.

"Show me, Dante. Show me what it feels like to drink blood from someone you love."

He bared his fangs on a sensual growl, bringing his wrist to his lips. I gasped when he punctured his own skin.

I gasped again as two crimson rivers glided down the pale skin of his inner forearm.

Then once more as he brought his wrist to my lips.

# ONE

## *Erin*

**M**y heart raced wildly, its beat thrumming in my ears.

*Thu-thump.*

*Thu-thump.*

*Thu-thump.*

"I'm yours, Erin," he said huskily. "Take from me. Drink from me."

I clamped my mouth onto his bleeding wrist.

I'd tasted the coppery tang of my own blood before, when I bit my tongue, or when I kissed Dante after he'd fed.

Dante's blood, though... This was different.

Different and...spectacular.

A soft and silvery smoothness, maybe even some vanilla.

Could I be imagining it? Or could it be my own vampire heritage helping me enjoy the unique flavor, the warm liquid on my tongue? The concoction wasn't sweet, wasn't savory, wasn't a flavor I could describe with any authenticity.

It was, simply, Dante.

The vampire I loved.

More liquid trickled into my mouth, and as I swallowed, his strength flowed into me, nourishing me. I might not require his blood physiologically as he did mine, but still a need existed—a nebulous wanting that he was awakening, and then sating, in me.

I slid my tongue over the smooth skin of his inner wrist, licking up each droplet of red gold. Red nectar, as Dante sometimes called it.

"Feels nice," he said. "Feels nice when you take from me."

I smiled against his wet skin, continuing to lap up his essence. A low growl emitted from him, and though I didn't hear it with my ears, it vibrated from his body into mine, like an inaudible drumbeat in a rhythm meant only for us.

I continued to drink, taking very little but savoring each drop.

Sweet and vanilla, like a honey cake with silver frosting. A touch of salt—just enough to give it a tingle on my tongue.

Salt.

More pronounced now.

More salt.

More...

No.

Something had changed.

I pulled back, licking my lips.

Dante's eyes were on fire...and not in a good way.

"Baby?" I said tentatively.

He pushed his wrist against my lips. "Drink. Drink from me. Become what you are meant to be."

I shuddered. "Become...what?" I said against his moist skin.

"Take it. Take it." He smashed his wrist into my mouth.

I pulled back and stood. "Dante? Are you...all right?"

"Only when you drink can you fulfill your destiny, Erin."

I inched backward. "Exactly what destiny are you talking about?"

"You *will* drink." He came at me forcefully. "You will take what I'm giving you."

"I've taken enough. It started to taste different, Dante. What's going on?" A sliver of fear lodged in my belly. Dante would never harm me. I knew that as well as I knew the sun would rise tomorrow. But what was going on?

"You will take it."

No. This wasn't right. Without thinking, I stood, scurried out of the room, and headed toward the stairs. As I stepped down—

"No!"

My foot didn't move. I performed the action in my head, but my foot stayed put.

Then, I slid backward, not moving my body voluntarily, the carpet rough under my feet. Backward, backward...until I was again in the bedroom facing him.

Facing a vampire.

I looked into this vampire's eyes.

And he was not Dante.

# TWO

# DANTE

*Let it consume you, Dante. Let it change you. You are becoming everything you are meant to be.*

*Everything I've trained you to be.*

*My blood has nourished you, strengthened you, and Erin's blood has brought you to the peak.*

*The fights have brought out the darkness in you, and the more you remember, the stronger this part of you becomes.*

*It is time, Dante.*

*Time...*

*Time...*

*Time...*

My wrist throbbed as the trickles of blood meandered over my skin. Erin had taken from me, fed from me, *made* me...

I'd brought her toward me using nothing but energy, nothing but my own mind, my own will.

I had no idea how I did it, only that I willed it, and it was so. I willed it because it was necessary. Necessary to my life, to my existence.

Necessary to what I was to become.

Something within me was rising, making me powerful.

*Darkness rising.*

Yes, darkness rising. I'd heard that somewhere before.

*Fight or die in the arena.*

In the arena, I had faced darkness, and I had emerged victorious...

I had emerged...

And then my reward.

*I used to dream of severed human heads.*

*They hung above me, their skin gray and pasty as the elixir of life flowed out of them. I inhaled, and the metallic scent of iron infused itself into my cells. It was the iron and other nutrients in blood that our bodies needed, but that wasn't the scent that drew us, the scent we craved.*

*Humans don't realize they each possess their own scent beyond perspiration and pheromones, a fragrance that comes from their very life-force—their blood.*

*From one neck, a drop of citrusy blond female fell onto my tongue. From another, the leathery and musky flavor of a brown-haired male, this one muscular and full of testosterone. A third fed me with the floral flavor of a female redhead. Redheads were rare, and their blood tasted better than the finest Bordeaux. Redheads with green eyes tasted the best—a lusty concoction laced with essence of lavender yet acidic enough to make a vamp's mouth water for more and more.*

*Then there were the dark-haired ones with light skin— those who, somewhere hundreds of generations ago in their family tree, were descended from a vampire. Their blood was the ultimate concoction, the Champagne of plasma. Bold and tannic yet fruity and divine. Peach, plum, blackberry. Leather, coffee, the darkest of chocolate. Tin, zinc, laced with violet and apple and estrogen. Even the men smelled of traces of milky estrogen.*

*All this plus the one-of-a-kind flavor unique to every human.*

*I lapped it up, gaining strength, finally able to pull hard enough to release my leather bindings.*

*I roared, flexing my muscles, ready to bolt—*

Then I always awoke.

Awoke to nothingness.

But now... Now I remembered.

The severed human heads, the heads that dripped red gold onto my tongue, were not a fantasy, not a dream. They were my reward for winning.

And as I drank, my strength returned.

Returned with a vengeance.

*Dante?*

*Dante, my love?*

Monster! I'd drunk from human heads. I'd taken her reward for victory in the arena.

And I still didn't know what had happened to the vampires I'd fought. Just as I was going to strike, to end it once and for all...

Everything went black.

Then I was tied down again, in a different room, and severed human heads hung above me.

Monster!

Monster!

Monster!

*Dante? Please! You're scaring me!*

The voice was familiar.

*Control, son.*

*Dante! Dante! Dante!*

*Control.*

Something existed that gave me control.

No... Some*one*.

Not my father, though he was here. I didn't see him, but his spirit was here, guiding me.

The woman.

Soft fingertips touched my cheek.

A blur of fair skin and dark hair.

*Dante, please.*

This woman. She was my control. She was what I lived for.

She was light.

She was love.

Love and light could chase out the darkness.

"Erin." My voice cracked.

"Thank God." She melted into my arms.

I wrapped my arms tentatively around her, embracing her warmth and her goodness.

*That's it, son. Remember what's inside you, what no one can touch.*

"But I..."

Erin trembled. "What?"

*But I drank human blood.* She *killed humans to feed me.*

Or did she? Did...*I*?

I squeezed my eyes shut, holding back tears that threatened to drop.

*I'm not a killer. I'm not a killer. I'm not a killer.*

But what if...?

I closed my mind to the possibility.

I was *not* a killer.

Because if I were, I would not deserve anything good. I would not deserve Erin.

And if I didn't have Erin, I would die.

## THREE

# Erin

I held on to him as hard as I could. Blood was still dripping from his wrist and smeared onto me, but I didn't care.

As I held him, I felt him. Felt Dante. The man I loved.

Still I trembled in fear. For just a moment, he'd been a stranger to me. His eyes hadn't been his own. Something had taken him over, something bad. Something almost sinister.

Something *dark*.

I wasn't the only one trembling. He was as frightened as I was.

I pulled back slightly. "Dante? Baby?"

He buried his face in my neck. "Stay. With me. Chase the demons away."

"I'll always be with you. Everything's okay."

He closed his eyes, wincing. "I don't want to remember anymore, Erin. I can't. I'm..."

"You're what?"

"Nothing. It's just... Please. Just hold me. Let's hold each other."

I snuggled into his arms, burying my head in the crook of his neck. I inhaled his spicy scent, now with a bit of silvery vanilla. His blood.

He'd gone away for an instant, like he had when he met my mother, like he had when...

"Dante?"

He didn't respond.

"Babe?"

He kissed the top of my head. "I know."

He knew? What did he know? Did he know what I'd been about to ask?

I shuddered against him. The question was stuck in my throat. I wouldn't ask it. I couldn't.

I was afraid of what the answer might be.

# FOUR

# DANTE

*T ell her, son.*

My father didn't appear, didn't even speak. Or did he? Erin didn't seem to hear him.

I'd been about to tell Erin that the darkness I'd perceived as following me actually *was* me. Was inside me, and sometimes it fought for control. She'd gotten angry, and then her scent...

Oh, God, her scent when she was angry...

No anger now, though. She was holding me, helping me, her love and light chasing away the darkness.

I'd said it before. She was my control. Erin. My love. With every last ounce of strength I possessed, I pulled out of her embrace.

"Baby?" she said.

"I'm okay. I'm so sorry, Erin."

She nodded and swallowed. "Where were you? For a split second, it was like you weren't *you*."

For a split second, I hadn't been. Or perhaps I *had* been, and that thought was even more frightening. Who was the real Dante?

*You know the answer.*

I gasped.

The thought in my head had two separate sources. My father...and her.

They each meant something vastly different.

I let my gaze drift over the beauty that was Erin. Her high cheekbones blushed a rosy pink, her full lips and chin tinged with the crimson of my blood. Her beautiful long dark hair curtained her shoulders. Her body, so fit and perfect, lean muscles and a slightly rounded belly. Her pussy, still glistening. Her long and shapely legs. Her perfectly painted pink toes.

And those eyes. Those dazzling peridot eyes. Eyes that looked upon me with love. With trust.

I owed her the truth.

I sat down on the bed and patted it. She sat beside me and took my hand, rubbing circles with her thumb into my palm. Her touch was soothing, like a warm fire on a snowy day—not that we saw much snow in New Orleans. Or like the first bite of a warm beignet in the Quarter.

"The third thing..." I whispered.

"It's okay. I wanted it as much as you did."

"What?"

"You were about to tell me, and then we got...involved." She smiled. "I have no regrets. I mean, I only regret that you went somewhere you didn't want to go. You need to fight *her*, Dante. You need to fight *her*. For us."

Yes. *Her* I could fight.

But could I fight myself?

"I don't understand, Dante. It was something with your blood. It started tasting different. Saltier. And then...something I can't describe."

*Darker.*

That's what Erin wanted to say. I already knew *she* had done something to my blood. I had a positive Rh factor that was genetically impossible for me to have. Had she found a way to alter the taste of my blood as well?

"I liked the flavor at first," Erin continued. "I wasn't sure what to expect. I knew I enjoyed kissing you after you fed from me, but this was *your* blood. Something different. It tasted like blood, but when I stopped to savor it, it had a silvery vanilla flavor, if that makes any sense. I mean, I've never tasted silver before, but it tasted like I imagine silver might taste."

"It makes perfect sense, baby."

"Does it?"

"Why wouldn't it? Taste is subjective. You're describing how it tasted to *you*."

"I just don't understand why the flavor changed. But it seemed to..."

She didn't need to finish for me to know what she was thinking. The taste of my blood changed when *I* began to change. When the darkness pushed itself to the surface.

"I'm so sorry I scared you," I said. "Please know that I'd—"

"I know. But that pulling me back in here with your mind was kind of—"

"Shit. What?"

"I ran away, and you... You don't remember?"

I closed my eyes. "Yes. Yes. I remember. It was..." I shook my head. "I'm sorry."

"Don't be sorry. Just work some more with your dad and learn to control this stuff that's happening to you. I know you won't hurt me."

No. I wouldn't. If something threatened to consume me

to the point that hurting Erin was a possibility, I'd take my own life, if necessary. But that wasn't what I needed to admit to her now.

"I will. I'll figure this out. Once Bill tells my dad what he read in the *Texts*, maybe we'll understand what's happening to me."

"I know. Now...the third thing?"

I sighed. Best to just come out with it. "You know the darkness I feel sometimes? That Bea said has targeted me?"

She nodded.

I cleared my throat. "Please don't leave me. We need each other now."

"Dante, I would never."

I kissed the top of her head. "Thank you."

"Just tell me. Please. Maybe it's something I can help with. The darkness hasn't gotten you yet."

"No. And it won't. I promise." Not as long as Erin was with me. She was my control.

"Okay. Is that what you needed to tell me?"

I sighed again. "No."

"Then what is it, babe?"

"The darkness. It hasn't targeted me."

She smiled and clapped her hands together. "Great! That's good, right?"

"Well...no. It's actually a *part* of me."

She widened her eyes. "What? I don't understand."

"I don't either, to be honest, but I feel it strongly, and my father corroborated it. Whatever darkness has seemed to be following me is actually coming *from* me."

Erin's soft cheeks went pale.

"I can control it, baby. I promise."

"But..."

"I know I scared you today. I'm sorry. But I came out of it. You helped me. You are my control, Erin."

"I don't understand."

"My love for you. My need for you. Our blood bond. It's my control. I can't explain any better than that, but I know in my heart that you give me something beyond nourishment, beyond strength, beyond perseverance, beyond love even."

"But how..."

"I don't know, but I promise you one thing. We will solve all of these mysteries. After we find Lucy and Em and the others, we'll figure out what's going on with me and between you and me. It's not something you need to fear."

"I know that. But sometimes you..." She shook her head slowly.

I cuddled her close to my body. "I know, baby. Believe me, I know."

"You said you didn't want to remember anymore."

"I don't. But I will if it's necessary. If we need my memories to figure all of this out. I promise."

"I don't want you to hurt."

"I know. But I've been to hell already, love. I don't fear it." My words were truthful. I didn't fear hell. I feared only myself.

"You were trembling today. You were afraid, Dante. Why?"

How could I tell her? It wasn't fear so much as facing something I didn't want to face. I'd drunk from dead humans, and I might have killed other vampires in the arena.

Why hadn't I turned my head away? Why had I succumbed to fresh human blood?

More secrets I had to keep from Erin, at least until I figured out what was happening to me.

Until I figured out if I could stay alive.

Protecting Erin was paramount. If I posed a danger to her, I would end my life.

Simple as that.

Only it wasn't simple at all.

If I took my own life, I might condemn her to the same.

# FIVE

# *Erin*

He didn't answer right away, just held my hand in his, squeezing it softly from time to time.

"Dante?"

He nodded. "I'm always afraid when I scare you. I don't mean to, Erin. I never mean to."

"I know that."

"I won't ever harm you. I'll do whatever it takes to keep from harming you. Please tell me you know that. That you understand that and believe me."

"I do."

"I realize this is more than you ever thought you were getting into," he said. "More than I thought *I* was getting into as well."

"My world has been turned upside down, but I honestly wouldn't change any of it. *You* are my world now, Dante. You and our love." She stood, still holding my hand. "I think we could both use a shower. What do you say?"

Within a few minutes, we stood together under the pelting warm water, embracing, kissing each other softly. Dante's teeth didn't descend, and though his dick got hard and I became aroused, kissing was as far as we went.

This shower wasn't about sex or lust or even love. It was removing the dirt from our bodies and cleansing the fear and darkness from our souls. After we'd lathered each other and then rinsed, we embraced once more.

*I love you,* I told him with the warmth of my body pressed against his. *I love you. I trust you. I believe you and I believe in you. You will protect me, and as God as my witness, I'll protect you too.*

And I would.

I had no power, only the love for him in my heart. But love was powerful indeed, and I would use everything within my control to drive out the darkness that threatened the man I loved.

*I vow to you,* I said silently, *that I will find this vampire bitch who harmed you and put her in a grave myself. I don't know how, but I will.*

*I promise you, Dante.*

⚜

I yawned, stretching. Darkness had fallen, and silver moonlight streamed in through my bedroom window. Dante lay beside me, still sleeping, a soft snore escaping his throat. I leaned over and kissed his stubbly cheek.

He opened one eye. "Hey."

"Hey," I said. "We need to get up."

"Already? Why?"

"We need to go to the bridge."

"What for?"

"To see Abe Lincoln. We promised him food for meals, remember? I saw him yesterday, and he was hungry. Plus, we need to see if he has any new information for us."

He sat up. "I'll go. I don't want you going down there at night."

I huffed. "We've been through this. Those vampires can't smell me when I wear the potion. Plus, I didn't say I was going alone. You'll be there to protect me. We can get River and Jay as added protection if you want. And your dad, even."

"For God's sake." Dante threw the covers off, displaying his magnificent body. "We don't need the whole posse."

His cock was fully erect.

Too much for me to resist.

"Maybe we'll go in a half hour or so." I leaned down and licked the bead of fluid from his cockhead.

He groaned. "God, baby."

I swirled my tongue over his length, raining tiny kisses down to and over his balls. "I don't think I've spent nearly enough time with your gorgeous cock in my mouth," I said against his inner thigh.

"Turn around then, and get on top of me. I want to taste you too."

He didn't have to ask me twice. I loved sixty-nine, and Dante and I hadn't done a lot of it. I planted myself on his gorgeous lips and then took his dick into the back of my throat. I shuddered when he swirled his tongue over the tip of my clit.

Yeah, this wouldn't take long.

I pulled back just until his knobby head was between my lips, and I tugged, sucking as hard as I could.

His groan vibrated against my slick pussy lips, nearly catapulting me into climax.

No. I'd wait.

Wait until I brought him just to the edge, so we could come together.

I hummed against his skin as I sucked him, harder and harder, and then traced figure eights with my lips down to his balls. They were already scrunched up, and he was on the brink. I inhaled the sweet musk of him, grabbing each cheek of his perfectly formed ass as I brought my mouth down upon him once more.

He chuckled against me, tickling my folds. "You'll get what's coming to you, baby." Then he thrust two fingers into me, massaging my spongy G-spot.

"Ah!" The orgasm hit me full force, my mouth still full of cock. I shuddered above him, relishing the fucking motion of his fingers. I plunged my mouth onto his cock again, mimicking his fingering movements.

*Come, Dante. Come in my mouth.*

As I exploded into a second orgasm, he obeyed my silent command.

He pulsed into my mouth, and I took everything, swallowing every last warm drop.

Then, as I pulled away from his erection, I—

"God, Dante!"

He sank his teeth into the flesh of my thigh.

He didn't need to feed. He'd had enough today. This wasn't for nourishment. This was for pleasure.

Pure pleasure. Mine as well as his.

The tugging of his mouth on my flesh catapulted me into my third orgasm, and in another second, we were floating off the bed.

Hovering about five feet above the mattress, and something inside me snapped, taking me to a higher peak than I'd ever dreamed of.

The jazzy tune drifted around us, cocooning us in an almost visible cloud of melodies and harmonies. The shield safeguarded me—no, safeguarded *us*—for we were no longer two separate entities. We were one being, joined and encased in a cloak of music and feelings and intensity. Relaxation bathed me like a soft massage. I reveled in it, in this moment that I didn't want to end.

As we floated downward, I resisted.

I wanted to stay in this beautiful cloud where we were together, where no one could reach us, where pain and darkness didn't exist. Only love and light.

*Nothing lasts forever.* The words rang true in my mind. This orgasm, like all others, faded until it diminished into thin air.

We landed softly on the bed, and Dante licked the wounds on my thigh, helping them to close.

I sighed as I tumbled off him and lay next to him on the bed. I crawled toward the head of the bed and snuggled into his shoulder. "I love you."

"I love you too, Erin. More than anything."

I smiled. "I know." I kissed his neck. "I wish we could stay there, in that place, floating, forever."

"You have no idea how much I wish that."

"But others are depending on us."

He nodded. "You're right."

"Beginning with Abe Lincoln. He needs money for meals."

"If the thugs haven't already fed him."

"If he's getting money from us, he has no need for the

thugs. Besides, they nearly drained him once. Remember when he ended up in the hospital?"

"I remember," Dante said. "But don't for a minute think they'll leave him alone if he's getting his meals elsewhere. These aren't nice people, Erin. They took Emilia and probably the others. They left my father's body naked. Forced me to look at him..." He shook his head. "And they wanted to take you. *You*, Erin."

"I know." I caressed his soft hair. "But I'm safe right now. We have to go see Abe. He might have information."

"He might have faulty information that he's been glamoured into giving us."

I sighed. "I know, but we have to try. Besides, we did promise to feed him."

"All right, baby." Dante sat up. "Let's get dressed and go."

❖

Midnight on Claiborne Bridge. The New Orleans night was clear and pleasant, the nearly full moon big and bright. As we walked toward the tent city, holding hands, a light breeze drifted over us.

"I wish you could smell other vampires," I said tentatively to Dante.

"I do too. But don't worry. If they're around, I'll hear them before I see them."

Newspapers shuffled in the breeze. Several dogs awoke as we walked by, growling but then letting us pass. A black cat, nearly invisible, whisked past my feet, making me jump.

"Easy, baby," Dante said.

"I have no idea where Abe would be," I whispered. "But we

can find Bea, if she's in her normal place."

We walked farther, and there she was, lying atop a stack of old magazines and covered with a dark fleece blanket. She was snoring softly but opened one eye as we approached.

"You're too late," she said.

"Too late for what?" I asked.

"For Abe. He went away. With *them*."

"Shit." I turned to Dante. "You were right. They took him."

"Oh, they didn't take him," Bea said. "He went willingly, a slave to their promises, as usual. I never met a man who would willingly open a vein for food. Until Red Rover, that is."

"Why would he? He knew we were bringing him money for food."

"Maybe he prefers their food. Maybe he likes giving them his blood." Bea smiled. "*You* like it, don't you, dearie?"

I shivered. Yes, I did like it, but Dante and I were bonded. We were in love. "I wouldn't give my blood to just anyone," I told her. The rest was none of her business.

"'Anger's my meat; I sup upon myself, and so shall starve with feeding.'"

Dante rolled his eyes. "Thoreau again?"

I shook my head. "Thoreau was a vegetarian. He'd never talk about meat."

"She's not talking about meat," Dante said. "She's talking about anger."

*Anger's my meat; I sup upon myself, and so shall starve with feeding.*

The words echoed in my mind.

"Oh, no," I whispered.

"What?"

"'Anger's my meat. I sup upon myself.' She's talking about

Abe. They're going to drain him. Where is he, Bea? Where did they take him?"

"I know not."

Dante scoffed. "I thought you had the sight."

"'Is this a dagger which I see before me, the handle toward my hand?'"

"For God's sake."

"Wait," I said. "I know that one. It's Shakespeare, from *Macbeth*. The dagger is a vision. It's not real, at least that's what most lit experts teach. What are you trying to say, Bea?"

"Sounds like she's saying she doesn't have the sight after all," Dante said. "If whatever dagger she's talking about was invisible."

"'Alarum'd by his sentinel, the wolf, whose howl's his watch, thus with his stealthy pace—'"

I jumped. "Wolf? What about the wolf?" My mind raced. "Of course. It's all a part of the same scene. Macbeth is thinking about killing the king. The dagger is a vision, and the murder becomes a separate entity in his mind, awakened by what he hears as a wolf's howl. That's it! A wolf's howl."

"What does any of this have to do with Abe Lincoln and the thugs?" Dante asked.

Nausea swam up my throat, and I swallowed, my heart racing. "Don't you see? It's Lucy. The wolf's howl. We have to find her, Dante. We have to find her now. They're going to drain Abe and kill her!"

# SIX

# DANTE

I bared my teeth on a low growl. "Listen, old woman, you need to tell us where they are. Now."

"Yes, please, Bea," Erin begged. "Is Lucy all right? Oh, God. Is she *alive*?"

"For now, but your friend has not been helpful. They have plans to eliminate her. Her time is running out."

"No!" Erin clasped her arms around me. "Dante, we need to find her. We need to find her now!"

"You haven't answered my question," I snarled at Bea. "Where the hell are they?"

"I know not," she said. "I know only this. 'Hell is empty and all the devils are *here*.'"

"Is that Shakespeare again?" Erin said. "I don't recognize it. It's not from *Macbeth*."

My mind whirled. I didn't recognize it either. The only Shakespeare I'd read was *Romeo and Juliet* in ninth grade English, and I barely remembered that.

But I knew exactly where I needed to go.

And I couldn't take Erin with me.

"Is that more Shakespeare?" Erin asked again. "Are you going to answer me?"

"*He* knows." Bea nodded to me.

"What is she talking about, Dante?"

Hell.

I'd *been* to hell.

Not the real hell, of course, if a real hell even existed.

Bea was telling me to go back. Back to where I'd been imprisoned, tortured, forced to fight for survival, and forced to drink her blood, and there I'd find Lucy, Emilia, and the others. The thugs and Abe Lincoln.

My uncle.

And *her*.

*Not only that, Dante. You'll also find yourself.*

I tilted my head to the side, as if the motion could cause *her* to fall out of my brain.

*I'll leave you now. For soon you'll return to me.*

I stomped my foot on the concrete, as if I were stomping *her* out of my head.

This time, though, *she*'d left of her own accord.

"I need to ask you something," Erin said. "Did you come to me in a dream? Tell me that the book we had was a fake? Give me a remedy for vampire morning sickness?"

Bea cocked her head. "I don't have the ability to infiltrate dreams, dearie."

"But do you have that ability when a ghost is inhabiting you?"

Bea lifted her fuzzy eyebrows. "Who says ghosts inhabit me?"

"Dante's fa—"

I nudged her as nonchalantly as I could, hoping Bea wouldn't notice. Was it possible the woman didn't know she was a medium? Or was she keeping something from us? In a second, she'd be spouting someone else's words again, and we'd have to figure out what the hell she meant.

But she stayed silent.

"Bea," Erin continued, "you've met—"

"Yes, I've met many ghosts in my day. Vampires, shifters, even a few demons."

"And you've never felt one of them...go inside you?"

"I had a werepanther lover once in the nineties. Since then, no one has been 'inside' me."

"That's not what—"

I silenced Erin with another soft nudge. Either Bea didn't realize she was a medium, or she didn't want to talk to us about it. Either way, we'd get no further.

And I had work to do.

I'd take Erin home, and I'd give her what she and I both craved—a forceful lovemaking using bindings and other toys. I'd feed from her, take her luscious blood and make it last, because I didn't know when I'd be able to drink more. Then I'd wait until she fell asleep, and I'd venture back to the alley behind Joseph's phony magick shop where my father had died. I'd felt strongly that it was near the place where I'd escaped.

I'd go quickly and heed Bea's warning, and hope I could get to the others before Bea's premonitions came true.

I'd find that place, find the loose manhole cover.

And go back into hell.

# SEVEN

# *Erin*

Dante held my hand and pulled me away from Bea.

"Wait! I have to pay her."

"She has my father's ashes. She told us that was more than enough payment for a long time, remember?"

"Oh. Right." I tugged on Dante's arm. "We didn't even say goodbye."

He seemed a million miles away.

"Dante?"

"I have to go on an errand," he said, barely above a whisper.

"All right. Where to?"

"Alone. I have to go alone, Erin. I was going to wait until you fell asleep, but I need to be honest. I've kept so much from you already, and I'm done with that."

I swallowed. I didn't like where this was headed. "Why alone?"

"I just have to."

"Sorry. Not good enough. I love you. You mean everything

to me. You at least have to tell me where you're going."

He stayed silent until we reached the car and got in. Then he turned to me, his dark eyes heavy-lidded and serious.

"You wanted to know what Bea meant by that last quote. I have no idea where it's from, whether it's Shakespeare or Thoreau or Mickey Mouse, but the meaning was clear to me. The devils are here. On earth. They have Emilia and Lucy. My uncle. The others. And I know exactly where they are."

I gasped. He meant to go back, back to where he'd been held captive and tortured. "No! I won't let you! You can't go back there." My heart thundered so hard I felt it everywhere in my body, the sound a drumbeat in my ears.

"I have to, Erin. I have to go back. Only then will I find the truth."

"Not without me."

"It's not safe for you there."

"It's not safe for you there either, Dante! For God's sake, she held you as a prisoner! Did horrible things to you that you won't even tell me about!"

"I know. But I'm different now. I can handle it."

His words dripped with strength and determination, but I wasn't buying it.

"Please, Dante. *No*."

"I'm sorry. I have to. It's the only way to find Em and the others. To put an end to all of this once and for all."

"But the *Texts*. Bill hasn't told your dad yet what—"

"Fuck Bill. Fuck the *Texts*. I have to do this, Erin. I have to. Try to understa—"

"I'll *never* understand!"

"Then at least... Oh, hell. I don't know what else I can say. I have to do this. It's the only way."

I hated crying, but the tears fell anyway. Soon I was sobbing, clinging to Dante's arm as he drove. "I can't lose you. I just can't."

"You won't, baby. Trust me. Trust that I have to do this." He sighed. "I can bear anything. Anything except your tears."

"Take someone with you at least. Your father. No one will be able to see him. He can spy for you. Figure out where to go."

"I have to do this alone."

"Why? You have so many people here who love you. Who care about you. Let us help!"

"No."

"Not even River?"

"Especially not River. I can't put him through this." He shook his head. "I can't."

"Why not? He loves Em and Lucy as much as anyone. And it's his father, for God's sake."

"That's why I can't put him through this. I saw my own father's body, what had been done to it. River's father is alive. I can't let his only son see him until I get him out of there."

"Why? Why only you? Why does it have to be you, Dante?"

He stared straight ahead. The headlights on the car shot two white beams across the desolate road as we neared home.

"Why?" I asked again.

"Because I'm the only one who *can*."

# DANTE

"*Y*ou've done well, Dante. You deserve your reward."

*Then...nothing. I was back in my dungeon, tied down with the enchanted—yes, they must have been—leather bindings.*

Fight or die in the arena.

*I'd fought.*

*I'd won.*

*I'd gone in for the murderous strike.*

*And then I always awakened back here, remembering nothing of the final blow.*

*My reward.*

*I looked up.*

*The heads. The severed human heads.*

*Though nausea erupted in my stomach at seeing death, my hunger for the dripping blood overcame any ambivalence.*

*I opened my mouth, let the droplets of sustenance feed me, soothe me.*

*Yes, a citrusy blond, a muscular male.*

*And then a vampire descendent, female, musky and dark*

*and truffly and tannic.*

*Delicious.*

*I lapped up the blood as it fell onto me, dripped over my lips and down my cheeks and chin.*

*Who were they, these lost souls who fed me? Who had died so that I might reap this reward? Pure human blood. Not bagged blood from the butcher. And not blood from* her.

*For a moment, I mourned the lives lost, gave thanks for their sacrifice.*

*I shouldn't drink. I knew that.*

Stop. Stop drinking.

*But I continued, letting the red nectar roll over my tongue and flow down my throat.*

*As I drank, I inhaled each fragrant and unique scent. Let them infuse me with their hormones and pheromones.*

*And I grew stronger.*

*This blood was fresh. These people had died recently. Recently as in within the last several hours.*

Stop. Stop drinking. Shouldn't do this.

*But I couldn't stop.*

*I* could not *stop.*

⚜

My plans to take Erin to bed—to bind her and claim her and make her obey me—were forced onto the back burner. Jay and River were at the townhouse, waiting for us.

"It's the middle of the night," Erin said to her brother.

"So what? We're all used to being up at night. Besides, it was River's idea to come over here right away."

"What for?" I said to my cousin, barely unable to unclench my teeth.

"Jay and I heard back from our buddy at the lab."

"In the middle of the night?"

"Well...yeah. He can't be doing this stuff during the light of day. It's totally off the record."

"What did he find out?" Erin asked.

River sat down on the couch. "As Jay and I suspected, most of the prints on the objects had no matches in the files."

"Okay," I said. "You said most."

"Yeah. I told Joey not to leave any stone unturned and to check them against the oldest files he had, just to make sure, and to hang the cost. I figured he'd go back twenty or thirty years. Turns out he took me a little more seriously than I anticipated."

"And...?"

"You won't believe it, Sis," Jay said.

"Believe what?" Erin said. "Just tell us."

"The United States began using fingerprinting for identification back in the eighteen nineties, but it didn't become mainstream until the FBI began using it in the nineteen twenties."

"Yeah, whatever," I said. "We don't need a history lesson."

"You kind of do," River said. "I never in a million years thought Joey would go through every file, even those from long ago. I guess he needs some money. We owe him big time."

"He'll get paid," I said. "Why would he go back so far?"

"Because I told him to. I didn't expect him to take me so literally. But here's the thing." River cleared his throat. "He found a fucking match."

Erin's mouth dropped open. "Who is the match?"

"That's the part that doesn't make a lot of sense," River said. "He found a sixty-eight-year-old female whose prints were taken in 1931 for a crime of petty theft. He says it's a perfect match. Problem is, that woman would be over a hundred and fifty years old by now."

"So she's a vampire?" Erin said.

"No, baby," I said. "We live slightly longer, but not that long, and men live longer than women, the opposite of humans. The longest known lifespan for a vampire is a hundred and thirty-two years, but most don't make it to that point."

"What about a vampire woman?" she asked.

"I don't know. Riv?"

"I don't know either. Bill would know. I don't think one has lived past ninety-five. At least not that we know of."

"More to ask Bill," I said. "And then we have to hope that he's truthful. Where did your guy find the prints?"

"On the little vodka bottle."

"Not Em's brush or other stuff?"

"Nope, just the bottle. None of the other prints had matches."

"But how?" Erin asked.

River shook his head. "Got me. The bottle is new. We've established that already. It was manufactured within the last couple of years. No way a dead woman could have handled it."

"This just gets fuzzier and fuzzier," Erin said. "Who do the fingerprints belong to?"

River sighed. "We don't know. The name on the card has been smudged off. It's illegible. All we know is the birthdate and that she's a female. No other identifiable information."

"Can a fingerprint be manufactured?" I asked.

"In this day and age?" Jay said. "Sure. But what are the chances of reproducing a fingerprint that is an exact match of a dead woman?"

"Good point." I rubbed my forehead. "So this isn't really any help at all."

"No," River said, "but it deepens the mystery. How did a dead woman's prints get on a tiny vodka bottle in Em's apartment? Em is pregnant, so we know she wasn't drinking. The bottle was left by whoever took her."

"Who also left the lapel pin with the weird fleur-de-lis on it," Erin said.

"Right, Sis," Jay agreed. "And we know they didn't mean to leave that. But did they mean to leave the vodka bottle? I'd say yeah, because if a couple thug vamps are drinking, they're not going to be drinking out of a tiny airplane bottle. That bottle was there for a purpose."

"Right, partner," River said. "They wanted us to find the bottle. Either that or someone else was with them who dropped the bottle by accident."

"And if they left it on purpose," Jay continued, "they had a reason for us wanting to find it. One reason could have been the prints on it, even though three of the sets had no match."

"But a dead woman?" I shook my head. "Something else has to be going on here. Why would they want to lead us to a dead woman?"

"Maybe they did it on purpose," Erin said. "To veer us off course."

"But how could they?" I asked. "How did they get a dead woman's prints on a brand-new bottle?"

"Cuz," River said, "I have no idea. But I can guarantee you one thing. We *will* figure this out. We have to. We have to find Em, Lucy, and the others."

*Come to me.*

I tilted my head. I did not need *her* in my mind at the moment.

*Come to me.*

Damn!

I jerked backward when my father appeared.

"Uncle Jules," River said. "We have some news."

"I was listening," he said.

"You eavesdropped on us?" River said.

"Yes. Not on purpose. I was about to materialize, but I got interested in your conversation. I can help you with one thing. The oldest female vampire was only eighty-eight when she passed. The longer-than-human lifespan really only pertains to vampire males."

"So whoever this woman is whose prints are on the bottle isn't a vampire then?" Erin said.

"She could be either," Jay said. "She's dead, no matter what. The oldest human female was some French woman who lived to be 122. She died in 1997."

"How do you know that?" Erin asked.

"I'm a wealth of trivia." Jay smiled. "Kidding. I looked it up after Riv and I got the call about the prints."

"The best explanation is that the prints were planted to throw us off track," River said. "Yet that still doesn't make sense, because why would they want to lead us to a dead woman?"

"You got me, partner," Jay said. "Though these people seem to do everything for a reason. Except for leaving the lapel pin. That seems to have been a genuine accident, at least according to your ghostly evidence." He nodded to my father.

"Can we figure out who this woman was?" Erin asked.

"Truly looking for a needle in a haystack. We'd have to research every woman born on that date in the US. Impossible."

"Yeah, I didn't think that through." Erin sighed. "Maybe just ignore this? We just really need to find Lucy and the others."

"Agreed," I said. "And I know how to begin."

# NINE

## *Erin*

I wanted to clamp my hands over my ears and drown out what was coming.

*I need to go back.*

I felt more than heard Dante's words.

Then voices. My brother. River. Julian.

All telling him *no*. No way was he going alone.

"I don't have a choice," Dante said. "I can't let any of you go there. It's horrific."

"You're forgetting one thing, son," Julian said. "I've already been there."

That jolted me.

Julian was dead. A ghost. Yet there were times that I thought of him as a living being. He had been alive, and he had been where Dante was. At least I assumed they'd been held at the same place. None of us had any way of knowing.

"I probably escaped the same way you did," Julian said to Dante. "I can help you find where you need to go."

"Wait, wait, wait," River piped in. "Exactly *why* do you need to go there? You think they're holding the women at the same place where they held you?"

"The priestess," Dante began. "She told me something. She said, 'Hell is empty and all the devils are *here.*'"

"Shakespeare," Julian said. "*The Tempest.*"

"We figured it was Shakespeare," I said. "I haven't read that one."

"I understand," Julian continued. "You have to go back."

Dante nodded. "Exactly."

I tugged on Dante's arm. "Please. Don't."

"I'm sorry, baby. I have to."

"You're not going without me," River said. "My father is there somewhere too."

"That's why you can't go," Dante said. "Do you want to see your father like that? Like you saw my father's body?"

"No. I don't want to see that, but I have to go. He's my father. He'd do the same for me."

Dante sighed.

"He's right, son," Julian said.

"I'm going too," Jay said.

"No." I rubbed my arms to ease the sudden chills that emerged on my skin. "No! Damn it! I can't lose all of you! No!"

"We have to, Erin," River said.

"Then I'm going too."

"No."

Four strong male voices.

In unison.

My lover, his ghost father, his cousin, and my brother.

Four men I loved. Four men I didn't want to lose.

Four men whose opinion I valued, who I'd listen to when necessary.

But not now.

"I'm just as all-in as the rest of you," I said, hands on my hips. "Lucy is my best friend. Dante is my...everything. Someone wanted me pregnant with his baby. I'm as much a part of this as the rest of you."

"Erin," Dante said, caressing my cheek. "You're my everything too, which is why you can't go. I can't be..."

"Can't be what?"

"I need to know you're safe."

"You'll be there. You'll all be there. You can protect me. Don't forget I'm pretty good at protecting myself too."

"You can be glamoured," Dante said. "And you too." He nodded to Jay.

"Aren't there some kind of glasses we can wear?" Jay asked. "To protect against that?"

"This isn't some vampire TV show, partner," River said with a slight laugh. "We can't protect you from being glamoured."

"Dante can," I said. "He reversed Bill's glamour that day in the courtroom."

"You can't depend on that, baby," Dante said. "I haven't been able to repeat it. I have no idea how I did it."

"You'd be able to do it to protect me," I said. "I know you would."

And I did.

I knew it.

Dante would protect me.

As long as he was alive.

I had no doubt.

Which was why I had to go along.

Plus, something was niggling at me. Something about the

dead woman's fingerprints.

"Could the rest of you excuse us?" I said. "Dante and I need to talk. Alone."

"Baby..."

"Please, Dante. This is important."

Julian vanished, so at least he understood.

"Sis, I'm with the guys on this one. You can't go."

"Sorry, Jay. Now leave, please."

Jay looked to River. "Nothing I can do when she gets like this. Maybe he can talk her out of it."

River nodded, and the two of them left.

I turned to Dante. His eyes were dark and smoldering.

I licked my lips. "I want to—"

"Upstairs," he commanded. "Now."

My nipples hardened as goose bumps erupted on my arms and legs. Between my legs, fire burned. But we needed to talk about this.

"No, Dante. We need to—"

In a swift movement I couldn't visually discern, I was in his arms and being carried up the stairs.

"Dante..."

"Not another word, Erin. Not another fucking word."

I shuddered, though my flesh was heating. I wanted him. Wanted him so badly.

But we truly did need to talk.

"Talk later," he mumbled.

Had I said anything out loud? At this point, I wasn't sure. It was the middle of the night, but my days and nights had glommed into one another since I'd taken my leave of absence from work. We worked nights and days, slept when we could. Always going... Always looking for something new... A new clue that would lead us where we needed to be.

Dante entered the bedroom and tossed me onto the bed. "Undress. Quickly."

I smiled a half smile and slowly began to unbutton my blouse.

I was teasing him. Trying to simmer him down. I wanted him as much as he wanted me, but we did need to talk.

He growled, baring his teeth. "Faster, or I'll tear it off you. You know I will."

I ripped my blouse down the middle, and buttons went flying. Then I scrambled out of my shoes, pants, and underwear.

He inhaled. Already I was ripe. Already I was ready. I could smell it as well.

"Lie face down. Grab the rungs of the headboard."

I obeyed without question. Whatever he had in store for me, I was game.

But still... We needed to talk.

Within a minute, he had strapped my wrists to the headboard. I tugged against the bindings out of instinct.

But truly?

I didn't want to be unbound.

I wanted to know where this was going.

I soon found out.

# TEN

# DANTE

This was what I'd wanted when we first got home.

To show her who was boss here. To show her she would obey me. That she would *not* accompany me when I went back into hell.

Erin was love and light and everything good in the world.

I could never take her into hell.

That place would change her. Show her the evil that existed in the world. She would learn things. She would learn things about *me*. Things I didn't want to learn myself.

No. Couldn't happen. She was mine. All mine. *Can't lose her. Can't lose Erin.*

She would learn that I'd drunk fresh blood from human heads. That people had died so I might feed.

She would learn that I'd fought and beaten other vampires in the arena, and most likely killed them.

She would learn that I'd succumbed to *her*. Allowed *her* to take my blood and force her own upon me.

She would learn all about me.

She would learn the truth.

We were bonded, and I loved her more than life itself. Needed her. Could not lose her. If she went with me, I would lose her. One way or another.

I could not allow that.

I fingered the leather paddle, soft on one side, firm on the other. No leading up to more today. I was going all-in.

*Whack!*

I brought the firm side down on Erin's perfect ass.

She cried out.

"Enough?" I asked.

"Just do it, Dante. Do whatever you feel you need to do. I understand."

"You understand?" A sound vibrated in my throat, part groan, part growl.

I brought the paddle down again.

God. The rosiness of her flesh. I could sink my teeth in one of those round ass cheeks right now and draw the sweetest blood.

But that wasn't why we were here.

*Whack!*

I brought it down again and forced the beautiful hum of her blood, the pop of her capillaries, out of my ears.

"You're mine!" *Whack!*

"Always mine!" *Whack!*

"Of course I'm—"

"Quiet!" *Whack!*

I brought down the paddle on her backside one, two, three more times.

My fangs were long, and I ground out a snarl. My cock was hard inside my jeans. So fucking hard. Diamond hard.

I couldn't see her nipples, but I knew they were poking through to the mattress.

I couldn't see her clit, but it was hard and swollen and red, redder than her ass cheeks after a fresh whipping.

I couldn't see her eyes, but they were a fiery green.

All this I knew.

I fingered the hard leather of the paddle.

Once more.

One more time.

*Whack!*

And as if the paddle were an extension of my hand, I felt the smack of her vessels as they burst, making her skin rosier.

I throbbed all over, from my toes to the top of my head, and inside my jeans my cock throbbed the hardest of all.

I undressed quickly. For what I was about to do, I wanted nothing between us. Then I fumbled in my box of toys and found the tool I required.

A butt plug.

Tonight, I'd take Erin in her forbidden place. A virginity for both of us. And I'd take her blood while doing it.

We would truly be one.

And no matter what happened between us in the near future, she would be mine forever.

## ELEVEN

# *Erin*

My ass stung from Dante's punishment. What had I done? Didn't matter. Whatever he gave, I would take. I would do anything to please him. Anything.

Except let him and the others go after the women without me.

He could paddle me a thousand times, beat me until my ass turned blue, and still I was going.

"You want more of that, baby?" he said huskily.

"I'll take whatever you want to give," I gritted out into the pillow.

"Good. Because we're far from done."

I gasped when something cold dribbled between the cheeks of my ass. It warmed as Dante's fingers rubbed my tight hole.

"You'll take what I give," Dante said. Then he inserted a finger into my asshole.

I gasped again.

"Easy," he said. "Breathe."

Until he reminded me to breathe, I hadn't realized I'd been holding my breath. As I let out a smooth exhale, the sharp pain of his finger stretching me relaxed into a simple invasion. In a few more seconds, a pleasant invasion, when he pulled out slightly and pushed his digit back in.

"Easy," he said again. "This is new for both of us."

New for him? I supposed it was. He'd been gone for so long, so he couldn't have had any experience with anal. Still, he was going slowly, helping me adjust.

He knew what he was doing.

Somehow, Dante always knew what he was doing.

"How's that feel, baby?"

"I...uh..." How could I answer? This was a sensation I'd never felt before, never imagined feeling. I settled for, "Good."

"Good. That's what I want. This will be good for both of us. I'm going to add another finger, okay?"

I nodded into the bed pillow.

"Okay, Erin?"

"Yes," I eked out.

"You sure?"

I nodded furiously into the pillow. I wasn't going to stop now. I wasn't ever going to stop with Dante. I was his. He could do what he wanted with me. I knew in my heart he would never hurt me.

Never.

I regulated my breathing. In. Out. In. Out.

Then I smiled into the pillow.

The jazzy music drifted over me.

All would be okay now. This was meant to be.

I winced when he stretched me farther, adding the second finger. *Breathe, Erin.*

I did, letting the breath out slowly, like I'd taught women during childbirth.

It helped.

Soon he was moving his fingers in me, and it felt... interesting. Almost good.

No. Wait.

It was good. Yeah. Good.

Everything with Dante was good.

A few minutes later, when I'd gotten used to and was actually enjoying the invasion, something cool touched my cheek. I jerked softly.

"Stainless steel, baby. It's a plug. I'm going to remove my fingers and put this inside you. It will stretch you. Make you ready for me."

Ready for...

His cock.

Of course. I knew that. That was what he was leading up to. Anal sex.

The thought frightened me...and turned me on.

My nipples were so hard, they were probably denting my mattress, and my pussy... Oh God, my pussy...

When his fingers were gone, I felt empty, until the cool pointy knob nudged at my asshole.

"Just a little more lube," he said.

The liquid, warm this time, trickled over me.

"Ready?"

"Sure." Though I was not sure at all.

He pushed the knob past my tight rim, and though I winced, it didn't hurt much. He'd stretched me nicely with his fingers. Once it was in, my rim softened.

"There. That will stay inside you while we do...other

things." He nipped at my butt cheek, scraping me with his fangs. "Beautiful, Erin. Your blood is at the surface from the paddling. I need a taste. Just a taste." He sank his teeth into my stinging flesh.

My skin was so sensitive from his whipping, and then the puncture with his teeth... My pussy throbbed. Every cell of my body became mobile, at least that was what it felt like, and I heated, cooled, heated, cooled. I tugged at the ropes binding me to the rungs of the headboard. Low moans emerged at the back of my throat, coming forth as husky gasps.

*More. Take more. Take all of me. I'm yours.*

Too soon, he withdrew his teeth and licked the small wounds. "Beautiful. So fucking beautiful." He inhaled harshly, the sound a melody in my ears. "Your scent is strong today. Almost as strong as when you were fertile, Erin. Something about you... Bringing your blood to the surface with the paddle. My God."

"Dante, please."

"Please what, love?"

"My pussy. I need you."

He pressed kisses up my back until he came to my neck. His hard cock nudged the butt plug, making it move slightly, making it drive me slightly insane.

So close. He was so close to thrusting inside me. So fucking close.

"Your pussy? What does your pussy need?"

"Your cock. Your fingers. Your tongue. You, Dante. It needs you." I slid my knees as far upward as they would go, hoping to entice him with my swollen wetness.

A swift inhale.

Yes. I was getting to him.

"Your scent gets inside me, Erin. Inside every cell of me. It's part of me. *You* are part of me."

"Please, Dante. Please."

Seconds passed. Then more seconds.

He was driving me to the brink.

Then the soft pressing of his lips down my back. Over the globes of my ass.

Downward...

Downward...

Downward...

Until he swiped his tongue over my wet folds.

I nearly shot into orgasm, but something held me back. I was waiting for more. More. More.

He thrust his whole tongue into my heat. I pushed backward, trying to get more of his tongue, lips, face all into me.

"Patience, love," he said against my inner thigh. "Patience has its reward."

"Please!" I cried out.

He nudged the plug. "How's this feeling?"

"Amazing. Please. I have to come, Dante. I have to."

"And you will, Erin. When *I* decide you will."

Intensity. Insanity. Need. Ache. All flowed together in one huge web of torment.

"Your scent is driving me crazy." He inhaled harshly once more.

Good. If I was insane, I wanted him insane too. I wanted him so hard and so full of aching need that he had to have me. Had to drive into me with a force so profound we'd both explode.

*Smack!*

His hand came down onto my already stinging ass, nudging

the plug further. God. God. I'd go crazy if I couldn't come.

Then the plug nudged again, but this time Dante was turning it slowly.

*God. God. God.*

Then he pulled it out, stretching me.

"Beautiful, baby. You're so ready. So ready for me to take you here." He swiped his tongue over my pussy once more and continued all the way over my stretched asshole.

"I need you," I cried into the pillow.

"I need you too. I'm going to fuck your ass, baby."

"Yes. God. Please."

"You're ready. I'm going to go in quickly to minimize the pain. All right?"

"Yes. God. Please."

"Ah!"

He was in.

So full.

So full of cock and everything Dante.

He stayed inside me, immobile, letting me get used to this perfect invasion.

After a minute, I could stand it no longer, and I pushed backward against him, willing him to move. To pull out. To thrust back in.

And he did.

He so did.

Inside me. Taking all of me.

And then—

The familiar sharpness as he sank his teeth into the flesh of my shoulder.

Truly joined.

Full. So full. And so good as he took me.

I longed to reach downward and touch my clit. Just one light caress, and I'd be flying. Flying so high.

But I was bound, and pulling at the ropes did no good.

"So tight, baby. God, this feels amazing. You feel amazing."

His thrusts increased, and the jazzy music floating around us crescendoed into a clashing of cymbals and a triumph of brass.

*Please. Please. Please.*

*Need to come.*

And then—

I was flying. Truly flying, still bound to the bed.

Colors swirled around me. Soft pink, neon blue, bright yellow, lime green.

"Yes. Yes. So good. So tight." He slammed into me with a low growl.

Yes, we were flying. But I was bound to the bed... Bound to...

Didn't matter. Didn't care.

"Dante! God, I love you. I love you, Dante."

"I love you too, baby. You're unbelievable. Un-fucking-believable." He ground into me, releasing every last bit of himself.

At least that was how it felt to me.

My climax roared to life again, and I drowned in the music, the menagerie of color, the kaleidoscope of feeling and pure, raw emotion.

When I finally came down, panting—

"Oh!" I gasped into the pillow, jarring as the bed hit the floor.

"Wow," Dante said above me.

I whimpered at the withdrawal of his cock.

I turned my head, craning my neck to try to see him. "You... You..."

"I know. Wow."

"You made the whole bed rise. The whole bed."

"I know," he said again. "I mean, I guess it was me."

"It sure wasn't me." I tugged at the bindings.

He moved forward and untied the ropes. "You okay?"

"Yeah. Yeah. I think so."

"It wasn't too much?"

"No. Not the sex. But you..."

## TWELVE

# DANTE

*I* *know.*

Feelings flooded me. Emotion I didn't even recognize. Erin had given me something she'd given no one. She'd let me whip her with a leather paddle, drink the blood that rose to the surface from the punishment. She'd let me take her in her most intimate place, and while we were joined, I'd somehow lifted the entire bed into the air.

A dark emotion whirled above me, invisible, but I knew it was there. Invisible but black. Invisible but...evil.

The part of me I had to fight.

How? Why?

Erin and I had just shared the ultimate intimacy. Why this torment now? Why this savage beast that threatened to destroy me? To destroy *us*?

*Because it is who you are.*

"No!"

Erin shuddered next to me. "Dante?"

"Nothing. I'm fine." I closed my eyes, swinging my arm

over my brow. "Thank you for that."

"You never need to thank me, Dante."

I opened my eyes.

She was so beautiful, her cheeks flushed with burst capillaries, her face shiny with perspiration, her lips full and beautiful.

My God. I hadn't even kissed those lips.

I'd been selfish. So selfish. That wasn't like me.

That wasn't *me*.

It was something else.

A part of me that both was me and wasn't me.

*Because it is who you are.*

*No!*

I sat up in bed and turned to Erin, taking her in my arms. I needed her. Needed to kiss those beautiful lips that I'd neglected.

I crushed my mouth to hers.

She opened for me as she always did, letting me take from her as I had only moments ago. So special. So giving. So much more than I deserved. She was mine. I knew that. She knew that.

I needed to be worthy of her love, of this bond between us. And to be worthy...

*No. Won't think of that now.*

Instead, I lost myself in her lips, her tongue, her sweet moans into my mouth. Kissing Erin. Immersing myself in Erin.

In Erin, I could find the truth.

In Erin, I could find myself. The self that was the true me. I could fight off everything else. I could fight.

*Fight or die in the arena.*

*No. Not now.*

Kiss. Only this kiss. Only this mating of mouths.

Our lips slid together. Our tongues tangled. My sharp teeth nicked her gums, and tiny droplets of her essence touched my taste buds, giving me strength, giving me so much more than I deserved.

I would be worthy of this kiss.

I would be worthy of Erin.

I had to be, and I knew just how to do it.

I would go back into hell. Back to *her*.

And I would end this once and for all.

❖

No more.

Please. No more.

*The goons had entered, and as they fussed with the electric prods, I forced myself to stay silent. To not beg for mercy. To not beg at all.*

*I breathed through my mouth to spare myself their noxious odor.*

*"Time for your punishment, shithead," one of them said.*

*Punishment? I'd just been rewarded.*

*Rewarded with the blood of innocents.*

*Why?*

*But I knew better than to ask. They had no answers for me. They simply did as* she *told them.*

*One of the goons stared down at me, his eyes crazed beneath his mask. "You think you're special, vampire? Think you're worthy?"*

*I said nothing.*

*"You do. You think because you—"*

"Quiet," the other said. "You'll only anger him."

Anger him? I was already angry. Angry that I was here against my will. Forced to feed a vampire woman I hated. Forced to take her blood. Forced to endure the torture of these sadistic garbage-scented humans. Forced to fight for survival in that damned dirt arena.

"Anger him? I couldn't give a shit. He's nothing. Not worth the dog shit on my shoe."

And the torture began again.

## THIRTEEN

# *Erin*

The kiss.

Oh, the kiss.

Dante was kissing me with a feral ferocity. Almost an *unusual* ferocity, as if he were trying to prove something. Trying to make amends for something. Trying to chase something away.

I didn't care. I relished the intensity, the strength of the kiss, of his tongue in my mouth, of his teeth scratching me, of the tangy flavor of my own blood from his lips.

I could go on forever.

We kissed and we kissed and we kissed.

Until, finally, I had to break away to draw in a deep breath.

I panted, wiping the sweat from my brow.

He gazed at me, his eyes still dark with desire, his chin glistening from our very openmouthed kiss. His lips were still tinged with my blood from our lovemaking.

He was so beautiful, so magnificent.

His shoulders so fair and broad, so rippled with muscles. His arms were taut and corded. His whole body was tense, as if he were ready to flee.

A spark of fear churned in my belly.

He was going to leave.

He was going to leave without me.

I reached forward and caressed his cheek, thumbing the stubble that I loved.

"I love you," he said gruffly.

"I love you too." I smiled. "Always, Dante."

Before I could say any more, the doorbell rang downstairs.

He rose. "I'll get it."

He pulled on a pair of jeans and nothing else and left the room. Hastily, I dressed in jeans and a tank and followed him.

He was already opening the door for my mother.

"Mom?" I hurried down the stairs. "It's the middle of the night."

She eyed Dante, raking her gaze over his naked upper body, his disheveled hair, his lips still tinged with tiny smears of blood. She went pale.

"Mom?" I said again.

"I came to tell you I'm leaving. Driving back to Ohio."

"In the middle of the night? Can't this wait until morning?"

"It's five a.m." She pointed to her watch. "It *is* morning."

"Oh. Still, it's awfully early."

"Erin, I can't stay here any longer. I need to get back to your father. I need to be around familiarity right now. I just need..."

I walked to my mother and hugged her. "I know, Mom. Believe me. No one knows better than I do that things are never what they seem."

She pulled back a little and met my gaze. "Honey, I hope you know what you're doing." She nodded to Dante. "He's..."

"What?"

"Is he...dangerous?"

Dante stiffened but said nothing.

"He's the man I love, Mom. He's not dangerous at all." Not dangerous to me, anyway. I was certain of that. To others? I wasn't sure, but I couldn't say that to my mother.

"But the way he—"

I held up my hand to quiet her. She'd seen Dante at one of his worst times. Unfortunately, those times seemed to be getting more frequent. The dark energy he spoke of—that darkness that lived inside him—could it take over?

Fear laced my mother's eyes.

"You don't have to leave," I said.

She nodded, gulping. "But I do. I need to be with your father. How am I going to tell him any of this?"

"The words will come. There's no hurry."

"Of course there's a hurry. We're going to be grandparents. If the cops can find that poor girl. What have you kids gotten yourselves into?" She clasped her hands together.

Dante remained eerily silent. I looked toward him, but he remained unresponsive.

I was starting to worry.

"I've spoken to your brother," my mother said. "He's promised to look after you."

Dark energy. Dante's teeth had descended. I wasn't looking at him, but I knew. I *felt* it. He didn't want anyone looking after me but him. I could almost hear the words he wasn't saying.

"Mom, I'm fine."

She nodded. "You're a smart girl. A strong girl. I thank

God for that. I want to stay here and look after you, but—"

I quieted her again. "I'm a grown woman, Mom, not a girl. I'll be fine. You leave if you need to. Be with Dad. Find some comfort. Then you'll be better able to deal with all of this."

She pushed a velvet pouch into my hand.

"What?" I unzipped it. The cut diamonds sparkled in the artificial light.

"For you and your brother."

"No, Mom, they're yours."

She patted my hand. "I haven't had the chance to get them appraised yet, but they must be valuable if my mother hid them. After you've gotten through all"—she glanced at Dante—"*this*, I want you to do something for yourself. Go to medical school. It was always your dream, and you'll make an amazing doctor, Erin."

Tears formed in my eyes, and I sniffed, trying to hold them back. "Are you sure?"

"Of course I'm sure. If we'd had these five years ago, that's what you would have done. Your father and I would have seen to it. After you've paid for school, give the rest to your brother to start a life for his child. His"—she gulped—"half-vampire child. I was a half-vampire child too, apparently. Perhaps it makes sense that my grandchild"—she cleared her throat, again eyeing Dante—"grand*children* will also be. That baby deserves everything your brother can give him or her."

Still no words from Dante. He stood stiff as a mannequin, his lips sealed. But inside his mouth, his teeth were long and sharp. I didn't have to see them to know.

He was not happy.

I hugged my mother and kissed her cheek. After she left, I turned to the vampire I loved.

"What was that about?"

He bared his fangs on a growl.

# FOURTEEN

# DANTE

"Your mother doesn't want you with me," I growled.

A duel erupted within me.

*Of course she doesn't want her daughter with you. Look at you. Blood on your face, half dressed. She doesn't understand yet, doesn't understand how much you love Erin.*

Then, the darkness...

*Doesn't matter what that woman wants. Erin is yours, always yours, to do with as you please.*

Erin approached me, her arms outstretched. "She just doesn't understand yet, Dante. You know that. This was a lot for her to deal with in two days. She will eventually love you. I'm certain."

"Doesn't matter."

"You're right. It doesn't. Because I love you, and I want to be with you."

Her words should have soothed me, calmed my anger, but they didn't.

Control. I needed my control.

The darkness inside me bubbled to the surface once more. *No! Must force it down. Must bury it. Must...*

Erin.

She stood before me, her hair a mass of dark brown, her feet bare. So beautiful.

She would always be the key to my control.

A heavy burden to bear for this woman I loved, but bear it she would. She was strong and determined.

Thank God she was here. Without her, I'd have already descended into the darkness.

"I love you," I said huskily.

"I know." She smiled.

Then a knock on the door. Erin walked back the few steps necessary and opened it.

An older gentleman stood there. I blinked. If he'd been wearing a robe, I would have mistaken him for Merlin or Dumbledore or Gandalf, with his long white beard and glasses. Santa Claus if he'd been overweight and wearing red.

But this man looked strong of body and wore a dark gray suit, complete with a burgundy-and-black tie.

"May I help you?" Erin asked.

"I'm looking for Dante Gabriel."

My teeth were still descended. I inhaled. Nothing. But that in turn meant nothing. I hadn't been able to smell anyone but Erin for months.

With the last shreds of my control, I forced my teeth to shorten into regular cuspids. I wore nothing but jeans, but I walked forward anyway. "I'm Dante Gabriel."

The man cleared his throat. "You're a difficult man to find, Mr. Gabriel. I couldn't find an address for you within the last ten years. Your last known address is a beautiful house in the

Garden District that has been vacant for a decade."

My father's house. Of course. After he went looking for me, Em went to live with Bill. That house now belonged to us. Funny that I hadn't given it a thought and that my father hadn't mentioned it.

"What do you want?" I asked.

"I need to speak to you. May I come in?"

"Not until you tell me who you are and what you want."

"Of course." He cleared his throat and turned to Erin. "Could I trouble you for a drink of water? I've come a long way."

She looked to me, and I nodded. She went to the kitchen. Seconds later, she handed the man a glass of water. He drank the whole thing and handed the glass back to her.

"Thank you, my dear." He turned back to me. "I've come in response to a query you sent to a website. I'm Lucien Crown."

I stopped myself from jerking in surprise. Erin, however, did not. She nearly jumped, her brows rising.

"You're Lucien Crown? From Nocturnal Truth?"

"One and the same. May I come in now?"

She looked to me, pleading. Was this man a vampire? Without my sense of smell, I couldn't tell unless his teeth descended. I could try triggering him by angering him, but most vampires could control their teeth. That I could not was due to being held captive for so long.

Whoever he was, I could most certainly protect Erin from an old man. "Sure. Come on in." I motioned to the living area. "Have a seat. Do you want more water?"

"Maybe in a minute. Thank you." He sat in one of the leather chairs.

Erin sat on the couch, across from him, and I sat beside her.

"What can we do for you, Mr. Crown?" Erin asked.

"I think we can help each other," he said. "I'm sorry. Who are you, dear?"

"I'm Erin Hamilton, Dante's...er... We live together." She grabbed my hand.

I entwined my fingers around hers.

"How nice." He cleared his throat again. "You sent a query to my website, Nocturnal Truth. I received it before the site crashed and was able to save it to a cache."

"Your site crashed?" I asked.

"It seemed to, but when I investigated further, I found that it was hacked and destroyed." He shook his head. "Years and years of research, just gone."

I sighed and raked my fingers through my hair. "Shit."

"You didn't keep backups?" Erin said.

"I did." Lucien Crown smiled and tapped the side of his head. "In here."

I resisted the urge to roll my eyes.

"I have a photographic memory. I'm an old man. I relied on my memory long before computers were a household item."

"Then can you help us?" Erin asked. "Can you tell us whether there's such a thing as a blood bond?"

Lucien cocked his head. "A blood bond? Funny. I had a query not long ago regarding something like that."

"Bill," I said softly.

"Who?" he asked.

"My grandfather. He used your site to get access to parts of—" I stopped abruptly. How much could I say to this man?

He smiled, and this time his teeth descended slowly. "You can speak to me freely. I am vampire. I know you and your lady are as well. You have no scent to me."

Erin stiffened slightly beside me. The potion masked her scent. As long as he thought we were both vampires, he would not try to glamour Erin.

"As we can speak freely," I continued, "it was my grandfather who made that query to your site."

"Do you know why?" he asked.

"I'm afraid I don't," I lied.

"Is that why you sent a query, then? To find out what he was trying to do?"

I shook my head. "My request was going to be more general. I need a translation of the entire *Vampyre Texts*."

"I see." Lucien drew in a deep breath.

"I can pay," I said. "I can pay what you were asking on the site."

"I wish I could grant your request. I certainly could use the money. But the full translation was lost."

I shook my head. "How could you not keep backups?"

"I told you. I never really got used to the world of computers, which is probably why my site was so easily destroyed. But I did have copies made."

"Where can we find them?"

"I had copies bound and printed and translated into English and French."

"We need one," I said. "Where do we find one?"

"Unfortunately, most of them were destroyed in a fire twenty-five years ago. However, I did manage to distribute a few to the more prominent vampire families outside of Louisiana."

"Wait!" Erin stood suddenly and ran up the stairs. In a flash she was back with the book her mother had given her. "Is this one?"

Lucien took the book, smoothing his fingers over the

leather binding. "It certainly looks like one." He fidgeted with the cover. "But it doesn't seem to open."

"It's been shielded," Erin said. "It will open when we need it to."

Lucien smiled. "Who told you that?"

"My mother."

"I see. You believe in magick, then?"

"I've seen enough to make me think about it," Erin said. "Don't you believe in it?"

"My dear, when you get to a certain age, you find that most things are possible. I've never been a student of the magickal arts myself, but I know such is prevalent here in New Orleans."

"Look, Mr. Crown—" I said.

"Lucien, please."

"Lucien, Erin and I have had the help of voodoo and magick in the last several weeks. I never believed in the stuff either, but I do now. By the way, ghosts are real too."

Lucien chuckled. "Yes, son. I know."

"And werecreatures," Erin added.

"Again, I know."

"Not to pry," I said, "but how old are you? Why aren't you on the council of elders with my grandfather?"

"So much you don't know," he said. "I guess I should begin at the...well, at the beginning."

# FIFTEEN

# *Erin*

"I'm one hundred and one years old," Lucien said.

"A year younger than my grandfather," Dante said. "He's supposedly the oldest living pure vampire male."

"I wouldn't know whether he is or isn't," Lucien said. "I was cut off from all vampire business decades ago."

"When you decided to translate the *Texts*," I said, more to myself than to Dante and Lucien.

"Yes, my dear. Exactly."

"What is in that book?" Dante demanded. "Why is my grandfather—" He abruptly shut his mouth.

"Why is your grandfather what?" Lucien asked.

"Nothing."

"Dante, if I'm going to help you, I need you to be up front with me."

"I will be," he said. "After you tell us why you're not on the council."

"I did say I'd start at the beginning." Lucien closed his

eyes for a moment and then opened them. "You remind me of myself at your age—so full of questions, so sure I could handle whatever I found out." He paused for a moment, sighing.

Then, "I fell in love with a beautiful vampire woman when I was still in my teens. We married young, but she and our son died during childbirth."

"I'm so sorry," I said.

"It was a long time ago," he said. "Back then, human women dying in childbirth was still fairly common. But I vowed then never to love another vampire woman. I couldn't risk such a loss again. Even now, I'm not fully recovered."

"So that's why you researched the *Texts*," Dante said.

"That is certainly part of it, yes. Many years passed before I allowed myself to even consider loving again."

"What did you do during those years?" I asked.

"I studied medicine."

"You're a doctor?" I said.

He shook his head. "No. Unfortunately, my license was rescinded by the medical board back in the fifties."

I clamped my hand over my mouth. "I'm sorry. Why?"

"On the record? Faulty record-keeping practices. But off the record?" He shook his head. "The vampire council didn't approve of my research."

"What research?"

"Vampire genetics, of course. I started the research to try to find a way to make pregnancy and childbirth safer for our women and also to increase their fertility. But I began exploring other avenues, and I found unanswered questions. So I turned to the *Texts*."

"And that's when the council took your license," Dante said.

"Exactly. They glamoured the medical board into taking my license and told me I'd never be a part of the council no matter how long I lived. At that point, though, I didn't care. I'd found love again with a human woman, and she was expecting our third child. My vampire heritage, though important to me, didn't matter for the survival of those close to me."

"So you gave up?" I said.

"No. I just lay low...and I continued my research into the *Texts*."

"Wait, wait," Dante said. "If all this is true, my grandfather should have known who you were when he found your name on the Nocturnal Truth website."

Lucien smiled. "There's a simple explanation for that."

"What?"

"I changed my name and identity. Your council has no record of a Lucien Crown. Lucien Crown is a human male born eighty years ago. I have a birth certificate and everything."

"Then...who are you?" Dante asked.

"My birth name is Alexandre Gabriel."

# SIXTEEN

# DANTE

"You're a Gabriel? But you..." I eyed him. He had the Gabriel height and build, but the white hair and long beard was throwing me off.

"That's right. I'm your first cousin twice removed."

Erin counted on her fingers. "That makes you Bill's cousin," she said.

"Yes," Lucien said. "Our fathers were brothers."

"So you know Bill. You know he made the query."

"No, not until you told me. He used a dummy account. But he paid, so he got what he paid for."

"You really gave him portions of the *Texts* that explained a blood bond?" I asked.

"I gave him portions of the *Texts* that referenced the key words he gave me. He didn't use the term blood bond. He must have gotten that from the documents I provided him."

"Bill has never mentioned you," I said.

"Of course he hasn't. Obviously, I'm the black sheep of the family. Besides, Alex Gabriel doesn't exist anymore. He disappeared into oblivion. Only Lucien Crown exists now. My wife and children took the new name, and my children were young at the time. As far as they're concerned, they were always Crowns."

"Logan," Erin said softly.

"What about Logan?" Lucien asked.

"He's a physician at the hospital where I work. His last name is Crown, and he's descended from a vampire."

"I have a great-grandson named Logan, but we're not in contact. He's the son of my grandson Hector, and he had a falling out with his father—my first son, James—years ago."

"So you've never met Logan?" I asked.

"No. I'd like to, but Hector won't have anything to do with his father or anyone associated with him. James passed away ten years ago, and as far as they all know, I'm dead as well."

"Do you know if it's possible for a human descended from a vampire to resist a glamour?" Erin asked. "Dante's cousin glamoured Logan for information, and he reacted...strangely."

"Why didn't you glamour him yourself, my dear?"

"She wasn't there," I interjected. "My cousin River told us the story."

Lucien sighed. "Many things are possible for our species. I learned that during my research."

"But Logan is human," Erin said.

"Yes, but he carries vampire blood." Lucien shook his head. "There is a lot I can tell you, but first I have to know. Why? Why are you searching for this information?"

"Because—"

River burst through the door, interrupting me. "You guys need to come with me. It's Bill. He's sick."

❦

My grandfather, the man who'd taught me so much and then become a stranger to me, lay in his bed, paler than usual, and refusing to go to a hospital or even to call Jack.

"I'll be more helpful to you as a ghost," he said, his voice weak.

"That's the dumbest thing I've ever heard." I paced around his bedroom. "What the hell is wrong with you?"

"I'm an old man, Dante. My time has come."

"Yes, you're old. But as a vampire male, you probably have another ten years if we find out what's wrong and get you treated. What's going on here, Bill, really? Why can't we call Jack?"

"I'm done fighting. I'm done, Dante. I can't fight both you and River. You're younger and more potent, and you... You are stronger than anything I've seen in my life. You're a danger to yourself, Dante, and as a ghost, I can figure things—"

"Bullshit. Your son is already a ghost. Have him figure this out if you think you need a ghost to do it. I'm not losing you too!"

"I wasn't sure you cared anymore."

"Of course I care."

"You've been so angry."

"That's because— Damn!" I paced some more. If something was truly wrong with Bill, now wasn't the time to give him hell.

Someone knocked, and I opened the door to Jack Hebert, the vampire doctor.

"Thanks for coming, Doc."

He entered swiftly, eyeing my grandfather.

"So, you old fool. What have you done this time?"

# SEVENTEEN

# *Erin*

"Do you think he'll be mad that you called the doctor?" I asked River, sitting in Bill's living room.

"I don't rightfully give a fuck. He's being stupid. He doesn't want to die and become a ghost. This is some other kind of trick. I can smell it a mile away. He's trying to pull something on us, and we're not stupid enough to fall for it."

"He sure looks sick," I said. "His temperature is a hundred. Low-grade fever for a human but high for a vampire, from what you've said."

"Maybe he has food poisoning or something."

"At his age, he should be in a hospital."

"Preaching to the choir, Erin."

"Where's Jay?" I asked.

"He's back at my place. There was no reason for him to come over here and deal with my idiot grandfather."

"The timing could have been better," I said. "Not that I think Bill got sick on purpose."

"What do you mean?"

"We rushed in here so quickly that neither Dante nor I had a chance to tell you. We had a visitor this morning. The guy from the website, Lucien Crown."

River's brows nearly shot off his forehead. "What? Where is he?"

"We left as soon as you called. He said he'd be in touch."

"And do you think he will?"

"Why wouldn't he? He came to *us*."

"Christ." River rubbed his forehead. "I smell a rat here."

"What do you mean?"

"Just as you guys are about to get information on the *Texts*, Bill gets sick and I show up and take you and Dante away from the meeting. Shit. No wonder Bill didn't want to go to the hospital or see Jack. He's not sick at all."

"He has a fever, River. I checked it myself."

"Maybe he held the thermometer under a lamp or something."

I shook my head, chuckling. "I used an ear thermometer from my bag. He definitely has a fever."

"Yeah? Well, still, something's not right. The old coot is up to something. It doesn't smell right."

"What do you smell?" I asked.

"Figure of speech."

"Oh. Yeah. Since you're a vampire and all, I thought you actually smelled something. My bad."

"I'm going up there." River stomped up the stairs.

My phone buzzed. Hmm. Not a number I recognized. "Hello?"

"Erin?"

"Yes? Who is this please?"

"Bella Lundy. I need the rest of my dough."

Sheesh. With everything else that had gone down, I'd forgotten about Bella and the copy of the *Texts* she'd sold to Jay and me. "I'm sorry, Bella. We've been busy."

"You said you'd be back with the rest of the money."

"It will be a little while longer. I've been dealing with—" I sighed. "Never mind."

"I need to feed those little boys," she said.

"I understand. But we gave you six hundred dollars a day ago. Surely that will—"

"I had to pay some bills. The kids are hungry."

"Didn't you buy them food? You said you needed milk. You were going to buy milk."

"After I paid the overdue bills, there wasn't much left for food."

I bit my lip to keep from yelling at her. Why wouldn't she buy food for her nephews? Ridiculous. This was the granddaughter of the ghost who was forcing Bill to keep council secrets.

I texted Jay quickly that she was badgering me for the rest of the money. I'd just hit *send* when River, Dante, and Dr. Hebert stalked down the stairs.

"Is he okay?" I asked.

"He's fine," Dante said. "Just trying to pull the wool over our eyes, right, Doc?"

Dr. Hebert, an older vampire male, nodded. "He'll be fine. He tried to poison himself. Luckily, I was able to administer an antidote."

"He tried to kill himself?" My mouth dropped open.

"Honestly, I'm not sure what he was trying to do. The amount he ingested wouldn't have killed him, but it would have made him miserable for a week or so. Even with the antidote, he's going to be feeling pretty bad for the next day or two."

"I know exactly what he was trying to do," River said, "and we fell right into his trap."

"I agree," Dante said. "Erin and I were just about to get information from Lucien Crown, and all of a sudden Bill has an emergency."

"Yup," River said. "What do you want to bet that Lucien Crown has now suddenly disappeared?"

"Did you tell them that Lucien is actually Bill's cousin?" I asked.

Dante shook his head. "I haven't had the chance to divulge that little gem yet."

River scratched his forehead. "Say what?"

"Apparently Lucien Crown was born Alexandre Gabriel. His father and our great-grandfather were brothers." Dante filled River and Dr. Hebert in on the rest of our conversation with Lucien.

"Did he leave any information with you?" River queried. "A phone number? Email?"

"No." Dante shook his head. "When you interrupted us with Bill's emergency, we hightailed it out of there."

"Damn him," River said.

"Would have served him right if he'd croaked," Dante agreed.

I touched his arm. "You don't mean that."

He met my gaze, his eyes dark and angry. "No, I don't mean that. But he's been nothing but a thorn in all our sides since I returned. He's been hiding stuff—stuff that would help us find the missing women."

"We need Lucien," I said. "We've got to find him. Plus, we

need to deal with Bella Lundy. She wants the rest of her money."

"So pay her," Dante said. "Five grand is nothing to us."

"Not to you, maybe—"

"Baby, nothing to *us*. What's mine is yours, remember?"

"I wouldn't have a problem if I thought she'd use the money to take care of those little boys. But we already gave her six hundred dollars, and she claims she didn't buy food. She paid bills instead."

"Just pay—" Dante paused abruptly. "She didn't buy food?"

"That's what she claims. I have no idea if she's telling the truth."

"All right." He took my hand. "Now that Bill's okay, and he's probably destroyed our chances of getting any information from Lucien Crown, you and I are going grocery shopping. We'll get some nutritious food for those boys and pay this woman the rest of the money—"

I opened my mouth to speak, but he held up his hand to silence me.

"—we owe her for the book. That way, we can make sure the kids are fed. That's what is bothering you, isn't it?"

I nodded.

"When we're done there, I need to rest."

I gulped. "Why?"

"I have things to do tonight. Things I have to do myself."

"Hey, cuz—"

"My*self*," he said adamantly. "My fucking self."

# EIGHTEEN

# DANTE

"*W*hy? *You dare to ask me why?*"

*I lay limp, knives of pain lancing through my body, my flesh buzzing from the electricity the goons had sent surging through me.*

*"Why?" I whispered once more.*

Why do you take my blood? Why do you force me to drink yours? Why do you have me tortured? Why do you make me fight? Why do you reward me with human blood that I can't resist? Why, after rewarding me, do you torture me again?

*All those questions, but all that came out was another weak, "Why?"*

❧

After we had dropped off four boxes of staples and fresh food—along with forty-four hundred dollars—to Bella Lundy, Erin and I headed home.

Lucien Crown, of course, was nowhere to be found.

Bill's ploy had worked.

Lucien wouldn't be back. Somehow, Bill—or someone else—had gotten to him.

But could he?

Lucien had changed his identity and had the *Texts* translated. He was as interested in all of this as we were. Maybe for different reasons, but he'd devoted his life to the *Texts*. And to medical research. He'd wanted to make childbirth easier for vampire females.

And he'd lost his medical license for it.

The fucking vampire council.

What was the council exactly? The elders. The keepers of our history and private census. That was what we were always told.

But I was beginning to understand that the council existed for a much broader purpose, and I wasn't sure all of it was good. They guarded their information with their lives, to the point that all members swore an oath to end their own lives if they divulged secrets.

What secrets were so powerful that the council couldn't risk them getting out to the vampire community, to the entire community?

And Bill... Bill knew something the council didn't—what he'd read in the *Texts*. Though he'd promised to divulge this information to my father, Bill was now ill and in no condition to do so.

I couldn't wait any longer. I had to act now.

Tonight.

Tonight I'd go back to hell.

Tonight I'd end this, once and for all.

"Hey, babe," Erin called from the kitchen. "I made you a sandwich for lunch."

I *was* a little hungry. We hadn't eaten breakfast. I hadn't fed either, but I'd fed more than once the previous day and night. I was doing okay.

I walked into the small kitchen and took a seat in front of the plate Erin had set. I ate the salami sandwich quickly and then turned to her. "Tonight is the night, baby."

She swallowed the bite of bread she was chewing, but she didn't say anything.

"I'm going alone. I haven't told River or Jay or even my father. But I can't keep this from you."

"Dante, please..."

"It's the only way. I won't be able to protect you there. I need you here, and I need River and Jay here to protect you while I'm gone. They'll take care of you in case..."

She shook her head vehemently. "No. No. Don't say it."

*In case I don't come back.*

The words sat in the back of my throat. I could never say them. I couldn't even believe them. If what Bill found out about our bond was true, we would each die without the other.

If I didn't return, I might be sentencing Erin to death.

For that reason alone, I had every intention of coming back to Erin. But my primary purpose was to find Emilia, Lucy, my uncle, and all the others. To free them. I'd give my life to do it if I had to, because I was the only person who could.

This all had something to do with me.

With me and with *her*.

If only we could understand the secrets in the *Texts*... But we were out of time. I felt it strongly in my bones. Bea was right. Erin was right. I had to act now.

"Keep trying to decode the *Texts*," I told her. "You're smart. You can do it."

"I don't speak French, and I certainly don't speak Old French."

"Hire a linguist."

"Any old linguist? I thought you guys were trying to lie low."

I shook my head. "No longer. The lives of innocent women are more important than guarding ancient vampire secrets. Get them deciphered, Erin, any way you can."

"Maybe I won't have to. Maybe Bea can remove the shield from my English version."

"Lucien said it could be English or French."

"Why would my grandmother have a French version? She wasn't French." She grabbed my hand. "Come with me this afternoon to see Bea. Please."

"Erin..."

"I won't try to stop you." She sniffled back a sob. "I won't, Dante. I know you have to do this. But maybe Bea can break the shield and you can go through the book before you do this. Please, Dante, for me."

For Erin.

I'd do anything for her.

She had saved me, had shown me I wasn't a monster. She loved me and nourished me.

Which is why I *had* to make it back.

If we truly had a blood bond and what Bill had found out was true, neither of us would survive without the other.

I stood. "All right. Let's go see Bea."

She rose as well and kissed me lightly on the cheek. "Thank you. I love you so much."

"I love you too." If she only knew how much.

She grabbed her purse and we walked to the door, when—

"What's this?" She stooped down and picked up a small white piece of paper near the doorway. "I didn't notice this when we came in."

"Neither did I." I looked over her shoulder as she unfolded it.

*If I don't make it back to you, you'll find what you need between the doors of perception. Have faith. –LC*

# NINETEEN

# *Erin*

*T*he doors of perception. I'd heard that somewhere before, but where?

"Faith," Dante muttered. "People always want me to have faith. Faith in *what*?"

I shook my head. "I don't know. I wish I did."

"He *knew*," Dante said. "Lucien knew this was a trick. He knew he couldn't come back. Why else would he have left the note?"

"When did he write it? He left right when we did, after we got River's call."

"He already had it written," Dante said thoughtfully. "He *knew*."

I nodded. Yes, he'd known we'd be interrupted. Or at the very least suspected and had come prepared.

"Do you think they took him?" I asked.

"Who?"

"I don't know. The thugs."

"That would mean Bill is working with them." Dante shook his head. "He couldn't be. He couldn't have allowed his own granddaughter to be taken."

"Or his sons. Or his grandson." I shivered. "But this is all connected somehow."

Dante nodded. "Yes. It is. I know it is. If I'd ever doubted it before, I have no more doubts now."

"Of course we don't know if it was those vampires, and if it wasn't, then Bill isn't working with them."

I said the words hoping they'd sound true to me.

They didn't.

⚜

"Out in the daylight, Mr. Vampire?" Bea took a drink from the bottle of water I handed her.

"Since you have the sight, Bea," Dante said, "you should know vampires don't burn up in the sun. Also, you've seen me during the day before."

"Yes, but you're more comfortable walking by night. It is a different season."

"The Thoreau quote again," I said. "Only you're condensing it."

"What do you mean the night is a different season?" Dante asked.

"You should know, vampire," she said.

"I should know what?"

"If you don't know, I can't help you."

This was going nowhere fast. I grabbed the book out of my tote bag. "Bea, we need your help. This book has been shielded. Can you remove the shield so we can read it? We have it on good authority that it is 'the most important work of all,'" I said, reminding her of the words she'd previously used.

"May I?" She reached for the book.

I handed it to her.

She caressed the supple leather cover and examined it at various angles. Then she tried to open it.

"Definitely shielded," she said.

"Thanks. We already knew that."

"No, you didn't. It could have just been glued together."

"My mother told me otherwise. She said her mother told her it would open for us when we needed it to."

"Then the shield has an ending. You don't need my help at all." She handed the book back to me.

"Bea, we *do* need your help. This is the *Vampyre Texts*, the 'most important work of all,' as you put it."

"You're gifted at shields," Dante agreed. "My grandfather couldn't touch the other book you shielded for us."

"Reversing a shield is much more complicated," Bea said. "It requires dark magick, and though I've dabbled in it once or twice, I try to stay away from it unless the need is dire."

"The need is dire," I said. "Women are missing. You yourself said there's a baby out there who needs my help."

"And you think the answers are in this book?"

"*Something* is in the book," Dante said. "Something my grandfather is willing to go to great lengths to keep a secret."

"And you feel this secret will help you find the women? Where is the logic in that?"

White noise clouded my mind. Did Bea have a point? Were we hearing hoofbeats and thinking zebras rather than horses?

"The book says something that my grandfather is willing to die for to keep a secret," Dante said. "Whether it will help us find the women is up in the air at this point. But it might explain what is happening to me. It might help us understand why the women were taken. We know vampires are involved in their abduction."

"How do you know that?"

"You tell us," I said. "You have the sight."

"You know glamouring was used. You know vampires took your sister, because they went back looking for something."

"So why are you asking us if we know?" I demanded. "This is a waste of time."

"'Oft expectation fails, and most oft there where most it promises; and oft it hits where hope is coldest and despair most sits.'"

"Shakespeare again?" Dante asked.

"I have no idea." I sighed. "Bea, are you saying we're expecting the *Texts* to answer all our questions, and we might be disappointed?"

"'You shall know the truth, and the truth shall make you mad.'"

"I'm already mad," Dante growled. "Fuming, to be honest."

"Huxley. Aldous Huxley."

I jumped at Julian's voice. Then he appeared before us.

"The previous quote was Shakespeare, from *All's Well That Ends Well*."

"You've been spying on us?" I said.

"Just listening in."

"What the hell is the difference?"

"Bea," Julian said.

"Yes, Mr. Ghost?"

"You can't reverse the shield on the book, can you?"

"Not without the darkest of magick. As a voodoo priestess

346

and practitioner, I prefer to stay in the light."

"And you will," Julian said, turning to us. "Bea is right. You two have put too much emphasis on what you might find in this book. It might not have the answers you seek."

"It has something," Dante said. "Something Bill doesn't want us to know."

"Have you considered that you might be better off not knowing? This isn't the first time I've posed this question to you."

"Julian," I said, "has Bill told you what he promised to tell you yet? What he read in the *Texts*?"

"Not yet. He's been playing other games, and now he's ill. Did it to himself, but you already know all about that."

"What is this about?" Dante demanded. "You've been behind us this whole time. Been behind our desire to get answers from the book."

"We just spent five grand on a copy, before my mother gave us this one. We need to know what's inside."

"And you will. Bea is only telling you to be cautious in your expectations, and that what you find out might cause madness."

"Madness?" Dante said. "You mean anger."

I closed my eyes to an image I'd seen before. Dante, his eyes dark and cold.

Madness. Dante had been on the brink of madness more than once since I'd met him. I'd tossed the image away, told myself he was recovering from being held captive. Told myself I could keep him happy. Happy and sane.

But this darkness that had rooted inside him was surfacing more frequently lately.

This was a warning—a warning that Dante could not read the *Vampyre Texts*. A warning for me as well, to keep him safely away from the book.

I met the gaze of his father, the ghost.

He knew. Julian knew.

And now so did I.

I gulped. "No, Dante. The other meaning of 'mad.' It's a warning. A warning for all of us. A warning for *you*."

# TWENTY

# DANTE

Not anger.

Madness.

Descent into an anger so deep it morphed to sheer insanity.

My teeth descended and sharpened with a snap, pain lancing through my gums. The rapid descension I'd experienced only a few times in the past. Mostly in the arena.

*Fight or die in the arena.*

Couldn't go there. Not now, at least.

"What is it, then?" I demanded of my father. "Do we decode the damned book or not?"

"I won't be able to speak to Bill until he has recovered from his attempt to poison himself. For now, what he knows about the *Texts* will remain with him."

"Then what do we do?" Erin asked.

"We wait for the shield to let you into your book," Julian said.

"Who knows when that will be?" Erin whipped her hands to her hips. "And according to Bea, we might be disappointed in what we find. So now what?"

"Now...we continue our search for the women," Julian said. Then to me, in a voice only a vampire could have heard, "May the light go with you, my son."

He knew.

He knew I'd be going back into hell.

I'd planned to go alone. I didn't want to put anyone, even my ghost father, through hell. But he'd already been there, and he was energy now, without a body that could be harmed.

*Need is weakness.*

Where had I heard those words? Didn't matter. I could go alone, but I wanted my father with me.

"Will you go with me?" I whispered.

He nodded slightly. "I will be there when you need me. I promise you."

Then he spoke so the others could hear. "We will find out what is hiding in the *Texts* one way or another. But at the moment, we must find Emilia and the others. We must find my brother."

"I agree," Erin said. "But—"

"What must be done will be done," Bea said. "Only then will you find what you seek."

"Shakespeare again?" Erin asked.

"Bea," she said, smiling, her yellow teeth not nearly as stark in the light of day.

"Bea is right," Julian said. "Dante must go back."

❧

*The masked vampire in front of me was by far the largest I'd encountered in her arena. A head taller than I and much broader in the shoulders, he stood still, his light-blue eyes a menace beneath a black mask.*

Fight or die in the arena.

She *had kept me alive for days, weeks, months, years...never allowing the torture to take my life or mar anything vital.*

*Still, though, would* she *allow this brute to savagely beat me? Kill me?*

*He was vampire. I smelled nothing but the moist dirt in the dank field of battle. Sometimes I could smell the fear of my opponents.*

*Not this time.*

*I did not frighten this vampire.*

*Nor did he frighten me.*

*I tilted my head slightly, sizing him up, trying to figure out his motives, his moves.*

*Usually I got some clues, but this one? He was a blank slate. I had no idea how or when he would strike.*

*I never struck first.*

*I waited. Always waited. And when my opponent struck, I was ready. I'd learned after my first time in the arena to be patient. To wait. To conserve my energy.*

*His teeth had descended, and a low growl emerged—so low I doubted a human could hear it.*

*But I heard it.*

*I returned it and bared my own long teeth.*

*His eyes widened slightly. Only slightly, but I noticed. My teeth had surprised him.*

*Why?*

*Why would my teeth surprise another vampire?*

*Still he made no move to strike.*

*So I waited.*

*And waited.*

Fight or die in the arena.

*Would I die in this arena?*

*Not today.*

*For the first time, I made the initial strike. I lunged forward and hammered with a vengeance.*

*I would win. Again. Then one day I would escape this hellish prison.*

*And I would never return.*

❖

*I would never return.*

How many times had I promised those words to myself? Dozens. Probably hundreds or thousands.

And now I would return to hell. I had to.

Erin and I arrived back home. She sighed and placed her book on the table alongside the much bigger and more ornate version she'd purchased from Levi Gaston's granddaughter.

"I just don't know what to do anymore," she said on a sigh.

"I do." I took her in my arms.

*I do.* My words had two meanings.

I had to return to her lair.

But first I would make love to Erin. Then I would take her blood, as much as I could, for I had no idea how long I'd be separated from her.

The blood bond.

If what Bill had researched was true, and we'd truly die without each other, was I condemning us both to death?

I couldn't allow her to come with me. She wouldn't be safe.

I'd deal with that later. Right now, my cock was hard and

my teeth were descended and I needed her.

Needed her so badly.

Our lips met in a frenzy of tongues and teeth. The kiss was raw and brutal, and I ached to take her to bed, tie her down, fuck her with raw force.

But I couldn't. Couldn't leave her with that as her last memory.

This would be sweet love, a passionate embrace, and then I'd feed from her, take as much as I could from her to stay with me in the darkest hour that might be coming.

Our mouths still fused, I swept her into my arms and carried her to the bedroom. Then I undressed her slowly, despite the urge to shred her clothes with my hands and teeth.

I laid her naked body on the bed—God, so beautiful—and then undressed myself, a lot quicker this time.

I inhaled. Her ripe musk sank into me, making my cock even harder and my lust for her blood that much stronger. I hovered over her, inhaling again and again, taking in her gloriousness, and then I thrust my cock into her heat and sank my teeth into her neck simultaneously.

She cried out at my invasion, her breath warm on my cheek and neck, and I pumped into her, each ridge of her vagina taunting my cock, threatening to make me explode.

As I pumped, I sucked her delicious blood, letting it trickle over my tongue and down my throat. The dark delicacy of it—the earthy truffles, bittersweet chocolate, lusty Bordeaux. I'd need as much as she could spare this time.

She writhed beneath me, moaning my name, urging me on, and I went willingly where she led me.

My last time inside her, my last taste of her red nectar...

I would return. I had to. Both of our lives depended on

it, and Erin's life meant more to me than my own. I'd decided previously that I'd die saving the others if I must, but that was no longer an option.

I would do what I had to do. I would free Emilia, Lucy, Braedon, and the rest.

Then I would return.

# $\mathscr{E}rin$

He sucked at my neck, the sweet tugging urging me closer and closer—

"Dante!"

The climax hit me like a lightning bolt, electrifying me and shattering my insides. Above me he thrust and sucked, and with each rhythmic push I flew higher and higher, the colors swirling in abstract imagery. And the music...the sweet jazzy music, like a melodic backdrop for the mainstage production that was *us*.

Still his teeth tugged at my flesh. He was taking more than usual, but I felt fine, the climax still whirling through me.

He needed sustenance for his journey.

His journey... Couldn't think of that now. Wanted only this moment. This tiny slice of perfection.

I rolled into another orgasm, and still he took from me, sucked my blood into his body.

I would always have enough for him. Enough for both of

us. We were bonded now, and my body had been created to feed him.

He increased the tempo of his thrusts, and we lifted off the bed, floating a few feet in the air. Magical. So magical and ethereal. How lucky I was that this man had come into my life, had bonded with me and I with him.

I would let him go. I wouldn't fight him.

He *would* come back to me.

One way or the other, I'd make sure of it.

⚜

Darkness had fallen when I awoke.

I rolled over, seeking the warmth of Dante's body.

He was gone.

I sat up abruptly. He'd left? Without saying goodbye?

I frantically turned on the light and searched for a note. Nothing. Then I spied the text notification on my phone.

*My love,*

*I had to leave without waking you. If I'd looked into those sweet green eyes, seen the ache within them, I wouldn't have been able to go. I have to do this. You know I do. I love you. You are everything to me. I will return for you. I promise.*

*Dante*

I sniffled, trying to hold back, but tears streamed down my cheeks anyway. He hadn't said goodbye. Well, he had, but a text was so impersonal.

I understood why he hadn't woken me. I truly did. Didn't

make it hurt any less.

I got up and showered quickly. Then I hastily dressed in jeans and a tank top and added a hoodie. I went downstairs and picked up the book my mother had given me.

"What secrets do you hold?" I said aloud.

"You'll know when you need to know."

I jumped. "Julian! Why aren't you with Dante?"

"I will be with him when he needs me."

"I'd rather you be with him at all times. Please?"

"If I know my son, and I do, he'd rather I be with you, making sure you're taken care of."

"I'm fine. The thugs can't smell me. River and Jay are around as well. They won't let anything happen to me."

"Yes, they will do what they can, but your safety depends on something else. Something River and Jay can't provide."

"What's that?"

"Dante. Or rather, the need to feed Dante."

"Yeah. The blood bond. He had a really big feeding a few hours ago. Took more than he usually takes."

"That will last him forty-eight hours. Perhaps seventy-two. He will need your blood."

"Do you want me to give blood for him? I could go to a donation center—"

"No, Erin. I've already spoken to River and your brother. They will be here in a few minutes. Right after I leave."

"Where are you— What?"

"I must get back to Dante, but I will leave clues for you. Rather, I'll have Dante unknowingly leave clues. The three of you are going to follow him."

TWENTY-TWO

# DANTE

Leaving without saying a proper goodbye to Erin felt all wrong, but I'd had no other choice. The magick shop was now closed, and a "for lease" sign hung in the small window. Joseph, the owner who'd admitted he was a fraud, had spoken the truth when he said he was closing up.

I skulked around the other shops on the street and into the dark alley behind the magick shop where my father had died. I was on high alert, fangs descended, body tense and ready to attack if necessary.

A shudder ran through me.

I still felt the residue of my father's body. This was where he'd swallowed the poison that ended his physical life and began his ghostly one. Then Decker and his vampire gang had stolen his body, stripped it, and buried it in St. Louis Cemetery One for me to find.

They'd wanted me to see it, wanted me to see what had been done to him.

My cuspids sharpened into fine points.

They would pay.

*She* would pay.

Another shudder, this one also of recognition—but recognition of a different kind.

I was close.

Close to the place where I'd risen from below the ground. Near Bourbon Street, but far enough away to stay in the dark.

The dark.

Dark energy crawled along my skin like tiny pinpricks. I closed my eyes and inhaled, drawing all my strength and control to tamp it down.

I couldn't be slave to anything but my own rational mind, my own light, if I wanted to find where I needed to be.

*Control. Must have control.*

I inhaled, but no scents stood out. Once I'd scrambled out of the manhole that night, all I'd been able to think about was sating my hunger. I'd been so preoccupied that I hadn't paid attention to the sights, sounds, and smells around me.

Of course I hadn't. I never thought I'd go back.

"No!" I said aloud.

The darkness circled me once more, threatening to invade my senses.

*Control*, I seethed. *Control.*

*Help. Can help.*

I stopped, scanning the area. Those last three words hadn't come from *her*. They'd come from the darkness.

They'd come from *me*.

*Let me in. Can help.*

Dark energy clawed at me, but not in a menacing way. It was still part of me.

Perhaps I needed it for this endeavor.

As long as I held on to Erin, held on to my control, it would not overtake me.

I closed my eyes, inhaled...and then unleashed the energy whose existence I'd been denying. Sweat protruded from my brow.

I opened my eyes abruptly.

I knew where to go.

After wiping the perspiration from my brow with a red bandana I'd hurriedly stuffed in my pocket before I left—Why? I didn't know—I shoved it back into my pocket and I headed to the right, down the alleyway, following the residue from my father's body. Of course. He'd come from the same place. My own body hadn't left any residual energy because it was still alive.

Why hadn't I felt this without the darkness?

Didn't matter. I could—*would*—control the darkness. Right now, I needed this part of me to find Em and the others.

Oddly, *she* hadn't spoken into my mind tonight. I lifted my brow. Easy. Because *she* was getting what *she* wanted. I was returning to *her*.

But I knew the truth. I was *not* returning to *her*. I was returning to free the women. To find my uncle. To solve this mystery once and for all.

"Dad?" I whispered. "Am I going the right way?"

No response. He hadn't joined me yet.

*Have faith.*

The words popped into my head. My father hadn't actually planted them there, but they existed because of him.

*Have faith.*

I was going in the right direction. I would find what I needed to find.

As I drew closer, the sounds of Bourbon Street registered faintly in my ears. Laughter, music, the buzz of automobiles. Yes, this was all familiar. I'd been here before.

A homeless man holding a cat sat underneath a ragged awning. "Spare some change, mister?"

I walked toward him and handed him a twenty.

"Obliged. God bless."

I smiled. In a way, I was paying back Abe Lincoln for giving me his clothes that first night.

A few more homeless slept, snoring softly, along the alley.

This was familiar. So familiar.

I scanned the ground, looking for the manhole cover. Nothing.

Had I taken a wrong turn?

*Keep going.*

The words came from the darkness. From me.

And it struck me, almost as if I'd always known. I didn't have to fear the darkness. It was part of me. Perhaps *she* had put it there, or perhaps it had always been there. I was still Dante.

I was still me.

I strode forward, my intuition my guide, walking over several manholes and knowing that none were the one I sought.

Until my foot met heavy metal that sent a wave of recognition through me.

This was it.

The entrance to hell.

# TWENTY-THREE

# *Erin*

J ay and River had arrived dressed all in black. I wore black leggings and a black long-sleeved shirt. Black gloves, black boots. A black bulletproof vest. A black ski mask Jay had brought for me.

Rather, the latter was in my pocket, as were theirs. A small backpack held a couple days' worth of protein bars, bottled water, and the book my mother had given me. I vowed to keep it with me at all times in case the shield lifted, meaning we needed the information inside.

We drove near Joseph's magick shop and found a parking spot.

"You up to this?" Jay said.

I nodded, exhaling. I'd do anything for Dante.

"He'd kill us if he knew we were bringing her," River said.

"I know." Jay opened the passenger door and slid out. "But his dad seemed to think it was important that she come along."

To feed Dante. I alone knew why I needed to come at all costs.

"Which way?" River asked me.

I led them to the small shop where I'd tried to purchase a masking potion. I shined my small flashlight on the "for lease" sign. "We have to go out back, in the alley behind the shop."

Once there, I scanned the area. "You guys are the detectives. Find us some clues."

River inhaled. "Nothing smells off here. Nothing sounds off either."

"Dante said this was close to where he'd escaped," I said. "This is where he would have started."

Jay kicked some stray rocks around. "I'm not seeing anything that indicates where we should go."

"Julian said he'd guide us," I said.

"I'm not sure how," River said. "Uncle Jules doesn't have a body, so how could he leave a clue?"

"He said he'd have Dante—" I shook my head. "Never mind. We'll just have to figure it out. Let's just walk around a bit and see if anything stands out."

They both nodded. I turned to the left while Jay turned to the right, and River stayed behind the shop, still sniffing around.

After I'd passed the next few shops, I headed back, shining my flashlight along the bottom of the buildings, in case I'd missed something.

Jay was several yards away, bent over. He stood up, holding something red. River and I hurried to him.

"What is it?" River asked.

"A handkerchief. A bandana," I said. "Let me see."

I held it to my face and inhaled. Dante. Dante's perfect masculine musky scent. "It's his."

"A red bandana?" River said. "Since when does Dante use a red bandana?"

"I don't know. I've never seen him with one, but I have a few in my underwear drawer. Maybe he took one. This smells like him. I swear it."

"I guess we found our first clue," Jay said, pointing. "We head that way."

We walked along quietly, looking for something, anything, out of place.

We found it. A homeless man was perched under an old green awning, eating a po' boy with fries and drinking from what was presumably wine in a bottle covered by a brown paper bag. An orange tomcat sat with him, munching what looked like tuna right out of the can.

"Evening," River said gruffly.

"Evening yourself," the man said with his mouth full.

"That's quite a meal you've got there," Jay added.

The man nodded. "Some guy came through here a few hours ago, slipped me a twenty." He patted his belly. "I can eat like the king himself tonight."

"Do you remember what the guy looked like?" River asked.

"Tall, dressed in black." He lifted an eyebrow. "Looked kind of like you, actually."

"Did you see which way he went?" Jay asked.

"Yup. That way." He pointed east down a darker part of the alley. "Probably headed toward Bourbon Street."

"Thanks for your trouble." Jay pulled his wallet out of his pocket and handed him a ten-dollar bill.

"Obliged," the man said, his mouth full of fries.

We walked several yards out of earshot of the vagrant.

"Dante said he was somewhere near Bourbon Street when he emerged from the manhole. We're on the right track."

River led the way through the darkness, and Jay stayed

behind me. They were both armed, but I wasn't. New item for my bucket list—learn to fire a gun so I could protect myself. I was sandwiched in the middle of two trained police detectives as I walked as stealthily as I could. Another block and the buzzing of Bourbon Street drifted toward us.

We were getting close.

Really close. My body was reacting in a strange way. Shivers coursed through me. I was frightened, of course, but the shudders were not from fear.

"You okay, Erin?" Jay said from behind me.

"Yeah. I'm good. We're near where we need to be. I feel it."

"Some manhole covers are ahead," River said, without shining his flashlight. Vampire vision must be truly remarkable. "We'll check each of them."

I scanned the alley with my light, looking for anything out of the ordinary, something that could be our next clue.

River knelt at the first manhole cover. "This one's locked down tight."

"Do you think he could have locked it down from the inside?" Jay asked. "He doesn't know we're coming. If he had any idea Erin—"

"I know, partner. I know. But Erin needs to be here. She and Dante are bonded." River placed his cheek on the cover, looking through a tiny opening with one eye. "Nothing that I can see."

"You want a light?" Jay beamed his flashlight over the cover.

"Nah, it won't help."

I stood in silence. No response from my body. This wasn't the right manhole. "Try another one," I said.

We walked until another appeared. No luck this time either.

Jay sighed. "Ever feel like we're searching for something that doesn't exist?"

"What do you mean?" River asked.

"I mean...what if the manhole is in another dimension or something?"

River chuckled. "Dude, I think you're in another dimension right now."

"I'm serious. Look at everything we've all learned in the last few weeks. Why can't an opening be hiding in plain sight?"

"Because it just can't," River said.

"Wait!" I tugged on River's arm. "He might have something. Lucien Crown left a note for Dante and me. It said we would find what we need between the doors of perception. Bea mentioned the doors of perception as well."

"That could mean anything," River said. "It most likely means the guy is nuts. We already know Bea is a little out there."

"Bea has been a huge help to us," I said. "And he's not nuts. He's an academic. He's studied medicine and the *Vampyre Texts*. He changed his name to hide from the council. He was trying to find—" I clasped my hand to my mouth.

"What?" Jay asked. "Are you okay?"

"Yeah. It's just that this is all starting to make sense now. Julian told me that dreams can be regressions or premonitions. It's dreams. It's got to be. Dreams are the doors of perception."

"You could just as easily say drugs are," Jay said. "That's what Aldous Huxley was talking about in his book of the same name."

"How do you know that?"

Jay shrugged. "Don't have a clue. I must have been listening one day back in high school."

"Say you're right," River said. "What do you suggest? That

we take a quick catnap so we can find the manhole? Maybe get high?"

I sighed. "I don't know. But doesn't it make a certain amount of sense?"

"Maybe," Jay said. "But we're looking for the manhole, not this Lucien Crown guy."

"No, we're looking for the truth. His note said we would find what we *need* between the doors of perception."

"He might be talking about something else. Another truth," River said.

"There is no 'other truth,' damn it. There is *the* truth. The truth about what's going on. What's happening to Dante. Why Lucy and the others were taken. About your father, River. Only one truth, and we need to find it."

## TWENTY-FOUR

# DANTE

The cover had been loosened, just as it had been the night I escaped. I moved the heavy iron disk to the side so I could slide in.

I didn't have a flashlight, but I didn't need one. My vision was perfect in pitch black, but more than that, this was familiar to me. Too familiar.

I returned the cover as best I could underground and descended steadily down the ladder.

Dark and dank.

Definitely hell.

Recognition flooded through me. Recognition I didn't want. But I knew. I was definitely in the right place.

My body knew.

My mind knew.

That part of me—that dark energy that had been born here—definitely knew.

At the end of the ladder, I landed on a concrete pad. Had that been there when I escaped? I wasn't sure. The path before me was not illuminated as it had been the night I'd left, but no matter. I could still see. I could also smell. Not people, but other things. Mold, mildew, dirt, grime.

*Forge ahead, Dante.*

I nodded and moved forward.

"I'm with you, son."

"Dad?" I looked around.

"I'm not going to materialize here, but my energy is with you."

"Thank you."

My father's nearness would give me strength, would help me keep control, help me to not succumb to the darkness.

Or to *her*.

"We need to find the women first," my father said. "Then my brother. They must be brought to safety before we think of anything else."

"Of course."

"Remember that, Dante. If you see anyone who was a party to your torture and captivity, you'll want to strike. Don't. Not until the others are safe."

"Dad, I would never—"

"You would."

I opened my mouth to continue protesting but then shut it quickly. My father was right. If I saw either of those two goons who'd electrocuted me regularly, I'd take them out.

"Control, son. The others depend on that."

I nodded.

The narrow pathway curved to the right, and I continued walking. A strange sound drifted toward me, like a baby crying.

A baby. Erin had dreamed of a baby who needed her help. Was that baby here somewhere?

The narrow hallway continued for what seemed like miles. Had I gone this far the night I escaped? I didn't know. All I'd been thinking of was getting out of there, not getting caught. I hadn't stopped to estimate the distance I'd traveled.

Again the baby's cry.

"Do you hear that, Dad?"

"I do."

"Erin's dream."

"Yes. A baby is here. At least we know the child is alive."

"Unless it's a recording," I said. "If only I had my sense of smell, I could tell if a human baby was here. I could smell Lucy and the others, all except Emilia."

"You don't need your sense of smell, Dante. All you need is your intuition and your strength."

"What about you? Can you feel Braedon?"

"No. I know only that he's still alive. I don't feel any connection to his body. Maybe as we get nearer, I will. I don't know."

"You said earlier that he didn't have a lot of time. Is that still true?"

"Unfortunately, yes. I feel it very strongly."

"If you can't connect to his body—"

"It's a bond between twins, Dante. I can't explain it any better than that. Unless you're a twin, you won't understand. My father never did. We drove him crazy with the 'twin thing,' as he called it."

I nodded. "Is this the same way you got out?"

"I don't recall, honestly. Your mother gave me detailed instructions in the dream, and I followed them on what now seems like autopilot."

I nodded again. "Neither of us knows where we're going, then."

"I'm afraid not, but when we get there, we'll know. I'm sure of that."

The baby hadn't cried for the last several minutes. At least when I'd heard the wail, I could follow the sound. Now? Nothing.

"Just keep going forward," I said under my breath.

"That's the only way," my father agreed.

On I trudged. At some points, the cavern became so narrow that my broad shoulders brushed the sides of the walls.

*The masked vampire in front of me was by far the largest I'd encountered in her arena. A head taller than I and much broader in the shoulders, he stood still, his light-blue eyes a menace beneath a black mask.*

How had that vampire gotten through this maze? He was way too big. Unless...

What if he'd *always* been there?

What if—

A shrill scream broke through the silence.

A woman's scream.

My ears perked. It wasn't Emilia. I would have recognized her voice. Wouldn't I have?

"Not your sister," my father agreed. "But definitely a woman. Follow the sound."

"There's only one way to go, Dad."

"No, Dante. Look ahead. The pathway forks off in the distance. Veer toward the left."

I squinted. He was right. And the scream had definitely come from the left.

*Keep going.*

My teeth elongated at a second scream.

Emilia.

That one was my sister.

"Yes," was all my father said.

I increased my pace, almost into a run, my shoulders hitting the dark walls as I went.

*I'm coming, Em. I'm coming, Em.*

*I'm coming.*

# TWENTY-FIVE

# *Erin*

The next two manhole covers yielded nothing.

"Did we take a wrong turn somewhere?" Jay asked.

"We're going in the direction the homeless guy told us," River said.

"Dante might have turned somewhere after he left that guy," Jay said.

"True."

I listened with one ear. What could we be missing? Another clue must be here somewhere. I shined my flashlight around, the beam moving like lightning against the darkness, as I scanned the area for the elusive clue.

"I don't know guys. There must—" I gasped.

No. This could not be *that* simple.

"What is it, Sis?"

I shined the light on a bedraggled sign hanging between two old wooden doors.

*Perception Hair and Nails.*

In the alleyway, situated between those two doors, lay a manhole, the cover slightly ajar.

"You're kidding," River said. "You were right, Jay. It's not another dimension, but it is an opening hiding in plain sight."

"I guess it's not dreams after all." I shrugged with a chuckle. "Or drugs."

"I'll be damned." Jay patted me on the back. "Between the doors of perception. Good work, Sis."

"If we hadn't been wondering if we'd taken a wrong turn, we could have easily missed that old sign," River said.

"This has to be it. Which one of you strong men wants to move that cover?"

River and Jay moved it effortlessly. I stared down into the darkness. A metal ladder descended downward, but after a few rungs, I could no longer see, even with my flashlight. My skin prickled.

But I had to do this. Dante needed me.

"You go first, since your vision is the best," Jay said to River. "Then Erin. I'll bring up the rear. That way Erin is protected between us."

"Roger that." River stepped down onto the first rung of the ladder. "Here goes nothing."

Once his head had gone under, I timidly stepped onto the first rung.

"Easy, Sis. Riv is ahead of you and will catch you if you slip. But"—he smiled crookedly—"don't slip."

I inhaled, gathering every ounce of courage I possessed, which, at the moment, wasn't a lot. I wobbled as my foot hit the metal rung.

I inhaled again and let the breath out slowly. *You got this, Erin. Don't fuck it up. Dante needs you. Lucy needs you. People are counting on you.*

My leg trembled as I went down another rung.

Then another.

Jay's foot was above my head.

I descended.

And descended.

For what seemed like forever, until River spoke.

"I've hit the bottom."

He took my arm as I eased down the last few rungs.

A chill wafted over the back of my neck. "Julian?" I whispered.

Nothing.

"He's not here," River said.

I swiped at my neck. "I felt something. A breeze or chill."

"We're underground, Sis. No breeze down here. It's just nerves."

I swiped again at my neck. He was no doubt right. My nerves were a ball of jitters.

"Where are we?" Jay asked, jumping down from the second-to-last rung.

"Got me," River said. "Underground. Way underground."

"Good thing I'm not claustrophobic," my brother said.

Neither was I, but his words had my nerves jumping even more.

"Looks like there's only one way to go from here." Jay beamed his light. "You're in the lead, partner."

I took my spot in the middle. We had to go single file, as the pathway was narrow. Dark and mysterious and narrow.

My heart pumped against my sternum, and my breathing intensified. "Is there enough oxygen down here?"

"Yeah, I think so." River touched the back of his neck. "You were right, Erin. Though it's not a breeze. Air is being circulated in here. Oxygen."

"So not a ghost either." I laughed nervously. "Just air to sustain life. That's good."

"See any other clues?" Jay asked.

"No," River replied. "But at this point it doesn't matter. Like I said, there's only one way to go."

We began. I rubbed my arms to ease the imaginary chills.

"You two better douse your lights," River said. "We don't know what we're heading into. I'll warn you if you need to look out for anything."

"What if I lose sight of you?" I quickly deposited my flashlight in the small backpack.

He reached backward. "Take my hand, and Jay, you take hers. We'll stay connected just in case."

The touch of River's gloved hand in mine gave me some solace, whether real or perceived, I had no idea. When my brother grabbed my other hand, the feeling intensified.

It made moving slightly more difficult in the narrow area, but I was glad for the contact, especially since, even as my eyes had adjusted, I was nearly blind here. My flashlight in my pack tempted me, but I couldn't reach it anyway. Both of my hands were occupied.

We walked. And we walked. Until—

"A baby!" I whispered urgently. "Did you hear that?"

"Yeah," River said.

"I didn't." Jay from behind.

"The baby from my dream. Patty's baby. Bea said I'd been lied to. That the baby wasn't where I thought she was. She's here. I know it."

"We'll go toward the cry," River said. "There's a fork ahead."

I followed along, gripping River's and Jay's hands as if my fingers were vises. Patty and the baby were here. I knew it in the marrow of my bones.

After another ten minutes or so, the path began to widen, until we could walk side by side, still holding hands.

I blinked, letting my eyes adjust once more. It was lighter here. And was that...?

"A door?" I said.

"Yeah," River said. "It's a door. And there's light beyond it."

Yes. The light I was seeing. It came from the bottom of the door. Just that tiny amount of illumination was like having two new eyes.

River drew his gun. "Get ready, partner. We're going in."

# DANTE

Fluorescent bulbs provided light in the oblong room. I hadn't been here, at least not that I remembered.

I edged around silently. "You here, Dad?"

"Beside you."

Then another door opened on the opposite end of the room, and a woman walked out. She was blond, tall, beautiful.

Unmasked.

Recognition flooded me. I knew *her*.

I'd never seen her without a mask, but I *knew* her.

"You've returned, just as I knew you would."

"Where are they?" I demanded. "Where's my sister? Where's my uncle?"

"They are safe. They are more valuable than the most precious gems."

"Then let them go," I growled, my teeth snapping downward.

She smiled. "Oh, you are magnificent. Truly. But then, you always were."

"Let. Them. Go."

"They are fulfilling a higher purpose, Dante. One you will understand soon."

"Are you torturing them? Taking their blood without their consent?" I advanced toward her. "You won't get away with this."

"Dante, I already have."

Anger coursed through me, a black rage that curtained my mind. Blood thrummed in my ears, and I clenched my hands into fists.

Control. I needed my control. Needed Erin.

But Erin wasn't here.

I snarled again, my teeth descending further.

"That's it. Show yourself, Dante. Show your *true* self."

I'd already unleashed the darkness. I'd needed it to find this place, to return to hell. But now it whirled through me, overtaking my logic, my light, like a gray cloud consuming a sunny day with a raging storm.

*I* was the raging storm.

A click. A door opening. All the while red noise penetrating my ears.

*She* stood before me, waiting, her arms outstretched.

*Go forward*, the cloud urged. *Go and be who you're meant to be.*

I grabbed fistfuls of my hair. *Must fight. Must fight. Must fight.*

*Dante!*

I jerked, looking backward toward the sound of a voice I knew. A voice I recognized.

A voice that meant something to me. A voice that exuded light.

Light...

But the black cloud edged out the light.

I squinted.

Three images. Two men, one woman. A daze swept over me. I squinted but could not see them clearly.

*Control, son.*

Another voice I knew, but it wasn't connected to anything.

My gaze was drawn back to *her*.

*Dr. Bonneville! I knew it!*

The feminine voice again. I blinked. Two men, one woman. I knew these people.

Knew these people...

Or maybe I didn't.

A duel of swords clashed within me between light and dark. Pain. Searing pain. I growled, letting my fangs sharpen to their most lethal points. I snarled toward the three images. I recognized them, as if I'd encountered them in a dream. Or a dream within a dream.

Or a nightmare.

*Dante!*

*Be strong, son.*

*Remember that part inside you, the part no one can touch.*

*Remember...*

*Remember...*

*Remember...*

*Re...mem...*

*Re...*

The voices became high-pitched buzzing, and the images...

They blurred into nothingness.

Nothingness...

Then I turned toward the blond woman, whose image was

so clear, as if she were outlined by fine black ink.

I dropped to my knees.

"I have returned, my queen."

# THE QUEEN

You have fared better than even *I* imagined, Dante.
You returned to me.
Now the real work can begin.

Continue The Blood Bond Saga with Volume Five

## *Undefeated*

**Coming Soon**

# ALSO AVAILABLE FROM
# HELEN HARDT

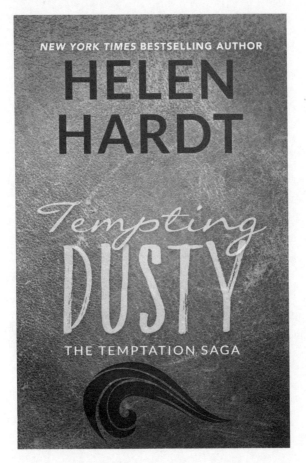

*NEW YORK TIMES BESTSELLING AUTHOR*
## HELEN HARDT

*Tempting*
# DUSTY

### THE TEMPTATION SAGA

*Keep reading for an excerpt!*

# EXCERPT FROM TEMPTING DUSTY

## BOOK ONE IN THE TEMPTATION SAGA

Dusty turned to face the man behind her, and her breath caught. Tall, though not as tall as Sam or Chad—six-feet-two, maybe, in his boots. Long black hair fell to his collar in silky waves. Broad shoulders clad in a black western shirt, and lean hips hugged by snug fitting jeans. The face of a god, chiseled and perfect with a strong jawline and straight Grecian nose. Full dusky lips. *Wow.* Then she noticed his eyes. One dark brown, one light blue. Those creepy eyes. Funny, they didn't seem so bad anymore. They worked with his movie star looks. They gave him a mysterious quality, like he could see into her soul.

He was magnificent.

"Zach McCray," she said in a breathless rasp.

"I hardly recognized you, Gold Dust," he drawled, eyeing her from top to bottom.

The smolder of his unique eyes warmed her from her head to her toes, and she was convinced he was somehow dissolving her clothes with his heated gaze. Her nipples hardened against the soft fabric of her bra, and she silently thanked God she'd chosen one with padding that morning.

Dusty looked down at his feet, shod in black ostrich cowboy boots. *Expensive* black ostrich cowboy boots. Here was money.

The McCray brothers no doubt owned McCray Landing now since their father had passed away a couple years ago.

"So"—she cleared her throat—"you're the man to talk to about riding this bull?" She gestured to Diablo, who snorted angrily.

"Darlin', I'll say it again. There ain't a woman alive who can ride that bull."

"I say there is," Dusty said. "And you're looking at her."

"She calls herself the Bull Whisperer, bro," Chad said.

Zach eyed her again, an amused smirk on his face. Was he looking at her chest? She crossed her arms.

"You think you can talk to bulls?"

"I don't exactly talk to them. It's not a literal whisper, Mr. McCray."

"Mr. McCray? Hell, that's my grandpa. You call me Zach, Gold Dust."

"Fine. It's not a literal whisper, Zach."

"Yeah, not a literal whisper." Chad's lips twisted into a wide leer. "She uses a flute and a turban. She's a regular bull swami."

The three men chuckled as Dusty rolled her eyes. Some things hadn't changed in seventeen years. Chad teased her as relentlessly as ever. She turned back to Zach.

"Look, I understand bulls, and they seem to understand me."

Zach rolled his head back in a sarcastic guffaw. Dusty tried not to think about his sexy golden neck and how good his pulse point would feel against her lips.

"Now that takes the cake, darlin'."

"I'm not your darling."

"Course not. Women's lib and all. I'd hate to be politically incorrect."

"Women's lib? This is the twenty-first century, not the seventies." Dusty tapped her foot with indignation.

"Sorry, darlin'. Oops, I mean Dusty, or Miss O'Donovan."

"It's *Ms.*"

"Oh, Christ." Zach rolled his eyes.

"So can we talk about Diablo or not?"

"Not," Zach said.

"Told you, twerp." Chad smiled. "Ain't no way you get to ride Diablo."

"But I need to, for the—" Dusty stopped herself. The McCrays didn't need to know the small Montana ranch she and Sam had inherited from their grandparents was in financial trouble.

"Look, Dusty, I don't want to hear any more about this," Sam interjected. "The subject is closed."

"You're not my father, Sam," she said, keeping her temper in check. "I'll do as I please."

"Not with my bull, you won't," Zach said.

Dusty regarded the three men, all stiff as statues in their indignant stances. Perhaps she was going about this the wrong way. After all, she'd catch more flies with sugar...

"Zach," she said sweetly, "maybe we could discuss this further over a drink, or even dinner. I'm famished, and it would be fun to catch up, don't you think?"

"That sounds like a plan," Chad agreed. "Let's go for some chow. There's a great steakhouse about a mile from here."

"The lady asked me," Zach said, "and I'll take her to dinner. Alone."

"They can come too," Dusty said. "I'd love for us all to chat. It'd be fun."

Zach's eyes raked over her. "Now why would I want to

share a pretty little thing like you with these two clowns?"

Dusty's cheeks heated. She couldn't think of anything to say.

"Okay, okay, bro." Chad said, backing away. "What say we go for a few beers and some chili cheese fries, Sam?"

."Uh, sure, but Dusty—"

"I'll be fine, Sam. I'll see you later at the hotel."

Her brother and his old best friend trotted off together, as if seventeen years hadn't passed.

Breathing deeply, she gathered her courage, turned to Zach, and looped her arm through his. "Shall we?"

**This story continues in**
**Tempting Dusty!**

# MESSAGE FROM HELEN HARDT

Dear Reader,

Thank you for reading *Unmasked*. If you want to find out about my current backlist and future releases, please like my Facebook page and join my mailing list. I often do giveaways. If you're a fan and would like to join my street team to help spread the word about my books. I regularly do awesome giveaways for my street team members.

    If you enjoyed the story, please take the time to leave a review on a site like Amazon or Goodreads. I welcome all feedback.

I wish you all the best!
Helen

**Facebook**
Facebook.com/HelenHardt

**Newsletter**
HelenHardt.com/Sign-Up

**Street Team**
Facebook.com/Groups/HardtAndSoul/

# ALSO BY HELEN HARDT

**Blood Bond Saga:**
*Unchained: Volume One*

*Unhinged: Volume Two*

*Undaunted: Volume Three*

*Unmasked: Volume Four*

*Undefeated: Volume Five*
(Coming Soon)

**The Steel Brothers Saga:**
*Craving*
*Obsession*
*Possession*
*Melt*
*Burn*
*Surrender*
*Shattered*
*Twisted*
*Unraveled*
*Breathless* (Coming Soon)
*Ravenous* (Coming Soon)
*Insatiable* (Coming Soon)

**Misadventures Series:**
*Misadventures of a Good Wife*
*Misadventures with a Rock Star*

**The Temptation Saga:**
*Tempting Dusty*
*Teasing Annie*
*Taking Catie*
*Taming Angelina*
*Treasuring Amber*
*Trusting Sydney*
*Tantalizing Maria*

**The Sex and the Season Series:**
*Lily and the Duke*
*Rose in Bloom*
*Lady Alexandra's Lover*
*Sophie's Voice*

**Daughters of the Prairie:**
*The Outlaw's Angel*
*Lessons of the Heart*
*Song of the Raven*

# ACKNOWLEDGMENTS

I hoped you enjoyed *Unmasked*! This was the most exciting installment yet for me as the author. Dante is changing, becoming more powerful, and now he risks returning to darkness. Stay tuned. I promise more thrills as we find out who will be *Undefeated*.

Thank you to my editor, Celina Summers, my line editor, Scott Saunders, and my proofreaders, Chrissie Saunders, Michele Hamner Moore, and Lia Fairchild. You each added your own special touch to this story, and I'm forever grateful.

Thanks as always to the team at Waterhouse Press—Meredith, Jon, Robyn, Haley, Jennifer, Jeanne, Kurt, Amber, Yvonne, Jesse, and Dave. Your belief in me and my work keeps me going.

To the women—and a few men!—of my street team, Hardt and Soul—you rock! The love and support you give me lifts me to new heights. Thank you for spreading the word about the Blood Bond Saga and for your wonderful reviews and general good vibes.

Thank you to my family and friends and to my two local RWA chapters, Colorado Romance Writers and Heart of Denver Romance Writers.

Most of all, thank you to all my readers. Without you, none of this would be possible. Thank you for always supporting my work, especially as I venture into new territory. You are the best!

# ABOUT THE AUTHOR

#1 *New York Times,* #1 *USA Today,* and #1 *Wall Street Journal* bestselling author Helen Hardt's passion for the written word began with the books her mother read to her at bedtime. She wrote her first story at age six and hasn't stopped since. In addition to being an award-winning author of contemporary and historical romance and erotica, she's a mother, an attorney, a black belt in Taekwondo, a grammar geek, an appreciator of fine red wine, and a lover of Ben and Jerry's ice cream. She writes from her home in Colorado, where she lives with her family. Helen loves to hear from readers.

Visit her at HelenHardt.com